BURIED

STRANGERS

BURIED
STRANGERS

Leighton Gage

Published by
Soho Press, Inc.
853 Broadway
New York, NY 10003

Library of Congress Cataloging-in-Publication Data
Gage, Leighton D.
Buried strangers / Leighton Gage.
p. cm.
ISBN 978-1-56947-514-0
1. Police—Brazil—Fiction. 2. Transplantation of organs, tissues, etc.—
Fiction. 3. Brazil—Fiction. 4. Mystery fiction. I. Title.
PS3607.A3575B87 2009
813'.6—dc22
2008028443

Paperback ISBN 978-1-56947-614-7

10 9 8 7 6 5 4 3 2 1

To Jes Norgaard Jensen
Remembering . . .

Days in Sydney,
Nights in Paris,
Long, languid afternoons in Rome
And that damned bar in the Martinez.

. . . they took counsel and bought . . . the . . . field to bury strangers.

MATTHEW 27:7

Chapter One

"SOMEWHERE AROUND HERE," HANS said, swinging his flashlight beam from the dark tunnel in front of them toward the thick wall of vegetation on the right.

Geraldo acknowledged with a wordless grunt, pulled the truck onto the high grass bordering the rutted dirt road, and hit the brake.

Hans clambered down from the passenger's seat and disappeared into the brush.

Twenty seconds later, he was back.

"Yeah, here," he said, "on the other side of that big tree."

"They're all big trees," Geraldo said.

"That one," Hans said, shining his light up and down the trunk.

Gilda Caropreso hesitated for a moment, reluctant to leave the warmth of the cab. The others started opening doors and unloading equipment. Geraldo slung on his camera cases, freeing his hands for the heavier work ahead. Fernando produced a thermos bottle of hot coffee. They stood around for a while, leaning against the vehicles, blowing into their hands, waiting for dawn.

Then they set out to recover the body.

Frost coated the *samambaia* ferns like a sugar glaze. Nocturnal animals rustled in the darkness. Gilda's breath came out in white clouds, spreading and vanishing in the windless air. Twice she heard gunshots punctuating the rumble of traffic on the nearby belt road. The temperature was two degrees below freezing. The location was a rain forest less than twenty kilometers from the largest city in the Southern

Hemisphere. The jungle that surrounded them was as thick as any in the Amazon.

Yoshiro Tanaka looked down at his feet and grunted. His weight had carried him beyond a crust of ice and into a thick ooze of red mud. The little cop stepped onto firmer ground, bent over, and started scraping at the gooey mass with a handful of dead leaves from the forest floor.

Tanaka, shorter than Gilda by half a head, was a *delegado titular*. A man in his position had no need to risk his shoes. In fact, he had no need to be out there in the rain forest at all. But within the confines of his domain, the area covered by his precinct, Tanaka could do whatever he damn pleased. And what pleased Yoshiro Tanaka was the adrenaline rush he got from visiting crime scenes.

Gilda took a lead from his misstep and leaped clear of the slime. Her two assistants, Fernando and Geraldo, burdened by the tool-kit, body bag, and stretcher (and in Geraldo's case the extra weight of the camera cases), were unable to follow her example. They squished their way through the mud, muttering imprecations as they went.

Beyond the rise was a clearing. On the far side, perhaps fifteen meters away, a ball-like object protruded from the ground. Hans stopped and waved his arms.

"I was right about here," he said, "when The Mop spotted me."

Hans—his last name was something Teutonic, and Gilda had promptly forgotten it—was about twenty-five, blue-eyed and blond-haired, clearly the offspring of German immigrants. The Mop, twenty years younger, brown-eyed and properly called Herbert, was an old-English sheepdog, owned by Hans's employer, *Senhor* Manfredo. To hear Hans tell it, the animal was an escape artist, the Houdini of the dog world. Hans claimed he spent half of his working life chasing after him.

"He picked up this big bone," Hans said, moving forward again and holding his hands apart as if describing the proverbial fish that got away, "and came running toward me with the damned thing in his mouth. I thought it was from a cow—until I saw *that*."

He pointed at the ball-like object.

By then, the skull was only a few meters away. Gilda could see both of the eye sockets, but the mandible was still buried in the earth.

Fernando and Geraldo put down their burdens. Fernando lifted the lid on the box and started unloading tools. Geraldo unpacked a camera and started loading film. Gilda knelt down for a closer look at the corpse. The bones were free of flesh. There was no smell of corruption. Some wisps of black hair still clung to the cranium. She took a pair of latex gloves out of the pocket of her jeans, blinked at the flash from Geraldo's first shot and selected a medium-sized brush.

Tanaka rubbed his hands together to warm them and said something to Hans that Gilda couldn't hear. Whatever it was set Hans to talking all over again. Most people become silent, almost reverent, in the presence of death, but not Hans. Hans was a talker.

He'd first missed The Mop, he said, just before lunchtime. He didn't have any idea how long the animal had been gone because it was a big yard, with bushes and shrubs where The Mop liked to hide. Besides, there were a lot of things that Senhor Manfredo expected him to do around the house, like washing the cars and cleaning the swimming pool. He couldn't be expected to keep an eye on the damned dog all of the time.

"And then I saw another hole under the fence. Every time

he digs his way out I drive stakes into the ground so he can't crawl through the same place again. But then he goes and digs somewhere else. I've got stakes all over the place. The back of the yard is starting to look like one of the forts you see in those old American movies, the ones about cowboys and Indians."

"Dog never came back on his own?" Tanaka asked.

"Never. He likes wandering around, pissing on other people's fences, sticking his nose into other dogs' assholes—uh, sorry, *Senhora.*"

"*Senhorita,*" Gilda corrected him without looking up.

"Senhorita," Hans repeated. "And running around after kids. The Mop is crazy about kids."

"Friendly, huh?"

"The damned mutt will go to anyone who calls him. Anyone. And then he slobbers all over 'em."

"It would make him easy to steal, I suppose?"

"You suppose right. From what I understand, he cost a bundle, and Senhor Manfredo is scared to death of losing him. If I see The Mop is missing, I'm supposed to drop whatever else I'm doing and go after him."

"Doesn't sound as if you like him much," Tanaka said.

Gilda, following the conversation as she gently dug around the skull with her trowel, had a feeling that Tanaka had only asked the question to get a rise out of the *caseiro.*

If that was the delegado's intention, it worked.

"Like him? *Like* him. Are you kidding?"

"So why don't you let him get lost—permanently?"

"Because Senhor Manfredo would have a fit, that's why. You should see the scene when he gets home from work. The Mop whining and licking, and Senhor Manfredo making little kissy-face sounds and stroking. I swear if The Mop learned how to cook, Senhor Manfredo would ditch Senhora

Cristina and marry the dog. I lose that animal, and the next one out the door is going to be *me*. Senhor Manfredo would fire my ass in a heartbeat. First thing he asked me when I applied for the job was whether I liked dogs."

"And you told him you did?"

"I wasn't lying," Hans said defensively. "In those days, I did. And then Senhor Manfredo calls The Mop, and The Mop jumps all over me, and I scratch The Mop behind the ear, and Senhor Manfredo gives me the job. Jesus, if I'd known what I was getting into, I would never have applied. Did you see all that hair? Senhor Manfredo wants it brushed every day. Every. Single. Day."

Tanaka had, indeed, seen the hair. In fact, some of it was clinging to his pants—as was a stripe of Herbert's drool— from earlier that morning when they'd stopped at the house to pick up their guide.

"You have my sympathy," Tanaka said, but not as if he meant it. "Let's get back to what happened. You picked up his leash . . ."

"Yeah, I picked up his leash and went out to look for him."

"But not right away?"

"No. I told you. I had lunch first. A man's got to eat, doesn't he? Didn't take long. Maybe twenty minutes, that's all."

"Go on."

"So there I am, walking around, walking around, for the next four hours or so, and then, just before dark, I hear him barking."

"And you knew it was your dog because . . ."

"It's *not* my dog. It's Senhor Manfredo's dog. And I knew it was The Mop because The Mop's bark is different. You heard it. He sounds like he's hoarse or something. Like some guy who just walked out of a stadium, somebody who screamed so much he lost his voice."

Tanaka smiled politely, as if it were the first time Hans had made the comparison.

It wasn't.

"So, like I said, I followed the sound, found the path, came into this field, and found him chewing on that bone. He only let me take it out of his mouth because he thought I was gonna throw it for him."

"So then you . . ."

"Took one look at the skull, put the leash on him, got the hell out of here, and called you guys."

Tanaka nodded and addressed Gilda.

"I decided to leave it until morning," he said. "Can you imagine trying to find this place in the dark?"

Gilda shook her head and stood.

"We're on a incline," she said. "The grave wasn't deep. She was probably uncovered by erosion."

"She?" Tanaka sounded surprised. "A woman?"

"Probably."

Gilda pointed to the black hair still clinging to the skull. It was long, unlikely to be a man's.

"She's been here for quite some time," she said. "Hardly any flesh left at all."

"The dog, maybe?" Tanaka said.

"Not the dog. Decomposition and insects. Most of the bones appear to be in place, but I'll only be able to verify that once we get her back to the IML."

The IML, the Instituto Médico Legal, was the headquarters of São Paulo's chief medical examiner and the place where Gilda spent most of her time. She was a slim brunette, who looked too young to be a full-fledged pathologist. When she neglected to pin on her name tag, visitors to the morgue often took her for a secretary or a medical student.

She was about to kneel down again when the sun crept

over the encircling rim of forest. Long shadows fell across the field, emphasizing irregularities in the carpet of green. In the altered light, row upon row of rectangular mounds suddenly became visible.

Gilda saw them first and narrowly avoided putting one of her latex-gloved hands over her lips. Han's mouth dropped open. Fernando and Geraldo looked at each other. Tanaka just stared.

Graves. Tens of graves, lined up row-on-row.

Herbert, The Mop, hadn't just found himself one corpse to play with. He'd found himself an entire cemetery.

Chapter Two

"WHAT'S THIS CRAP ANA handed me?"

Nelson Sampaio raised his jaw and looked pugnaciously at Mario Silva. Sampaio was the director of the Brazilian Federal Police. Ana was his long-suffering personal assistant. What he was referring to as crap was a request for two round-trip airline tickets, Brasilia/São Paulo/Brasilia.

Ana had served five directors in succession, one more than Silva, and averred that Nelson Sampaio was the worst of the lot. The director was a pink-faced, prematurely balding man with suspicious blue eyes. Mostly, his eyes were enlarged by spectacles, but this morning he was trying out a new set of contact lenses. He kept blinking at Silva, while his hand remained splayed over the form in front of him. The two men, Silva and Sampaio, were on opposite sides of Sampaio's desk in his spacious office in Brasilia, the nation's capital.

Everything in the room had been chosen with an eye to making a statement: The national flag demonstrated Sampaio's patriotism; the portrait of the president bespoke party loyalty; the photographs around the walls assured visitors that they were in the presence of a man who rubbed elbows with Brazil's movers and shakers; the triptych on his desk (his wife flanked by his two daughters) showed that he was a good family man; the sports trophies (Silva suspected that at least some of them were bogus) revealed that he'd been an athlete in his youth; the awards for public service attested to his social conscience; a couple of knickknacks (fashioned by schoolchildren) indicated that Sampaio hadn't lost the common touch; and the two (Brazilian) paintings established his artistic sensitivity. Even the view made a statement: The window behind him overlooked the Ministry of Culture.

"You mind telling me what's so important that you have to take a couple of days out of your schedule and go gallivanting off to São Paulo when there's so much to do right here?" Sampaio continued.

"It's all there on the form," Silva said, patiently. "And, with respect, Director, it's not gallivanting."

"Oh? What is it then?"

"You've seen today's newspapers?"

"Of course, I've seen today's newspapers," Sampaio snapped. "I read three of them every morning. So what?"

Nelson Sampaio had been a successful attorney before he entered government service. A political appointee, whose ambitions went far beyond his current post, he was a man who'd never been to a crime scene and had never smelled a corpse. When he spoke of reading three newspapers, Sampaio meant the front pages, the editorial pages, and the social columns. The majority of the articles that attracted his attention were those dealing with the Machiavellian world of Brazilian national politics. They were unlikely to be the same ones that interested Mario Silva.

"Then perhaps you read about that clandestine cemetery in the Serra da Cantareira?" Silva said, making the statement a question.

"What about it?" the director said, neither confirming nor denying his awareness of the article in question.

"There were children in some of those graves," Silva said, plunging on in the face of his boss's apparent lack of interest. Silva, childless after the death of his son from leukemia at the age of eight, could get particularly passionate about the murder of children.

"Kids, adults, what's the difference?" Sampaio said. "I asked you a simple question: What's so important? Don't you think you have enough on your plate right here in Brasilia?"

"I wasn't aware that I had—"

"Not aware? *Not aware?* Mario, for God's sake, what about Romeu Pluma?"

Romeu Pluma was a former journalist and the current press secretary for the minister of justice, Sampaio's immediate superior. Pluma and Sampaio loathed each other.

"I told you, Director, we haven't been able to find anything in Pluma's background to suggest—"

"And I told *you* to keep digging. Everybody has *something* to hide. You, him, even me. I want to know what Pluma's hiding. Is that so much to ask?"

Sampaio was a believer in using the powers of his office to forward what he considered to be good causes, and foremost among all good causes was the continued advancement of Nelson Sampaio.

Romeu Pluma had the ear of the minister. He'd been whispering into it, questioning Sampaio's competence and criticizing his effectiveness. And, even worse, he'd been expressing those same opinions to the press. Pluma was quoted as being an "unnamed government source," but that didn't fool Sampaio. He always knew who was out to get him. He desperately wanted something to hold over the press secretary's head, and he expected Silva to get it for him.

"With all due respect, Director, the children in that cemetery deserve—"

"There you go again," the director said, cutting him off. "You remind me of Vulcano."

The director owned a *fazenda* where he raised cattle. He didn't do it for the money. It was more in the nature of a hobby, and it was an activity that interested him far more than apprehending criminals. Vulcano was his prize bull. Comparing Vulcano to Silva was as close as Sampaio ever got to paying him a compliment.

"Just like you," Sampaio explained, "Vulcano is always charging off whenever he gets wind of something he thinks is threatening his territory. But you're not a street cop anymore, damn it! You're my chief inspector for criminal matters. You've got people to do the legwork."

"But—"

The director held up a hand. "What's more important? That damned cemetery or your investigation into the background of that *filho da puta* Pluma?"

Silva looked at his lap.

"Exactly," Sampaio continued, as if he'd successfully made his point. "The corpses will wait. Pluma won't. The bastard makes me look bad every chance he gets. If he has his way, I'll be out of this job right after the election and *that*, as I don't have to remind you, is less than two months away." Sampaio glanced at the huge desktop calendar where he'd penciled in a countdown to election day. "In fact, it's only fifty-two days. Forget the cemetery. Or let your buddy Arnaldo handle it."

"I need—"

"Or get that hotshot nephew of yours, whatshisname?"

"Hector Costa."

"Yeah, him. Get him to work on it."

"He's already working on it, Director, but he needs all the help he can get."

Sampaio showed no sign of having heard him.

"Pluma is an ex-journalist for God's sake. All those guys smoked marijuana or used cocaine at one time or another."

"I hate to be insistent—"

"Which you're being."

"—but I feel that we have to go. How about if we leave tonight and we're back in the office on Monday morning? Will that suit you?"

The director stared at Silva for a while.

Silva didn't blink.

Finally, Sampaio said, "That's two round-trip tickets plus hotels, plus per diem. It's gonna cost at least three thousand Reais. Don't you think we have better things to spend our money on?"

"We can economize on the hotels," Silva said. "I'll stay with my sister. Arnaldo has family in São Paulo. He can stay with them."

"And you can take the midnight flight. It's cheaper."

"Alright. We'll take the midnight flight."

"Deal," the director said, and reached for his pen.

Chapter Three

AT ELEVEN O'CLOCK ON the following morning the prevailing smells in the corridor of the São Paulo morgue were of formaldehyde, tobacco smoke, and putrefying flesh, mostly putrefying flesh.

"They're in here," Dr. Gilda Caropreso said, stopping at a heavy metal door, "and so is Yoshiro Tanaka. He's been waiting for you gentlemen."

"Who's Tanaka?" Hector asked before Arnaldo or Silva could.

"The delegado titular of the precinct in which the bodies were found."

"How come he showed up himself? How come he didn't just send one of his homicide detectives?"

"I'm told that he takes a personal interest in the murders that occur in his district," she said, assessing Hector out of a pair of gray-green eyes.

Considering the years she would have needed to get a medical degree, and the postgraduate work required to qualify as a pathologist, Dr. Caropreso had to be—Hector did the calculation in his head—almost as old as he was. But she sure as hell didn't look it. If he'd passed her on the street, he might have taken her for a teenager, twenty or twenty-one at the most. He dropped his eyes to her left hand. She wasn't wearing a wedding ring.

"You're going to find it a little warm down here," she said. "I'm afraid the lack of air-conditioning only makes it worse."

She wrinkled her nose—and a most attractive little nose it was, Hector thought.

The "it" she was referring to was the smell. On a stainless-steel table next to the door, there was a jar of what appeared to be petroleum jelly. Dr. Caropreso picked it up, took a dab of the contents on her right forefinger, and spread it above her upper lip.

"May I?" she said, removing another dab and pausing in front of Hector.

"Please," Hector said.

Even before her finger got anywhere near his nose, he took in the strong smell of camphor. She applied the jelly, focusing on his upper lip. His eyes watered. He blinked—and could have sworn she blinked back.

Arnaldo reached over, took a dab of the jelly and applied it with the practiced gesture of someone who'd done it a hundred times before. And if it was taking the young doctor a lot longer to perform the service for him, which it was, Hector wasn't about to complain. When she finally finished, he glanced at his uncle, a man who didn't miss much, and flushed.

Silva was looking back and forth between the two of them. Without missing a beat, Dr. Caropreso met the older man's eyes and offered him the jar.

"Perhaps you'd better apply it yourself, Chief Inspector. Your mustache . . ."

She left the rest of her sentence unfinished and pulled a pair of rubber gloves out of the pocket of her white coat.

Silva smeared some of the jelly between his nostrils, carefully avoiding his mustache. He was a tall man, who gave the impression of being even taller because he held himself erect, as if he were trying to maintain contact between his neck and the back of his collar. That day, as on every other workday, he was dressed in a gray suit. Despite the lack of sartorial variety, Silva invariably looked dapper, as if he were expecting to have his picture taken, which—as he was Brazil's top cop—it often was. His most striking feature was his eyes. They were jet black, just like Hector's.

Dr. Caropreso finished putting on her gloves and depressed the steel lever, opening the rubber seal on the door. The stuff under Hector's nose was supposed to over-power the smell of death, but it didn't. Some of the corpses in the room were far too ripe for that. He'd need a bath after this. They all would. A short man with oriental features looked up from one of the coffins that covered the floor and came toward them with an outstretched hand. He offered it first to Silva.

"Your reputation precedes you, Chief Inspector. I'm Tanaka, *Policia Civil.*"

Silva shook his hand and introduced Arnaldo and Hector. "This is *Agente* Arnaldo Nunes, temporarily attached to our headquarters in Brasilia."

Tanaka nodded at Arnaldo.

"And this is Delegado Costa, from our São Paulo field office."

"Ah, yes. Your nephew," Tanaka said.

Hector *hated* it when people brought that up. The impli-cation was that he owed his position to nepotism. The truth was that his uncle had never wanted him to be a cop in the first place and was more demanding of him than he was of anyone else on the force. But he could hardly hope to explain that to Tanaka or to anyone else.

As if she sensed his embarrassment, Dr. Caropreso deftly intervened: "We'd prefer to use the floor space for only the most desiccated of bodies—or not at all—because that would keep the smell down, but it doesn't usually work out that way. This place was built thirty years ago, for the needs of thirty years ago. The number of cases has more than tripled since then. We never have enough space in the lockers."

Hector nodded, as if it were the first time anyone had told him that.

"The bodies you came to see are these." Gilda swept her hand over a long row of plastic coffins, all of them open. "Not much point to refrigerating them. There's hardly any flesh left at all."

It wasn't as horrific a sight as Hector had been expecting. Most of the bodies were no more than skeletons, piles of bones crowned by grinning skulls.

After they'd given each of the remains a token inspection, Gilda knelt down and stroked one of the smaller skulls with her forefinger. She did it gently, as if she were caressing a cat.

"The victims are of both sexes and varying ages," she said. "Children, like this one, were never buried alone. Sometimes they were interred with one adult, sometimes with two. When it was one, the adult was always a female. When it was two, there was one of each sex."

"Family groups?" Silva said. "Mothers with their children? Mothers and fathers with their children?"

"That would seem to be a logical conclusion, but you know how my boss—"

"Hates speculation. Yes, I know."

"We're doing DNA testing."

"Good. What else can you tell us?"

Gilda rose and, as she did so, moved closer to Hector. So close, in fact, that he imagined he could feel the warmth of her body. She responded to his uncle without answering the question he'd posed.

"Let's go across the street to Dr. Couto's office," she said. "He's waiting for us."

Chapter Four

DR. PAULO COUTO, GILDA'S boss and an old friend of Silva's, was São Paulo's chief medical examiner. He had his lair in the bowels of an ancient redbrick building that also housed the Municipal Revenue Service. The union of the two in a single location had given rise to the cops' nickname for the place: Death and Taxes.

Most meetings in Brazil begin with a cup of coffee, and most offices have their *copeiro*, a man whose principal duty it is to prepare and serve that coffee. Dr. Couto's office was no exception.

"With sugar," Silva said.

The copeiro picked up the pot containing the presweetened mixture and filled the last cup on his tray.

"Water, Senhor?"

Silva nodded. The tiny cup of coffee and a tumbler of water were placed in front of him. The copeiro left Dr. Couto's office, balancing his heavy tray. Silva reached out for the cup, but a touch told him it was too hot. He withdrew his hand.

"Ouch," he said.

"I've been telling you for years, Mario," Dr. Couto said, brandishing an enormous mug, "you should drink it my way."

Few people called Chief Inspector Silva by his first name, but Dr. Couto was someone who did. Their fathers had gone to medical school together. Their mothers had been close friends. Dr. Couto, as a little boy in knee pants, had frequented Silva's childhood home.

In his youth, the chief medical examiner had spent a year

at Harvard. Ever since then he'd drunk his coffee as weak as the Americans did, lacing it with vast quantities of cold milk. His mug, too, was American. I Don't Do Mornings was emblazoned on the side that faced the federal cops, red letters on white porcelain.

Dr. Couto took a mouthful of his lukewarm beverage and smacked his lips.

"Your way ruins the taste," Silva grumbled.

"And your way ruins the lining of your stomach."

It was an old debate. They rattled off their words without passion, as if it were a ritual, which in a way it was.

To look at Dr. Couto, one would never guess he spent his days cutting up corpses. He looked more like a clown without greasepaint, without humor, a rotund man who seldom smiled. When puzzled about something, or lost in thought, Couto would fix his eyes on the wall of his office where three of his five grandchildren, serious as their grandfather, stared at visitors out of a silver frame. Silva saw him doing it now, but it didn't last long. With no apparent effort, he suddenly broke his reverie and glanced at his watch, a cheap Japanese model that he wore with the clasp turned outward, the face on the inside of his wrist.

"There's a gentleman," he said, "waiting for me across the street with what appears to be a bullet hole in his head. I've promised to give one of Delegado Tanaka's colleagues some answers by two o'clock this afternoon. Let's get down to business, shall we?"

There were nods and murmurs of assent.

Dr. Couto swiveled around in his chair and took a file from his credenza. "The magnitude of this horror far outweighs a single shooting, of course, but Delegado Tanaka's colleague has expressed a certain degree of urgency in the other case."

"Who is this colleague?" Tanaka asked.

"Delegado Marto from the twenty-seventh."

"Marto is a pain in the ass," Tanaka said. "Let him wait."

Dr. Couto cleared his throat, but didn't disagree with Tanaka's assessment of Delegado Marto. He ran his index finger down the first page of the report, verifying the numbers.

"In total, there were thirty-seven corpses," he said, "some of them interred in common graves." The finger moved on. "Only thirteen were adults."

"Twenty-four were kids?" Hector said, looking back and forth between Dr. Couto and Gilda, but mostly at Gilda.

"I'm glad at least one member of your family knows how to count," Dr. Couto said, glancing at Silva. When his friend didn't rise to the bait he continued, "The youngest, a female, was no more than six when she died, the oldest child, another female, was about fourteen."

"Sick fuck," Arnaldo said. "Killing kids."

Arnaldo had two teenage sons, one of whom had just turned fourteen, both of whom he deeply loved.

"Sick fuck or fucks," Dr. Couto agreed. "I see no reason to exclude multiple perpetrators."

"*Desaparecidos?*" Silva asked.

The generals who'd run the country during the most recent dictatorship had been hard on almost everyone whose political persuasion was to the left of Attila the Hun. They'd labeled such people Communists, arrested them wholesale, and made them disappear. Hence the term, desaparecidos, disappeared ones. One thing they'd never been known to do, however, was to kill children.

"Definitely not desaparecidos," Dr. Couto said.

Silva leaned forward in his chair. He was accustomed to hearing Dr. Couto qualify his remarks with words like "possibly" and "maybe." "Definitely" was a word seldom used by São Paulo's chief medical examiner.

"The bodies hadn't been in the ground long enough," Dr. Couto continued. "Our estimates range from seven years, maximum, to three years, minimum, definitely not three decades or more. Couldn't have been desaparecidos. No way. Something else, too: the children were invariably buried in common graves with adults. Sometimes there was only one adult, other times there were two."

"Gilda mentioned that," Hector said.

Dr. Couto raised a critical eyebrow, but if it was because his assistant had offered the information without consulting him or because the youngest of the cops had referred to her as Gilda, and not Dr. Caropreso, wasn't clear. After a short pause, he continued: "It's also worth mentioning that corpses in common graves were always encountered in exactly the same state of decomposition."

"Meaning they were buried at the same time?" Silva asked.

"Meaning exactly that," Dr. Couto said, and took another sip of his coffee.

As he considered the implications of what his old friend had just said, Silva felt a chill on the back of his neck. He turned around and looked for a vent that might have been expelling cold air. There wasn't one.

Tanaka stroked his chin. "Are you suggesting, Doctor, that someone might have been murdering entire families?"

Dr. Couto looked at him over the rim of his mug. "I am suggesting nothing of the kind. I have no basis for such speculation. Whether the victims are related or not will be resolved by DNA testing. That testing is already under way."

"But they *were* murdered?"

Dr. Couto took another sip of his coffee. "I can't think of any other explanation," he said. "We appear to be dealing with one of Brazil's all-time great serial killers, or perhaps a gang of them."

Silva picked up his coffee, tossed it off in one gulp—and grimaced.

"I hope that expression on your face," Dr. Couto said, "is not reflective of the quality of our coffee."

"The director is going to go ballistic," Silva said.

"Would you care to elaborate on that?"

"No," Silva said.

"I've never met Director Sampaio," Dr. Couto said, "but I've heard he's somewhat of a publicity hound."

"There are those who say that," Silva admitted.

Dr. Couto had hit the nail squarely on the head. With a crime as high-profile as this one, Sampaio would be sure to regard anything other than a rapid solution and a quick arrest as bad publicity. And one thing he hated even more than Romeu Pluma was bad publicity.

"What else have you got?" Silva asked, breaking the lengthening silence.

The medical examiner shook his head.

"Not a hell of a lot. *Doctor* Caropreso"—he stressed her title, looking at Hector while he did it—"and her people excavated to a depth of thirty centimeters under each body. All of the victims were buried without a stitch of clothing. We found no bullets, no foreign objects. There was hardly any flesh to test for toxins and no trace, either, of anything lethal in the hair. Now, we're starting on the skeletons."

"What causes of death can we rule out?" Silva asked.

Dr. Couto took another sip of his coffee.

"We haven't run across any fractures of the hyoid bones, so I think we can rule out strangulation, but not suffocation. The skulls seem to be in good shape, so it's unlikely to be blunt trauma."

Gilda leaned forward. "There is one curious—"

Dr. Couto raised a hand to cut her off. "And it would be

premature," he said, "to elaborate any further at this time. Give us a few more days, and we may have something to add."

Silva shot his look back and forth between Gilda and Couto—and then focused on Couto.

"Come on, Paulo," he said. "I need it now. Out with it."

Dr. Couto shook his head. "You're going to have to wait for it, Mario." He gave Hector a significant look. "And don't try leaning on my assistant in the meantime. You'll be wasting your time. Her social life is her own, but her professional loyalties belong to me."

Paulo Couto was also a man who didn't miss much.

Five minutes later, the meeting broke up, Gilda remaining with Dr. Couto, the four cops heading for the street, Silva leading the way.

HE PAUSED in the reception area just inside the front door.

"Taken on a yearly basis, how many people are reported missing in this city?" he asked Tanaka.

"I don't know," Tanaka said. "I'll find out and call you."

"Just give me a rough estimate."

Tanaka took out his notepad and started making calculations. He spoke aloud while he was doing it. "If I multiply the total number of *delegacias* . . . by the figures for my own . . . I come up with . . . something like . . . thirty-two thousand cases. Mind you, those would be reported cases. Lots of them turn out to be false alarms. Girl runs away from home, for example; parents report her missing; she comes back. Sometimes, they don't bother to inform us. We haven't got the staff to keep doing follow-ups, so we just keep her on the books."

"What if we make an assumption?" Silva said.

"We don't do assumptions in this building," Arnaldo said in a pretty good imitation of Dr. Couto's gravelly voice.

Silva ignored him. "Let's assume the DNA verifies the suspicion that we're dealing with family groups."

Tanaka nodded.

"I get your drift. If we go after individuals reported missing, we'd have thousands of cases to deal with, but if we limit ourselves to families there'd be damned few. I've never had a case like that myself. If I did, I would have remembered."

"And so, I think, would everyone else. Can you go back seven years? Get all the reports filed up until three years ago?"

Tanaka shook his head.

"Recently, we've been managing to get everything into a centralized computer system, but three years ago that wasn't the case. All those reports are going to be buried in paper archives. Different archives, in different delegacias. It could take us months to find them all."

"But, as you said, you would have remembered. I'm willing to bet any other delegado would, too. You could talk to those men personally. Anybody who's retired, dead, or otherwise unavailable, you talk to their deputy."

"That I can do. Give me a week."

"Tell us more about the graves," Hector said. "How is it possible they went undiscovered for so long?"

"You know anything about the Serra da Cantareira?"

"Only that it's a park."

"Most of it. Not all. They call it the world's largest urban forest. Read that as rain forest, which really means jungle."

"Thick jungle?"

"I'll give you an example: a small plane on its final approach to Congonhas Airport went down back in 1963. Three people on board. They knew it was somewhere in the Serra. They drew a reverse vector from the end of the runway, spent almost a month searching for two kilometers to either side of that line. They sent in men and dogs, used a helicopter for four days straight. No dice. A biologist doing a study on monkeys finally stumbled across the wreckage in 1986, twenty-three years later. The pilot and both passengers, what was left of them, were still in the fuselage. People get lost in the Serra all the time. Nowadays, most people who venture off the paths carry a radio. You're crazy if you don't."

"You said most of the place was a park, but not all. What else is up there?"

"A few houses, a few condominiums, all of them pretty isolated. It's the kind of place that appeals to people who have to work in São Paulo, but who'd rather be living in the Amazon. So they went out and bought themselves pieces of the park."

Hector was the only one who looked surprised. He often affected cynicism, but he was still young, still learning. "They *bought* pieces of a city park?"

"So what else is new? You can buy just about anything in this town if you've got the money."

"Yeah, but Jesus, a city park."

"Same thing with the graveyard," Tanaka said.

"Wait a minute," Silva said, narrowing his eyes. "You mean to tell me those graves were on private property?"

"Uh-huh. Surrounded by park on all sides. The law would have given the owner access through the park if he'd asked for it. He never did."

"And who is this owner?"

"Was, not is. His name was Eduardo Noronha, and he conveniently died not fifteen days after he got title to the land. He willed it to a niece who's somewhere in Europe. His lawyers claim they're still looking for her."

"How long ago did this Noronha die?"

"Eleven years last January."

"Eleven years! And the land hasn't reverted to the city?"

"Nope."

"Who's paying the taxes?"

"A bank account is being held in escrow for the niece. It also feeds the lawyers and gives them power of attorney to resolve taxes and assessments."

"Sounds like a setup."

"Sounds like indeed."

"You speak to the lawyers?"

"I did. Got nowhere. I don't think they're being obstructive. They just don't know anything."

"This . . . cemetery? How isolated is it exactly?"

"Pretty isolated. The closest homes are six kilometers away, but you only get to drive five of those six. Then you have to cut through the rain forest. Ferns taller than you are, leaves a meter across, parrots, monkeys, snakes, beetles the size of your hand, the whole business. Once the jungle swallows you up, you feel like you're in the middle of the fucking Amazon."

"And people build houses in the middle of that?"

"Hell, no. Not in the middle of that. The houses are in a closed condominium. And the condominium is surrounded by a wall three meters high. You get inside that wall and you could be anywhere. Big green lawns, landscaped gardens, swimming pools, it looks like Alphaville."

Alphaville was a series of luxury condominiums, numbered 1 through 14, stretching from the suburb of Barueri to the suburb of Santana do Parnaiba. The walls that surrounded each project, and the guards stationed at their gates, guaranteed a degree of isolation from the otherwise harsh realities of the city.

Alphaville and the other closed condominiums were like small towns in the United States, an ersatz paradise only a few *Paulistas* could afford.

No crimes ever occurred in closed condominiums, at least

no crimes that any of the home owners would be willing to talk about.

"And that's where that *caseiro* lives, the guy who was searching for the dog? In a closed condominium?"

Tanaka bobbed his head.

"It's called Granja das Acacias. There are thirteen houses. We talked to nine of the owners and at least one employee from every house. They've got drivers, gardeners, caseiros, maids, all of them live-in because there's no city bus line that gets anywhere near the place. Nobody recalled any suspicious activity. None of the owners would admit it if they did. Property values, you know. It gets around that there's criminal activity in the neighborhood, the prices plummet. Those people are scared to death of that, almost more than they are of the crooks. And they're so cut off from the world that they could as well be living on Mars. They only come out from behind their walls to work, or to shop, or to go to a restaurant or a show. Otherwise they sit around their pools and talk about their servants, or whatever else it is that rich folks talk about."

"So no help there," Arnaldo said. He sighed. "I guess we're going to have to talk to the *buceta*."

Tanaka looked mystified at this use of the vulgar term for the female genitalia.

"Talk to the *what?*"

"A nickname," Silva said. "Godofredo Boceta is our profiler. He's going to want photos of the corpses *in situ* and of the site overall."

"Some nickname," Tanaka said. "I'll bet it pisses him off. Photos shouldn't be a problem. Dr. Caropreso's assistant must have taken a hundred of them. I'll ask her to send you copies."

"I could take care of that," Hector said, "call her directly, save you the trouble."

"I'd appreciate that," Tanaka said. "I have quite a bit on my plate at the moment." He glanced at his watch. "Now, if you gentlemen will excuse me, I have to get back to my delegacia. I'll keep in touch. You can count on it." He shook hands with them, turned on his heel, and hurried away.

Silva watched his retreating back for a moment, then turned and looked at his nephew.

"Your professional zeal is praiseworthy," he said.

"What?" Hector asked, innocently.

"Your generous offer to unburden Delegado Tanaka of the onerous task of calling Dr. Caropreso."

"I don't know what you're talking about," Hector said.

But of course he did.

Chapter Five

TANAKA LIED TO THE federal cops. He had no intention of going back to his delegacia.

His staff was accustomed to see him disappear at lunchtime on Friday and resurface on Monday morning. So accustomed, in fact, that he no longer bothered to inform them of his impending absences. They not only took those absences for granted, they followed his example. Friday afternoons at Tanaka's delegacia had taken on the aspect of Saturday mornings. There were empty desks throughout the building.

His plan on that particular Friday was to catch the three o'clock replay of the match between São Paulo's Corinthians and their nemesis from Rio de Janeiro, Flamengo.

But it was not to be.

He drove directly to his apartment, parked under the building, pressed the button for the elevator, and waited. And waited. He pressed the button again, and put his ear to the door to see if the damned thing was moving.

It wasn't.

"Piece of shit," he mumbled to himself and made for the stairs.

Tanaka's front door opened directly onto his living room. He turned on the television, went to the kitchen to get a beer, and found himself standing face-to-face with his own nemesis: his wife, Marcela.

Marcela was the daughter of Sicilian immigrants, one of those women who, when they stop getting taller start getting wider. For almost twenty years she'd outweighed Tanaka by a considerable margin, an attribute she used to good advantage when their spats turned physical. Her husband had learned to be wary of her fierce temper and took care not to provoke her. It was embarrassing to show up at the office with a split lip or a black eye, an occurrence so frequent that Tanaka had long ago run out of excuses to explain his injuries.

His hand had barely closed around one of the cold bottles in the refrigerator door, when he realized there was something amiss. His wife was seated at the kitchen table, attacking a cauliflower, ripping off the outer leaves, tearing pieces off the core, occasionally looking up at him with angry eyes.

From long experience, Tanaka knew that if he didn't confront the situation right then and there, Marcela would follow him into the living room, turn off the TV, and start haranguing him. He decided to get it over with, harboring the hope that he could appease her before the game began.

"Bad day, *querida?*" he said tentatively.

She narrowed her eyes in exasperation.

"Nilda Ferreira was here," she said. "They have *another* new car."

Nilda Ferreira, a svelte brunette some fifteen years younger and thirty kilograms lighter than Marcela, was the second wife of Inspector Adilson Ferreira. She and her husband lived in a spacious apartment in one of the tonier areas of the city, an apartment that was a far cry from the tiny two-bedroom affair that Tanaka shared with his spouse and two daughters. Nilda and Adilson were people who frequented all of São Paulo's better restaurants. They often took shopping trips to Miami. Once, they'd even been to Europe.

Nilda's passions were fine clothes and expensive jewelry, but to Tanaka it seemed as if the woman lived for the sole purpose of raising his wife to Olympian heights of jealousy. Marcela didn't begrudge Nilda's trim figure or high cheekbones. But she deeply coveted Nilda's income.

Neither Adilson nor his wife had been born to wealth. Nilda, like Marcela, didn't work outside the home. Tanaka was a full-fledged delegado titular, while Adilson was only a section head. But Adilson was the section head of the unit charged with investigating white-collar crimes.

And that made all the difference. When it came to augmenting a municipal cop's meager salary, there was no better assignment than the white-collar unit.

The unit consisted of only seven men. And one woman.

The woman hardly counted. She'd been on the job for a little over four months and was expected to continue for another six, after which there's be a new vacancy. Her name was Eleni Soares, and she was the daughter of Lieutenant Soares. Her father was the brother-in-law of the state secretary for public safety. Eleni's position was a stopgap measure, an opportunity to save money for her upcoming marriage.

The men were in a different category altogether. On the rare occasions when one of them retired, or died (those being the only reasons a male ever left the white-collar unit), new appointments were hotly contested and candidates had to fulfill at least one of the two requirements, preferably both. Adilson had: he'd been able to scrape up the cash necessary to grease the requisite palms, and he had an uncle in the hierarchy, a man who had considerable influence when it came to making appointments.

Adilson's sinecure hadn't come cheap. It had cost him twenty thousand reais, but he'd once told Tanaka that it was the best investment he'd ever made. He'd earned his money back within three months, and by the end of that year there were already eighteen businessmen that had Adilson to thank for being out on the street, instead of sitting in jail, accused of crimes like embezzlement.

Bribes were a way of life in the policia civil. Not *all* of the cops took them, of course. There were exceptions, but none of them worked in the white-collar unit. While other men spent their days shaking down petty criminals and traffic offenders, the white-collar cops moved from one rich prospect to the next, milking them for a percentage of their ill-gotten gains.

"Justice through enrichment" was the way Adilson liked to put it.

Some said true justice would have entailed fines rather than payoffs, would have entailed giving the perpetrators their day in court, putting them in front of a judge.

Adilson wouldn't have it. Judges, he reasoned, would simply do as he did. They'd take a bribe. Ergo the money had a zero chance of ever winding up in a government coffer. What's more, judges were a hell of a lot more expensive than cops, so Adilson was actually doing his "clients" a favor by keeping their costs down.

And, besides, what would happen if the money, by some remote chance, actually wound up in the hands of the government? What would happen then? The politicians would steal it, that's what.

The paltry sums of cash Tanaka was able to extort from the people who passed through his delegacia were a mere pittance compared with the bounty that Adilson reaped, and when Marcela compared the Ferreira's union with her own, Tanaka invariably came out as The Great Loser and she as The Great Victim.

It was a comparison frequently made, and one which invariably brought down the wrath of The Victim upon The Loser.

"That's the second new car in the last three years," she said, continuing to commit mayhem on the cauliflower. "What kind of a provider are you? Answer me that!"

"Not a very good one, I'm afraid," Tanaka said meekly.

He didn't really believe that. It wasn't as if he were an ordinary beat cop. He was a delegado titular for Christ's sake, in charge of an entire precinct. It was just . . . well, it was just that he hadn't had the breaks. And he sure as hell didn't have an influential uncle down at headquarters. But he knew that another attempt to explain himself to Marcela would not only be fruitless, it could also result in physical pain.

He backed out of the kitchen, put the bottle of beer down on the Formica-topped table next to the front door, and crept out of the house. He was already driving away when he looked in the rearview mirror and saw her standing up on their miniscule terrace with her hands on her hips. He had no doubt that she had a scowl on her face, but the distance was too great for him to see it.

THE THIRTY-THIRD Delegacia da Policia Civil, the domain ruled over by Delegado Titular Yoshiro Tanaka, hadn't been built to serve the needs of law enforcement. Even people unaware of the building's history could easily figure that out, because the original owner's name, and the year 1923, were still up there on the gable.

The name, Johann Fuchs, had belonged to an exporter of coffee who'd spent most of his life in Brazil, but who could never bring himself to give up his German nationality or his intention to die and be buried in his home town of Bremen.

But Fuchs suffered a sudden and fatal heart attack in 1944, and by that time Brazil was at war with Germany, so there was no chance of having his body shipped back to the *heimat* for internment.

Two years earlier, largely as the result of Johann's insistence, both of his sons had gone off to fight for *Volk und Vaderland*. Neither son came back. No survivors came forward to pay the taxes. In 1946, the city confiscated the property. Two years later, they turned it into a delegacia, and a delegacia it remained. The building was brick with small windows and a tiled roof, gloomy both inside and out. Its one remarkable feature was the holding cell for female prisoners. Remarkable, because it was painted a color called shocking pink.

When Tanaka took over, in 2001, the cell had been a drab place, its walls battleship gray, designed for short-term incarceration. But the Brazilian justice system being what it was (slow), and the availability of space being what *it* was (limited), the cell had become overcrowded, so much so that only half the women could lie down at any one time. "Short-term" had also become a flexible concept, generally meaning no less than three months. The crowding led to squabbles about space and ultimately to something far more serious.

Tanaka hadn't been in the job a week when a certain Maria Aparecida do Carmo, a prostitute jailed for rolling drunks because she'd grown too old to attract anyone who wasn't desperate for sex, had been strangled by one of her fellow inmates. The crime occurred at night. None of the women in the cell would admit to having witnessed it. The case wasn't going to be solved. Ever.

If Maria Aparecida had been a man, her death probably wouldn't have attracted much attention, but a female was something else. It was potential news. An enterprising reporter managed to get his hands on a twenty-three-year-old mug shot of Maria Aparecida. She was white, and back then she hadn't looked half bad.

Two days after the murder, the photo appeared in the *Jornal da Tarde*. The accompanying article implied that the policia civil were a bunch of bunglers, incapable of preventing the murders of hot-looking chicks like Maria Aparecida, even within one of their own delegacias.

Tanaka's boss, the delegado *regional*, didn't like the article one bit. Neither did *his* boss, the state secretary for public safety.

The obvious scapegoat was Tanaka.

He found himself contemplating the possibility of losing the cushy job he'd worked so long and so hard to get. Tanaka knew the bitches were bound to murder another of their number before long, and when they did, it could result in the sudden termination of his flourishing career. He desperately sought a solution, however cosmetic, that would keep his superiors off his back.

He found it, of all places, in his own bathroom. Marcela had left one of her magazines next to the toilet. One morning before work, bereft of other reading material, and faced with the necessity of remaining seated for a while, Tanaka started leafing through an article on household decoration.

Certain colors, it seemed, could have a soothing effect. Tanaka didn't quite believe it, but liberal journalists, the only kind who cared about some dead whore, and the ones that proliferated at the *Jornal da Tarde,* ate up that psychology stuff. Tanaka's mind was seldom far from his job, and the idea to paint the female holding cell came to him in a sudden flash of inspiration. He could already picture the headline: Caring Policemen Make Inmates' Lives Better.

His first problem would be funding the project. He solved it by passing the hat and pressuring all of his subordinates to contribute money for the brushes and the paint.

He left the choice of color to the prisoners. That was something else the men and women of the press would look kindly upon: treating the inmates with some degree of dignity, letting them make up their own minds about the decoration of the cage they lived in.

After some biting, scratching, and hair-pulling, the bitches settled upon shocking pink. It wasn't on the list of soothing colors mentioned in the magazine article, but Tanaka wasn't particularly concerned about that.

The prisoners themselves did the painting. When they were done, Tanaka called in the press. It was a slow news day, and the journalists thought a shocking-pink holding cell was interesting enough to merit pictures and video footage.

The delegado regional loved it. So did the state secretary for public safety.

The violence continued, but by the time someone stuck a hairpin through the eye, and into the brain, of a petty thief by the name of Marlene Quadros, the murder of a female prisoner had become old news, and Tanaka's superiors had other things to worry about. It helped, too, that Marlene Quadros was black and that she was ugly as sin, and always had been, even in her youth.

IN THE first week of his new posting, Delegado Tanaka had appropriated the largest room in the building as his office. He still had it. It was one flight up, directly above the (now fading) shocking-pink holding cell and beyond the detectives' squad room. And it was to that sanctum Tanaka fled to escape the hostility of his wife.

Still musing about the outcome of the Corinthians/ Flamengo game, and the attendant consequences for the national championship, Tanaka sat down in his chair and started going through paperwork. The third item in the pile caught his eye. He summoned his sergeant, Abilio Lucas, for an explanation. Fortunately for Lucas, it was one of the few Friday afternoons he'd elected not to take off.

"What's this about a family disappearing from Jardim Tonato?" Tanaka asked, tapping the report with his ballpoint pen.

A *jardim*, literally garden, usually meant a rather upscale neighborhood with handsome houses set on spacious lots. Jardim Tonato had neither. Jardim Tonato was a *favela*, a shantytown, a community of self-constructed shacks occupied by the poorest of the poor. Unless they happened to live in one, most people didn't give a damn about what happened in favelas like Jardim Tonato.

Sergeant Lucas certainly didn't. He seemed surprised that Tanaka did. Lucas moved closer and Tanaka, a nonsmoker, wrinkled his nose. The sergeant smelled strongly of tobacco.

"That one, huh?" Lucas said, craning his neck to see the report. "Nothing important, Senhor. Not worth your attention. Four nobodies. A stonemason, his wife, and two daughters. You know how it is with those people. They move around." He coughed a phlegmy cough.

"I've got some questions for the couple who made the complaint," Tanaka said.

The sergeant reached for a cigarette, realized where he was, and returned the pack to his pocket. Lucas wasn't a street cop. He was an office drone who worked from nine to five, Monday through Friday. Complications on this, the last day of his work week, could lead to overtime and Lucas hated working overtime. As a sergeant, he wasn't compensated for it.

"What kind of questions, Senhor? Maybe I can—"

"You can't," Tanaka snapped. "Get them both in here, Sergeant."

He held out the report.

Lucas hesitated for a beat before he took it.

"Tuesday okay, Delegado?"

"Sooner. This afternoon, if possible. Monday morning at the latest."

* * *

THE COUPLE Tanaka asked Lucas to track down was named Portella, Ernesto and Clarice. Ernesto was a carpenter with no fixed place of work. His wife was a *faixineira*, a cleaning woman, and divided her days among various clients.

The Portellas, like their missing friends, lived in Jardim Tonato, and Jardim Tonato, like all favelas, was a place without telephones. To be absolutely certain of being able to present the couple by Monday morning, Lucas was going to have to work late, or he was going to have to cut some time out of his weekend.

He elected to work late.

By the time the Portellas got home, Lucas had already been waiting for about three hours. It was past 8:00 pm, and he was nervous about being in a favela, no place for a policeman after sunset. He was also royally resentful about the shambles that had been made of his Friday night.

"About fucking time," he said.

"Oh, *pardon me* for having to earn a living, instead of sitting around behind a desk and sucking on government tit," Ernesto said.

"You better watch your mouth," Lucas said, and then, when Ernesto didn't respond: "My boss wants you people down at his delegacia on Monday morning at seven o'clock sharp."

This time it was the woman who gave him some lip.

"What for?" she said.

Lucas looked her up and down. She appeared to be the bossy type. If there was one thing he'd learned as a cop, it was you didn't give people like that any rope. "Fucked if I know," he said. "Be there."

"But we both work—"

He didn't let her finish. "Seven am," he said, "And not a

minute later." He turned his back and walked away before she could say anything else.

Lucas knew Tanaka wouldn't be in until nine, but the fucking Portellas, by coming home so late, had trimmed three hours from his Friday night's drinking.

And now they were going to suffer for it.

Chapter Six

ON MONDAY MORNING, AT six forty-five, Clarice Portella dragged her muttering husband through the front door of Tanaka's delegacia and approached the corporal behind the desk.

"I'm Clarice Portella. This is my husband, Ernesto. Sergeant Lucas said—"

"Yeah," the corporal said. "He called me. I know all about it. Wait over there."

"I told the sergeant. We both work. We—"

"Over there."

Before Ernesto could raise his voice, Clarice grabbed his arm and led him to one of the plastic chairs that lined the wall.

Lucas showed up at quarter to nine. By that time the corporal was fed up with hearing Ernesto's complaints, and Clarice was livid.

"Hey, you, Sergeant," she began, waving a hand to catch his attention.

"Won't be much longer," Lucas said, and strode by without breaking his pace.

AT NINE o'clock, Yoshiro Tanaka bustled through the squad room and opened the door to his office. Lucas was standing by the window.

Tanaka sniffed the air. "Have you been smoking in here, Sergeant?"

"No, Delegado."

It was a lie and both of them knew it.

Tanaka went straight to the wastebasket and looked inside.

There was no trace of cigarette ash. Lucas was stupid, but not that stupid. Tanaka went to the window. It was one of those that swung out on a hinge, and it was slightly ajar.

Insufficient evidence.

"What are you doing in my office, Sergeant?"

"Waiting for you, Delegado. Those people you wanted to see? They're outside."

"Ah." The stern look on Tanaka's face vanished.

Luca's curiosity ratcheted up a notch. Tanaka didn't do anything to satisfy it.

"Bring them in," was all he said.

"BUT WE already told everything to the sergeant," Clarice Portella said a couple of minutes later. She turned and looked at the door behind her, as if she were expecting Lucas to come back and join them.

"I'm sure that's what you think," Tanaka said.

The woman was hunger thin, a *mulata* with bad teeth, far past the age of childbearing. Or maybe not. Favela people, Tanaka thought, always looked older than they were. And they bred like rabbits, which had a way of aging them still further. This one probably had ten kids at home.

She didn't look very smart, either. Matter of fact, she looked downright stupid, the way she sat staring at him with her mouth agape. Tanaka figured he'd better spell things out, take it slow and easy.

"Most people think that," he said. "Most people think they've told us everything after they tell it the first time, but it's been our experience that—"

"The sergeant wrote it all down, and then he typed it and we signed it."

"I know. I read it."

Clarice glanced at the clock on the wall. She wasn't wearing a watch. "Both of us have to get to work," she said.

Tanaka smiled, trying to put her at ease. "I'll be happy to give you a note for your employer—for *both* your employers," he corrected himself, shifting his gaze to her husband.

"A lot of good that's going to do," Ernesto Portella said, his tone surly.

He, too, looked like he needed a good meal. He was wearing a beat-up blue cap with the logo of the PCB, Brazil's Communist Party. The hat was cheap and fraying around the brim, obviously a promotional piece from the last election. Dirty blue jeans and a filthy T-shirt completed his ensemble. The little finger on his left hand was missing, probably severed in some kind of work-related accident. An ugly scar ran from the old wound across the back of his hand and halfway up his bare arm.

"They pay us by the hour," he said. "They don't give a shit if we show up late or not. We're the ones who suffer, not those fucking capitalist bloodsuckers."

Tanaka frowned. Fortunately for Ernesto Portella, membership in the PCB was no longer illegal.

"You want to do the right thing for your friends, don't you?" Tanaka asked. "The Lisboas *are* your friends aren't they?"

Clarice nodded her head in agreement. After a moment her husband did, too.

Tanaka had almost said *were* your friends.

Ernesto took a cigarette and a pack of matches out of his breast pocket.

"No smoking in here," Tanaka said.

"Then I'll go outside."

He got up.

Tanaka slammed a palm down on his desk.

"No, you won't," he said and pointed at the chair. "You'll sit right there until I tell you you're free to go."

Clarice seemed startled. Ernesto wasn't as easily intimidated. "You can't—"

His wife interrupted him. "Ernesto," she said, "shut up."

Ernesto resumed his seat, crossed his arms, and stared out the window.

Tanaka took up where he'd left off, this time directing himself exclusively to the woman.

"As I was saying," he said, "it often helps to go over everything again with a different interviewer. Sometimes we pick up small details that didn't come to light the first time around. And small details can be of great significance. Let's start again from the beginning. There are four of them, right? The father, Edmundo—"

"Edmar," she corrected him.

Tanaka glanced at the first page of Lucas's report. He picked up his pen, crossed out Edmundo, and wrote Edmar before continuing.

"You see? Even policemen make mistakes."

"Even policemen," Ernesto echoed, his voice dripping with sarcasm.

Tanaka elected to act as if he hadn't heard him. "The father, *Edmar,* the wife, Augusta, and their two daughters, Mari and Julia."

"Yes. Mari is Mariana. Everyone calls Julia Juju."

"And Edmar Lisboa is a stonemason, is that right?" He looked up from the report and waited for her to nod. When she did, he said, "This job he was offered, how did it come about?"

"I already told that to Sergeant Lucas."

Tanaka sighed. He hadn't overestimated the woman's intelligence, or rather lack of it.

"Senhora Portella, please. Forget Sergeant Lucas. Make believe you're telling me the story for the first time."

"Oh, yes. I see. Well, Edmar was building a wall. A man came up, watched him work and then he said he was looking for a stonemason to work on a fazenda. He was offering good money. He was even offering a house. Edmar liked the country. He was raised in the country. He only came here because he couldn't get work back home in Pernambuco. You know how it is up there."

Pernambuco was a state far to the northeast, tucked in between Bahia and Ceará. Tanaka did, indeed, know how it was up there. Everybody did. No industry, great poverty, some cities with twice as many women as men because of mass migration southward to where the jobs were.

And that's why my town is filling up with a bunch of fucking Nordestinos *like you and your friends,* Tanaka thought. But he didn't say it. Instead, he said, "So he took the job? Just like *that?*" Tanaka snapped his fingers.

She gave a little jump.

Not only stupid. Nervous, too.

She shook her head.

"No," she said, "Edmar isn't like that. He said he'd have to talk to Augusta."

"He's a pussy," Ernesto said. "Guy has no balls at all. She pushes him around."

"Shut up, Ernesto," she said.

The way she said it reminded Tanaka of his wife, Marcela. Ernesto went back to looking out of the window.

"So then what?" Tanaka asked, identifying just the least little bit with her husband.

"The man came to talk to her."

"To your friend, Augusta?"

Clarice nodded.

"He showed her pictures in a book."

"What kind of pictures?"

"Of the fazenda."

"And she bought the idea?"

"She what?"

"She agreed to go?"

Clarice nodded her head. "She quit her job," she said, "and Edmar quit his, and the man came to take them away. That was a week after his first visit. The street was too narrow to bring the truck up to the house. We had to carry everything down to the corner. Once the truck was loaded, the family went in a van."

"So there was a truck and a van?"

"That's right."

Tanaka made a note. "And that was the last time you saw them?"

"Last time," she said.

"You mentioned a letter." Tanaka put a forefinger on Sergeant Lucas's report. "Where is it?"

"Here." Clarice opened her purse, took out an envelope, and handed it to him. It was still sealed and quite thick. He bent it back and forth between his fingers.

"What's in it?"

"Augusta worked for Dona Inez Menezes," Clarice said. "Dona Inez owed Augusta some money. Augusta asked me to send it to her. I bought a postal money order and wrapped some paper around it so it wouldn't attract attention."

Tanaka scrutinized the front of the envelope. There was a stamp in red ink: RETURN TO SENDER.

"How did you get it?" he asked.

"Get what, Senhor?"

This is like pulling teeth, Tanaka thought.

"This address," he said.

He showed her the front of the envelope.

"Oh. That. The man wrote it for me."

"What man?"

"The same man who got Edmar the job."

"And the same man who took the family away?"

"Yes. He drove the van. He brought another man with him to drive the truck."

"Can you remember his name?"

She closed her eyes and pursed her lips. Tanaka waited, tapping his fingers on the desk. "Roberto . . . Something," she said at last. "He's a *carioca*."

It didn't surprise Tanaka that she could identify the man as a carioca, a native of Rio de Janeiro. He wouldn't have had to tell her where he was from. She would have heard it, heard all those sibilant s's that littered the speech of everyone who came from there. As to the name, Roberto, it wasn't going to help. There were only a few names more common.

"You'd recognize him? If you saw him again, I mean?"

Clarice nodded.

"Me, too," Ernesto said. "I helped load all of their stuff onto the truck, and some of it was heavy. The lazy bastard just stood there, giving orders. He didn't lift a finger. Typical fucking carioca."

Cariocas, most of Brazil agreed, were indolent. This time, Clarice didn't tell her husband to shut up. Apparently, she agreed with his evaluation.

"Describe this carioca," Tanaka said.

"He has black hair. I think he puts oil in it."

"Taller than me?" Tanaka asked.

"Yes."

That was no surprise. Almost everybody was taller than Yoshiro Tanaka.

"Show me," he said. "Show me how big he was."

She stood up and hesitantly held up a hand, palm downward, about thirty centimeters above her head.

"Beard? Mustache?"

She sat down again.

"Mustache."

"Eyes. What color?"

"Brown . . . I think."

"He wears a chain," Ernesto said, "with a big fucking medallion from Flamengo hanging on the end of it. Can you beat it? Flamengo. Here in São Paulo. Cheeky bastard."

Tanaka grimaced. The medallion was an affront. The team was anathema to fans who hailed from São Paulo, and those fans included Yoshiro Tanaka. The medallion was also new information, something Lucas hadn't put in his report. Tanaka made a note of it.

"The address?" he asked. "He wrote it himself?"

She nodded.

"Do you still have the paper?"

"No. I threw it away after I copied it into my address book. Did I do wrong?"

"Can't be helped," Tanaka said. "You're sure you got it right?"

"Augusta's oldest daughter, Mari, has a friend," Clarice said, "a girl named Teresa. She came to see me. Her letter was returned, too. What Teresa had, and what I had, was the same."

"And the Lisboa girl hasn't written to this . . ."

"Teresa. No. And she promised she would. There has to be something wrong."

"Just because your letter was returned? Just because neither of them have written?"

Clarice opened her mouth in surprise.

"You mean Sergeant Lucas didn't write up the part about the shop?"

Tanaka was puzzled. "Shop? What shop?"

Clarice lifted her eyes in exasperation.

"But that was the whole *point*," she said. "*That's* why we came here in the first place."

Chapter Seven

THEY'D BEEN SHOPPING FOR a cupboard. Actually, Clarice was doing the shopping, and Ernesto was tagging along to make sure she didn't go overboard on the price. It was late Saturday afternoon, just before six o'clock, three weeks to the day after the Lisboa family's departure.

Ernesto was weary and footsore. He wanted to go home, take off his shoes, loosen his belt, and pour himself a tall glass of beer, all of which was exactly as Clarice had planned it. *Armarios*, priced like the one he'd found "far too expensive" that morning at ten, he'd deemed "reasonable" by two and a "pretty good deal" by five thirty. All she had to do was to keep him on his feet for another half hour or so, and he'd be ripe for the picking.

"How about this one?" he said, giving the price tag on a squat, triangular cupboard only a cursory glance.

She shook her head.

"No," she said. "I want a taller one, like—"

"Like the one Augusta has," he sighed. "Yeah, you told me."

Ernesto sat down on a cane chair with a torn seat, took off his shoes, and started to massage his feet. Clarice, as if hers weren't hurting at all, moved forward into the gloom.

The secondhand furniture shop had, at one time, been three adjoining houses. An enterprising merchant had purchased them, knocked holes in the intervening walls, and created one huge space piled high with tables, chairs, bed frames, cupboards, and cabinets. There were only a few sales people. The entire area was dimly lit.

Clarice stopped in front of a dining table.

It couldn't be.

She bent over to examine the surface. In the near darkness, she could just make out the cigarette burn; the one Augusta tried to remove with steel wool and shoe polish. She looked for the ring-shaped stain that Mari had made with a can of Guaraná. And found it. The chairs were there, too, even the one with the broken back. She was about to call Ernesto when she spotted the cupboard. She walked around a sofa with stained upholstery, moved a small table out of the way, and examined it more closely.

Ernesto got up and came over to join her. "There you go," he said, tapping the front door, "An *armario* just like Augusta's."

The relief on his face would normally have pleased her, but not this time. A worried frown crinkled her forehead.

Ernesto fingered the price tag tied to one of the knobs. "Not a bad price, either. Let me see if I can talk the guy down a little."

Footsore or not, Ernesto Portella was a tough man to separate from his money. He was about to go in search of the shop owner when she put a hand on his arm.

"Ernesto," she said, "Augusta's cupboard had a hole on the inside."

"Clarice, why are you always—?"

She tightened her grip on his arm. "Pay attention. She used to keep her rice in plastic sacks."

"Plastic sacks?" He scoffed. "How dumb can you get? Everybody knows rats—"

"—can chew through plastic. And chew through wood. And one did, right through the back of her cabinet."

"And you think . . . ?"

She took her hand off his arm, opened the door, and pointed.

"Right there," she said.

The hole was almost seven centimeters in diameter.

It must have been a huge rat.

"WE LOOKED through the rest of the shop," Clarice told Tanaka, suddenly more garrulous than she'd been at any time during the interview. "Her bedside tables were there, too."

"Sure of that, are you?"

Clarice bobbed her head. "I remember the day she bought them. I helped her carry them home. Believe me, Delegado; something terrible must have happened. Augusta wouldn't have sold those things. I'm her friend, and I know. I asked her about the cupboard. I wanted to buy it myself, but she said she'd never sell it. It was her mother's."

Tanaka let her run out of steam, and then he stood up. "I'm going to that shop," he said, "and I want both of you to come with me."

"*Merda*," Ernesto said.

Chapter Eight

ON THAT SAME MONDAY morning, while Tanaka was interviewing the Portellas, Arnaldo and Silva were meeting with the federal police's criminal profiler, Dr. Godofredo Boceta.

Boceta was a man in his midforties with a receding hairline and horn-rimmed bifocals that looked as if they'd come out of a 1950's catalog. He never used one word if he could use two, never employed a shorter word if he could think of a longer one, and always took detours before he got to the point. He was one of those people who could break up a friendly office conversation around the watercooler just by putting in an appearance. To say he was boring was an understatement. Dr. Boceta's verbosity drove Arnaldo nuts.

The profiler sat upright in a chair across from the two federal cops. He was looking at one of the photos, the one that showed the overall view of the burial ground in the Serra da Cantareira. His mouth was puckered, as if he were sucking on a lemon.

"Do you know anything about Alzheimer's?" he asked.

"I had an uncle who died of it," Silva said.

"In an institution or at home?" Boceta asked.

"An institution."

"Did they use art as an activity for the patients?"

Arnaldo released a long breath, almost a sigh.

"I don't recall," Silva said. "Why?"

"Sometimes institutions hold exhibitions of patients' artwork," Boceta said, ignoring the question.

Arnaldo shifted in his chair. He was a bulky man, and his movement caused a considerable rustle. Silva kicked him under the table.

"Ouch," Arnaldo said.

"And?" Silva said.

Boceta looked back and forth, finally decided to ignore the interjection, and continued to address Silva.

"*And* if you look at the art of Alzheimer's patients, you'll notice something curious. Not all the time, but often."

Arnaldo couldn't contain himself. "What the hell has this got to do with what we should be talking about?"

Dr. Boceta pulled his glasses down to the end of his nose and stared unblinkingly at Arnaldo. His stare reminded Silva of that of a fish.

"If you'll contain your impatience," Boceta said, "I might tell you." He removed his glasses and rubbed his eyes, stretching out the moment.

Sometimes Silva thought Boceta knew exactly what he was doing to people. He was determined not to let the man get to him.

"Alzheimer's patients often draw trees and domiciles," Boceta said. "And as the disease progresses, the windows and doors of the domiciles tend to diminish in magnitude. One day they disappear."

Silva threw Boceta a conversational bone: "And the trees?"

"Ah, yes, the trees. The trees lose their leaves, extend longer and longer roots. Mostly, the patients choose to draw those roots in black."

Arnaldo let out another long, slow breath. Silva kicked him again, more gently this time. Arnaldo didn't react. Boceta put his glasses back on and resumed his study of the photograph.

"I'm telling you this to illustrate the correlation between

artistic expression and diseases of the mind. Now, take your serial killer. A disturbed individual often shares common characteristics with other disturbed individuals with the same malady. That, gentlemen, is a good deal of what criminal profiling is all about."

"I see," Silva said, hoping that Boceta was finally getting to the point.

"I'm sure you're aware that serial murderers, people who have a compulsion to kill, tend to demonstrate a lack of affect, often take trophies, and tend to specialize in certain kinds of victims. By certain kinds of victims I mean little boys, little girls, women, young men if the killer is a male and has homosexual tendencies."

"Yes."

"There are always exceptions, of course. Most serial killers are men, but there have been women, notably a prostitute in the United States named Aileen Wuornos, a lesbian who demonstrated a distinctly masculine approach to homicide."

Arnaldo stood, looked as if he were going to say something, but didn't. He walked to the credenza and poured himself a glass of water. Boceta waited until Arnaldo had resumed his seat before continuing.

"The expression, I might almost say *artistic* expression, of serial killers often extends to the way they bury their victims. Sometimes they pose them, as if for a photograph. Most commonly, they don't bury all of them in one central location. If they do, it's generally in their home, under the porch, for example, or under the floor."

"But there *are* cases where they set up their own little cemeteries?" Silva asked, his interest awakening.

"Indeed there are. And in most of those cases, the first victim is buried at the apex of a triangle with the other victims radiating out from there."

"*Most* cases?" Arnaldo might as well have said *what help is that*, because that's the way it came out.

Boceta bristled. "This isn't an exact science," he snapped. "We're dealing with statistical probabilities. Every serial killer is insane in his own insane way. There are always exceptions. Always. But they're always insane. That's why the Americans' criminal trials of serial killers are so ludicrous. Serial killers don't belong on their death rows. They belong in institutions. Their legal definition of insanity, and the aberrations that stem from it, are an abomination. Any fool can plainly see—"

"Conclusions, Godo?" Silva interrupted, trying to get the profiler back on track.

"Yeah, and sometime within the next twenty minutes, if you please," Arnaldo said.

Boceta sniffed, as if Arnaldo emitted an odor that offended him. "Alright, here's what we know," he said, addressing himself exclusively to Silva. "The killer shows no apparent preference for sex or age; he buries his victims side by side, indicating he doesn't give particular importance to any one victim; sometimes he buries them in a mass grave, adults and kids all heaped in together, not taking any care to arrange them, just disposing of the corpses. My conclusion is that he doesn't attach any aesthetic value to what he's doing, that he isn't milking it for a vicarious thrill, that he is, in short, not acting out of any inner compulsion. He's not your standard serial killer. I say *he*, but only to avoid repetition. I don't want to waste your time."

"Perish the thought," Arnaldo said.

Boceta narrowed his eyes and opened his mouth to reply, but Silva deftly cut him off. "So we could be dealing with a her, or a them, instead of a him?"

Boceta kept looking at Arnaldo. He looked so long that

Silva was arriving at the conclusion that he'd have to repeat his question. But then the profiler said, "Exactly."

It was probably the most succinct answer that Godofredo Boceta had ever given to anyone.

Silva pressed his advantage. "Okay, but I'm not sure I get it. What you're saying is—"

"I'm saying that I sense some utilitarian purpose here."

"Utilitarian purpose? What do you mean by a utilitarian purpose?"

"Well . . . genocide, for example."

"*Genocide?* You call genocide a utilitarian purpose?"

"In the mind of the perpetrator, or perpetrators? Of course it is. Haven't you heard the term *ethnic cleansing?* The people who practice it actually believe that they're making a positive contribution to their societies. Think of the Turks and the Albanians, the Hausa and the Ibo, the Bosnians and the Serbs, the Nazis and the—"

"Enough. I take your point."

"In all the cases I've cited, and many more that I *could* cite, the killers attached no great significance to the disposal of the bodies. Burning, dissolving in acid, burying, tossing into rivers, it was all the same to them, a simple problem of disposal where ritual played no role. There are consistencies between what they did and the behavior we see here."

"So you'd rule out ritual killings?"

Boceta waved a finger in Silva's face. "I never said that. Don't put words in my mouth. I merely suggested a hypothesis. There are, of course, other explanations."

"Ones in which ritual might be involved?"

"Of course."

"Give me an example."

Boceta thought for a moment. Then he said, "A use for body parts, perhaps."

"Like what?"

"Some believe that the eating of human flesh conveys benefits. That, by consuming another human being, you take on some of their life force."

"Now we got cannibals in São Paulo?" Arnaldo said. "Fat chance."

"I wasn't talking to you, Agente. Whether cannibals are active in São Paulo or not is no concern of mine."

"No? So why are you suggesting it?"

Boceta shot Arnaldo a beady-eyed stare before turning back to Silva.

"You might want to inquire, Chief Inspector, if the skeletal structures of the victims were intact."

"Why?"

"In ritual killings, the murderers often go after specific bones or body parts containing those bones. If the skeletal structures are incomplete, that could tell you something. Mind you, it would only be significant if the same mutilation took place in every case."

Arnaldo turned to Silva. "Remember when Dr. Couto cut that assistant of his short? Maybe she was gonna say something about missing parts."

"Maybe," Silva said. "And I'm sure Hector would be delighted to call her up and ask her."

Chapter Nine

SERGEANT LUCAS KNEW TANAKA was not a man to be moved by the disappearance of a family of nobodies from a favela. There had to be something else driving him, and in Lucas's experience, one of Tanaka's principal motivators was money. Lucas, too, was not averse to earning a few reais on the side. If he hung around and kept a close eye on his boss, he hoped some of the crumbs might fall to him.

When he heard Tanaka's door open, he kept his head down, picked up a pile of paperwork, and dropped it on top of the newspaper he was reading.

"Sergeant?"

Lucas looked up. "*Às ordens*, Delegado."

"Get me a car."

Lucas repressed a smile. Tanaka drove himself to and from the office. On all other occasions, he took advantage of his seniority and had himself driven. The person who normally did the driving was Sergeant Lucas.

Lucas stood up. "Right away, Delegado."

Tanaka looked at the surface of Lucas's desk. The paperwork didn't quite cover the sports pages of the *Diário Popular*.

"And since your hands are so full this morning," he said dryly, "I'll dispense with your services and drive myself."

THE SHOP was on a crowded street in Bom Retiro, a place of broken and narrow sidewalks, rumbling trucks, and crumbling facades. Once, years ago, it had been a residential neighborhood, lower-middle class even then, going downhill ever since. The shop's proprietor had moved a number of his bulkier and cheaper pieces into the open air, completely blocking the space between the shop and the curb. Tanaka had no doubt that the man was slipping a few reais to the cops on the beat to get away with occupying so much of a public thoroughfare.

He parked in front of the hardware store next door. The guy arranging a display in the window gave the police car an apprehensive glance. He looked relieved when the people who got out of it started walking toward his neighbor's establishment.

Next to one of the rolled-up metal doors was a sign, black letters on enameled metal, identifying Avri Cohen as the proprietor.

"Dead these two years," a balding man with a paunch told Tanaka as the delegado stood there, making a note of it. "I own the place now. Name's Goldman."

Tanaka produced his policeman's identity card.

"Hang on a second," Goldman said. He took out a pair of reading glasses, gave the card a careful inspection, and then said, "What can I do for you, Delegado?"

He didn't strike Tanaka as being nervous.

"For the moment," Tanaka said, "you can just follow along. Lead the way Senhora Portella."

Clarice navigated her way through the warren of furniture and stopped in front of a cupboard. Stained a walnut brown, with two latticework panels for ventilation, the triangular cupboard had been designed to fit into the corner of a room.

"This one," she said. "And that's the dining set over there." She frowned and looked around. "I don't see the bedside tables. They were right there, between the sofa and the wall."

"Formica tops?" Goldman asked.

"Formica tops," she confirmed.

"I sold them. What's this about?"

Tanaka turned a cold eye on the merchant.

"Stolen goods," he said.

Senhor Goldman held up his hands, palms outward, as if he were pushing something away from him.

"I had no idea," he said. "I swear. No idea."

"No?"

"No. I run a legitimate business. I pay my taxes."

"Yeah, I'm sure you do," Tanaka said. "No cash deals, right?"

Goldman reddened. "Well, yeah, sure," he said. "A lot of my customers haven't got bank accounts, much less credit cards. I wanna do business, I have to sell for cash. But I declare all of it."

"Uh-huh," Tanaka said skeptically.

"And I never buy for cash. I pay by check."

"Do you now?" Tanaka said. "So you've got a record of who sold you this stuff? The cupboard? The bedside tables with the Formica tops?"

"Sure I do. All part of the same purchase. I've got the canceled checks in the back. Probably even have an itemized receipt with the guy's name on it. I'll go have a look."

"Not alone, you won't," Tanaka said. "Does this place have a back door?"

Tanaka's caution was unfounded. Goldman had no intention of making a run for it. And he'd been telling the truth. He had both a canceled check and an itemized receipt, signed by someone named Roberto Ribeiro.

"That's it!" Clarice said when she heard the name. "That's the name I was trying to think of, Roberto Ribeiro. He's the one who offered Edmar the job. The carioca. The one who took them away."

Tanaka's heart lifted when he saw the logotype on the check, lifted even more when he saw the endorsement on the back. He, Ribeiro and Goldman all shared the same bank: Bradesco, Brazil's second-largest and least exclusive banking institution. It meant he wouldn't have to go through official channels. He could track the man down without leaving a trail.

"I may be here awhile," he said to Clarice. "You can go now. If I find any trace of your friends, I'll be in touch."

"Who's gonna pay for the bus?" Ernesto said.

"You are," Tanaka said.

Before Ernesto could open his mouth to reply, Clarice took his arm and led him toward the exit. Tanaka thought he heard him say the word "fascist" as they went out the door. He turned back to Goldman. "You remember what this guy Ribeiro looked like?"

"Mulatto," Goldman said promptly, no longer nervous. "Big mustache, hair slicked back with oil, wearing a chain with a Flamengo medallion. Can you beat that, somebody running around São Paulo with a Flamengo medallion? He's lucky he's so goddamned big. If he wasn't, somebody would beat the crap out of him."

"That somebody would have to get in line behind me," Tanaka said.

Goldman protested when Tanaka told him he was taking both the check and the receipt. "I need that stuff for taxes," he said. "Couldn't you just make a note of—"

"No," Tanaka said.

"But—"

"If you want to stand here talking," Tanaka said, "maybe we can discuss the merchandise you've got out there blocking a public sidewalk."

Goldman, to his credit, blushed. "The guys on the beat know all about it." he said.

"The guys on the beat," Tanaka said, "report to me."

"How about a cup of coffee, Delegado?" Goldman asked immediately.

"Coffee would be fine," Tanaka said.

TANAKA WAITED until he was behind the wheel of the car before taking out his cell phone and calling Ricardo Fortunato.

"What can I do for you today, Yoshiro?"

Tanaka and his bank manager were on first-name terms. A few years earlier, when inflation had been running at upwards of 30 percent a month, Tanaka had spent more time on the telephone with Ricardo Fortunato than he had with his current mistress. In those days, you had to invest your money in the overnight market or you might wind up scratching for food at the end of the month. The people who manipulated the investments were the bank managers, people like Ricardo Fortunato. It was all done on the basis of verbal commitments; paperwork following after the transactions had been made. Relationships of trust were created, relationships that persisted long after hyperinflation had become history.

"I need some information, Ricardo."

"Not about your own account, I take it?"

"No. And you know how it is when I have to go through channels. Takes too goddamned long."

"I understand," Ricardo said, his voice softer than before.

Ricardo didn't have an enclosed office. His desk was right in front of the long counter where the tellers worked. Tanaka imagined him looking over his shoulder to make sure no one was listening.

"I'm holding a canceled check," Tanaka said, "paid out of one Bradesco account into another. The recipient's name is Roberto Ribeiro. Got that?"

"Got it. What do you want to know?"

"I want Ribeiro's address."

"Easy."

"The check was issued by—"

"Don't need it. Just give me the numbers: the payee's account at the lower left and whatever's written on the back."

Tanaka did.

He heard Ricardo clicking away at his keyboard.

"Here it is," the bank manager said. "Got a pen?"

Tanaka couldn't believe it was going to be that easy.

Chapter Ten

BOCETA HAD MORE TO offer, but as usual, he was going to make them work for it. If people didn't listen to him around the watercooler, they sure as hell had to sit still when they asked him for an opinion—no matter how long it took. He settled back in his chair.

"Remember Villasboas?" he said.

"Oh, Jesus Christ, here we go again," Arnaldo said.

Boceta took off his glasses. "You are becoming tiresome, Agente."

"Me? Tiresome? You should have to listen—"

Silva put a hand on Arnaldo's arm and squeezed. "Villasboas," he said. "I was working in São Paulo then. I remember, but I'm a little foggy on the details."

"Who the hell is Villasboas?" Arnaldo said.

"Not who," Boceta said, taking his usual satisfaction at the opportunity to correct someone. "Your question should have been *what*. Villasboas is a what. More specifically, it's a town in Pará."

Pará was the state that embraced the mouth of the Amazon River, a huge area, much of it remote jungle.

"Alright," Arnaldo said, letting out a long sigh of defeat. "You got me. I'll bite. What happened in Villasboas?"

Boceta's smile was more like a smirk. He took his time about answering. "Some bodies were found," he finally said, "probably only a small percentage of the victims, but enough to excite interest. They were all young, all male, and all of them had their genitals removed. One of the perpetrators confessed. He was a medical doctor. The other people he implicated, another doctor, a few lawyers, some prominent local businessmen, denied involvement. It appears that he and his coreligionists all signed an oath in their own blood: lifelong obedience, secrecy about the rituals—"

Arnaldo tried to hurry things along. "Coreligionists? So they were members of some kind of cult?"

Boceta, running true to form, refused to be hurried. "Can you imagine any other reason why I might call them coreligionists?"

Arnaldo sighed. "No," he said.

"Of course you can't," Boceta said. "Yes, it was a cult, a satanic cult. They believed that the devil wanted anyone with certain characteristics . . ." He paused and looked at the ceiling.

"What's the matter?" Silva said.

"I forgot some of the characteristics. I'll go to my office and look them up."

He started to rise. Arnaldo put the heels of his hands over his eyes.

Silva motioned the profiler back into his chair. "That won't be necessary, Godo. Look them up later. Put them in your written report."

"Ah, yes, my written report. Alright. Where was I?"

"The devil wanted everyone with certain characteristics . . ." Silva prompted.

"To die. And the members of the cult were to be his instrument. To reward them for their obedience, he'd send a spaceship to rescue them from the destruction of the earth."

"And they truly believed that crap?" Arnaldo asked.

"Enough to murder at least fourteen people," Boceta said.

Chapter Eleven

CLOSING IN ON RIBEIRO had been far simpler than Tanaka had dared to hope. In addition to the address, Ricardo had supplied the man's telephone number.

Tanaka's call was answered by a sleepy male voice.

He hung up and immediately called for backup. An hour later, he and Detective Danilo Coimbra rousted Ribeiro out of bed in his surprisingly neat and clean two-room flat. Overriding his protestations of innocence, they cuffed him and hauled him off to Tanaka's delegacia.

In the early stages of his interrogation, Ribeiro demonstrated a self-confidence that bordered on arrogance.

"Hey, Delegado, you didn't have to drag me all the way down here. I woulda taken care of you, and that partner of yours, too, without going to all of this trouble. I mean, time is money, right?"

"Is it? Is time money? Are you trying to bribe me, Ribeiro?"

"I got a good friend on the force. Maybe you know him. Lieutenant Soares?"

"Yeah, I know Soares," Tanaka said.

It was true. Tanaka *did* know Soares—and so did everyone else in the policia civil. Soares was the brother-in-law of Adolfo Mendes, the secretary for public safety, and Mendes was the top law-enforcement official in the state's government.

Soares was a man who'd made a fortune by being a cop. It was said that most of his earnings went to his brother-in-law and the governor, but Soares did very well with what was left for him. He drove a Lexus, and the parties at his beach house in Guarujá were said to be fantastic, although Tanaka couldn't confirm that from personal experience. Even though he was only a lieutenant himself, Soares would never think of inviting a mere delegado titular.

Soares wouldn't invite a lowlife like Ribeiro either, but he *would* help him get out of jail, for a price.

"Why don't you just call the lieutenant?" Ribeiro said. "He'll vouch for me. I'm sure he will."

"I'm sure he will, too," Tanaka said. "But maybe we don't have to do that."

Ribeiro smiled. "Well, I'm glad to hear that," he said. "Means there's more to go around."

"More of what?"

"Come on, Delegado. You know what I'm talking about."

"Money?"

"Yeah, money."

"So what have you done, Ribeiro, that you feel you have to offer me a payoff?"

"Nothing. I haven't done anything. It's just the . . . convenience. Your time is valuable, right? So is mine. So let's cut to the chase. What do you think you have on me, and how much is it gonna cost to make it go away?"

That was when Tanaka hit him with it. He told him he didn't want his money. He told him he knew about the furniture and the Lisboas. He told him he had a canceled check from Goldman, that he had witnesses who could identify the furniture, who could put him at the scene on the day the family disappeared. He told him about the corpses down at the Instituto Médico Legal. And then he tied it all together: he accused Ribeiro of kidnapping entire families—and killing them.

"And now," he said, "all I need to know is why."

Ribeiro denied knowing anything, but from that point on he stopped talking and started avoiding Tanaka's eyes.

That was what he was doing now, five minutes into what had become a hostile interrogation. He sat with his shoulders slumped, staring at his hands. They were pudgy hands, like big, brown gloves, and they were splayed palm downward on the surface of the steel table. When Ribeiro moved them, they left spots of moisture on the cold metal. The air-conditioning in the interrogation room was cranked up high, but it didn't dispel the pungent odor of sweat generated by years of interrogations like this one.

Ribeiro was on the point of cracking. Tanaka knew this, because he'd known hundreds of men like Ribeiro. But then Tanaka did something that surprised Ribeiro: he stood and abruptly terminated the interview. He could see incomprehension written all over the carioca's face, but only because he was looking for it. Almost immediately, incomprehension was replaced by a crafty expression. Ribeiro, the stupid bastard, was thinking that he'd actually pulled it off, that his stonewalling had brought Tanaka to a screeching halt. It would never have occurred to him that Tanaka didn't *want* a confession. All he'd wanted to know was where Ribeiro worked and for whom. Now he did. The delegado waved at the one-way mirror on the wall. The door opened, and a uniformed guard entered.

"Bring me the tapes of this interrogation," Tanaka said, "both the audio and the video. As for Senhor Ribeiro here . . ." he paused, relishing the look of optimism on his prisoner's face, "take him back to his cell and lock him up."

Ribeiro's face fell as the realization hit him that there was more, and probably worse, to come. His forehead was still creased in a frown, partly fear, partly confusion, when the guard pushed him into the corridor.

Chapter Twelve

"BOCETA'S CONCLUSIONS," SILVA SAID, pushing a thin document toward Arnaldo's side of the desk.

It was the afternoon after their meeting with the profiler. They were alone in Silva's office.

Arnaldo picked up the report and hefted it.

"One of his usual weighty tomes," he said.

Silva nodded.

"Four pages," he said. "Took me less than five minutes to read it."

Boceta was known for talking long, but writing short. He loved the sound of his own voice, but found composing reports an onerous task.

"I had enough of him to last me a month," Arnaldo said. "Why don't you summarize?"

"He speculates that a cult or cults from Pará or Amazonas may be networking with a cult in São Paulo."

"And?"

"And nothing. The rest is a detailed account of what happened in Villasboas. He didn't add a damned thing to what he said yesterday."

Arnaldo grunted and shook his head in disgust. He was still shaking it when the telephone rang.

As it continued to ring, Silva got up and opened the door to his office. His new secretary, Camila, wasn't at her post. He returned to his desk, punched the appropriate button, and picked up the instrument.

"Silva."

"Answering our own phone, are we?"

Silva recognized the voice: Ana, Nelson Sampaio's secretary.

"I think Camila found another boyfriend in the building," he said.

"She did. This time, it's that tax accountant down on the second floor, the cute one with the blue eyes."

"Maybe she'll get married and leave me."

"You can always hope."

"Not to interrupt the pleasant chat, but why are you calling?"

"He wants to see you."

"Now?"

"Now. He's got the minister of tourism with him."

"The minister of—"

"Where the hell is he?" Sampaio said from somewhere in the background.

"On his way, Director," Ana said sweetly. And hung up.

BRAZIL'S POOR had put the current president into office and then sent him back for a second term. An ex-union leader, he spent much of his time attending to their needs. The reduction of poverty had accordingly become his first priority. His second priority was extending Brazil's influence throughout South America. His third priority was making Brazil a permanent member of the UN Security Council. Tourism came near the bottom of the president's concerns, somewhere below ribbon-cutting and baby-kissing.

That left Caio Cavalcante, the minister of tourism, with little to do and a tiny budget. He was the smallest cog in the wheel and everyone in Brasilia knew it. But he was a minister. He had the ear of the president. And possessing even a tiny piece of the president's ear was enough to cause Nelson Sampaio to treat Caio Cavalcante with deference. Sampaio firmly believed that if you aspired to be a minister, you had to be seen to associate with ministers.

The director of the federal police had targeted Cavalcante because, as the least important man in the president's cabinet, he should have been the most accessible.

That much was true. Cavalcante had little official business to occupy his time, but the two men had no common interests, no mutual friends, no long-term history. And even the Least Important Man In The Cabinet had a myriad of people vying for his attention. Cavalcante chose his lunches with care, limiting them to men of potential and men who were in a position to tell him things he wished to know.

Nelson Sampaio was twice blessed. He was marked as a man on the rise, and he always prepared an interesting story or two with which to regale the minister prior to picking up the tab. Generally, *just* prior to picking up the tab, because Cavalcante tended to abandon his loquaciousness only when he got well into the Macieira, the Portuguese brandy he consumed to crown his repasts.

Before being appointed to his present lofty post, the minister had spent nineteen years as head of the (twenty-thousand-member strong) Restaurateur's and Hotel Owner's Association, a position that gave him access to many of Brazil's movers and shakers. He was seen as an expert on the hospitality business, which, in fact, he was not. But in Brasilia, appearance beats substance every time, and appearance was something the minister had in spades. He always dressed well, was carefully groomed, appeared comfortable at the podium, kept his mouth shut at cabinet meetings, and carefully concealed his true nature from the public. His appointment was regarded favorably by almost everyone in the president's political party.

He sat now on the couch in Sampaio's office. The director

hovered over him with an open humidor of cigars in one hand and a cutter in the other. Sampaio, who kept the humidor on the credenza behind his desk, liked to smoke a Montecristo Number 2 after lunch, but he never offered one to Silva.

"Sit down," the director said when his chief inspector appeared on the threshold. He nodded to a chair that faced the couch from the other side of a low coffee table.

The minister chose one of the cigars, clipped off the end, and held it out for a light. Sampaio put down the humidor, performed the service with a long wooden match, took a seat at the other end of the couch, and busied himself with preparing a cigar. Once he had it lit, the two of them sat there, puffing away, looking at Silva through the smoke. The smell of aromatic tobacco filled the office.

The minister withdrew the Montecristo from his mouth and gazed upon it affectionately, giving it a look that most men of his age reserved for their grandchildren. "You know, the Americans ban the importation of these things?" he said.

"It's those so-called exiles in Miami," Sampaio said. "Exiles," he snorted, "like they're planning on leaving America and going back."

"More power to them," Cavalcante said. "Let the Americans smoke that Dominican crap. Keeps the price of the good stuff down. Supply and demand and all that."

They smoked awhile in silence.

Silva waited.

"You've met Minister Cavalcante?" Sampaio asked, finally getting down to business.

"Never had the pleasure," Silva said.

The minister took the cigar out of his mouth and extended a hand. Silva had to rise from his chair to take it. Cavalcante's hand was soft and dry. He applied just the right amount of pressure. Not so weak as to demonstrate frailty, nor so strong as to imply he was a bully. Silva immediately recognized that he was in the presence of a master hand-shaker. The guy could have earned money by giving lessons to young politicians.

"The minister, as you know, is from São Paulo."

Silva didn't know any such thing, but he nodded and resumed his seat.

"The subject of that cemetery in the Serra da Cantareira came up at lunch. The minister expressed concern."

Silva opened his mouth to say something, but a look from Sampaio caused him to shut it again.

"I told him," the director went on, "that I share his concern, that I had dispatched you and Arnaldo to São Paulo, that I had already assigned our profiler to the case. Minister Cavalcante had some time before his next appointment, so he came back here with me to read Boceta's report and discuss the issue."

Before Silva could formulate a polite way of asking why the hell the minister of tourism was sticking his nose into a murder investigation, Cavalcante took his cigar out of his mouth and leaned forward.

"This Boceta guy," he said, "I think he's full of shit."

He returned the cigar to his mouth and leaned back on the couch.

"Could you elaborate on that?" Silva asked.

Sampaio responded for his guest. "The minister feels there's no substantiation for Boceta's speculations."

"About a satanic cult?"

"Exactly. He feels, as I do, that there could be all sorts of other explanations for that cemetery. In the old days, for example, they used to have private cemeteries on the big estates. It could be one of those."

"There were no tombstones, Director."

"Who's to say they used tombstones? Anyway, that's just a hypothetical example. Remember that big flu pandemic after the First World War? There were millions of deaths worldwide. Whole families were wiped out. Something like that fits right in."

"No, Director, it doesn't. The forensics indicate that the graves weren't that old."

"But they weren't from last week, or last month, or last year either," Sampaio insisted. "You could almost call them ancient."

"I don't think I'd go quite as far as that, Director."

"So how far would you go?"

"Dr. Couto, the medical examiner in São Paulo, estimates that the graves are between three and seven years old."

Again, the minister leaned forward and took the cigar out of his mouth. "Let's not quibble about how long those people have been in the ground," he said. "When I say this guy . . ."

"Boceta," the director filled in.

" . . . is full of shit, I mean that there's no justification for him to assume, as he does in his report, that the deaths are linked to a satanic cult."

"Not necessarily, no," Silva said.

The minister leaned back and nodded.

"The minister," Sampaio said, "is concerned about the repercussions of the satanic-cult theory."

"Repercussions?"

Cavalcante saw the puzzled look on Silva's face. "Let me explain it to him, Nelson. You can't expect him to see the big picture unless we show it to him, right?"

"Right," Sampaio said.

"My concern," Cavalcante said, turning to Silva, "is to

make this country an attractive place for tourism. That's the mandate given to me by the president. What kind of attraction is there, I ask you, in a satanic cult that murders people?"

The question was rhetorical. Cavalcante had no intention of ceding the floor. He continued with hardly a pause. "Now a serial murderer is another matter entirely. Serial murderers don't seem to have a negative effect on tourism. Look at America. Look at all the serial murderers they've got, and people still flock to Disney World and Las Vegas by the millions. And France. And the UK. Even little Belgium for Christ's sake. You see all of that shit that went on with those kids in Belgium?"

Silva nodded. He kept up on international developments, particularly anything that involved crime. Cavalcante took the nod to be an agreement with his thesis. "There. You see? Madmen can sprout up anywhere. Eventually the guy is captured, or dies, and that's it. End of story. If he hasn't been captured, and the crimes have stopped, isn't it logical to assume that the guy who's responsible for that cemetery in the Serra da Cantareira is dead?"

"There have been cases when a killer goes dormant—" Silva didn't get any further than that. The minister cut him off.

"Now a cult, that's something else," he said. "A cult is lots of people. A cult doesn't stop doing what it's doing just because one member died. If it was a cult they'd still be at it, right?"

"It's possible, but—"

"But nothing. You just got finished saying there are no recent bodies in those graves. Nothing from last week, or last month, or last year. The killer is out of business. No doubt about it. People who do things like that never stop, do they? Not as long as they're alive. So he's dead. That's the only logical conclusion. I've read the books, seen the movies. The last thing the tourist industry in this country needs is for a fucking academic theorist like this . . . this . . ."

"Boceta?"

" . . . to come up with some crazy theory that there's a gang of madmen out there waiting to snatch people off the streets. The Americans would panic. They'd never come near us."

They aren't coming near us now, Silva thought. But he didn't say it. What he said was, "We can't be sure there isn't another cemetery out there someplace, one with more recent graves."

"Any more than we can be sure it's a cult," the minister said.

"WHO THE hell does he think he is?" Arnaldo said an hour later. "Since when does the minister of tourism get involved in murder investigations?"

"Since the director invited him in," Silva said.

"And what's his problem with a line of inquiry that links them to a satanic cult?"

"That's what I can't figure out."

"So what do we do now?"

"After Cavalcante left, Sampaio called in Boceta and had a go at him, told him he didn't think much of his theory."

"Uh-huh. And how did Boceta react to that?"

"You know of any other organization in this country that hires criminal profilers?"

"No, just us."

"So how do you think Boceta reacted?"

"The little weasel stressed it was just a theory? Said he'd give it some more thought?"

"Uh-huh. And he asked the director to thank the minister for bringing the lack of continuity, the absence of more recent murders, to his attention."

"I don't know why I bothered to ask. What now?"

"Now, Sampaio wants us to get back to what he calls the important stuff and leave the investigation of the graves to the people in São Paulo. Only he wants me to call them first and suggest that the line of investigation involving a possible cult is a dead end."

"And by the important stuff you mean?"

"Trying to dig up some dirt on Romeu Pluma."

"Okay. That's what the director wants. But what you're really going to do is follow the cult thread and maybe look into why Cavalcante doesn't want to investigate it."

"Uh-huh."

"So how are we gonna do it without Sampaio—"

"Or Cavalcante."

"Or Cavalcante getting wise to what we're up to?"

"We're going to tell Hector to go ahead, but to keep it out of his written reports, and I'm going to have a chat with Tarcisio Mello."

Chapter Thirteen

TARCISIO MELLO WAS A private investigator who'd retired from the federal police after a thirty-year career. He'd been a vigorous fifty-five at the time, and had been casting around, trying to find something to do with the rest of his life.

One day, after being turned down for a security job, he got a call from a childhood friend who was running for office in Tarcisio's native state of Santa Catarina. The friend asked him to look into the background of his political rival, a long-standing federal senator. The senator was a born-again Christian, a moral pillar of the community, and an odds-on favorite for reelection.

Mello's investigation uncovered that he was also carrying on an affair with his personal assistant. Brazil is a tolerant place, and the senator's love life might well have been perfectly acceptable to the electorate, if the senator hadn't been married and the assistant had been female.

Mello's friend was elected. Word got around. Mello let it be known that his services were available to others, but that he'd only accept work from one candidate for any given office. Homosexual liaisons weren't the only things that Brasilia's politicians wanted to hide. Some hired Mello because they hoped to repeat the success of the new senator from Santa Catarina. Others hired him out of fear, hoping to avoid the fate of the new senator's predecessor. Within a year, Mello had opened an office in Brasilia; within five, he had a staff of sixty-three and representation in five state capitals.

Mello received Silva in a book-lined office. Back when he was a federal cop, he'd been in the habit of bringing paperback novels along on stakeouts. Two of the shelves were lined with books of that type, their well-thumbed spines contrasting sharply with the expensive jacaranda wood. When Silva came in the door, his old friend came around his desk, gave him a firm embrace, and led him to the couch in the corner.

"How have you been, Mario?"

Mello knew about Silva's wife, Irene. He knew about her drinking problem, about the long-standing depression that had plagued her since the death of her only child.

"Good, Tarcisio, good," Silva said, knowing exactly what Mello was getting at by asking the question.

"She's better, then?"

"Oh, yes, much better."

She wasn't, but it was sometimes kinder to lie.

They passed the time in chat until the coffee was served. Tarcisio had three daughters and two grandchildren, and he loved to talk about them, but he wouldn't have brought them up if Silva hadn't. He was a sensitive man and a kind one, unusual traits in someone who'd seen as much of the bad side of human nature as he had. His recital over, he put down his coffee cup and got down to business.

"How can I help you, Mario?"

Silva filled him in on the case, starting with the discovery of the graves and telling him about Boceta's theory.

Mello's lip curled when he got to the part about the curious meeting with the minister of tourism. "What's Cavalcante trying to hide?"

"That's what I want to find out."

"You came to the right place."

There was no discussion of money or fees. Mello's business depended entirely on the ability to access information. Often, that information was something that his former colleagues at the federal police were able to provide. He never offered to pay, since payment could have been construed as bribery. But he was always willing to return favors.

"Let me see if I already have something on him," he said, and got up to call his secretary.

A shapely brunette soon appeared and put a dossier down on the coffee table in front of them. The brunette flashed a smile at Silva, turned, and walked out without saying a word. Mello picked up the folder, leaned back in his chair, and started scanning it. After a minute or two he looked up.

"Cavalcante never ran for public office," he said, "but he headed up the Restaurateur's and Hotel Owner's Association for almost twenty years. That's an elected position. During his tenure, he built the association a building in the center of São Paulo, put up a training school for chambermaids and waiters, and installed a dentist and a doctor so members could get dental and medical care in exchange for their dues."

"Sounds like he did a good job."

Tarcisio scanned some more of the document and stroked his mustache. The mustache was a pygmy compared with Silva's.

"He played to the people who owned *cantinas*, roadside *churrascarias*, little inns in the countryside, surrounded himself with yes-men, got to the point where he was running the joint like a fiefdom. In time, he turned into an egomaniac."

"Power corrupts . . ." Silva said.

Tarcisio smiled. "And absolute power corrupts absolutely. Do you know who said that?"

"No idea."

"An English lord, name of Acton. More than a hundred years ago."

"Not much has changed."

"I can attest to that. Anyway, getting back to your friend Cavalcante, a couple of years ago, the owners of some of the more elite restaurants and hotels got together and tried to topple him. They hired us."

"And?"

"And we couldn't find anything truly damaging."

"No sexual peccadillos? No corruption?"

"No sexual peccadillos. Not recently, anyway. The guy's seventy-six."

"Seventy-six? Jesus, he doesn't look it."

"He lies about it. But so what? His health's good for a man of his age. Nothing to impede him from doing the job he had then or the job he has now."

"And corruption?"

"Not an easy thing to prove, corruption. Nepotism for sure. While he was running the association, he put his wife, all three sons, and one of his two daughters on the payroll. Various nieces and cousins as well, but the association members knew about it and nobody complained. He spent a lot of the association's money flying back and forth between São Paulo and Brasilia and between São Paulo and Orlando in the American state of Florida. In the first case, he claims he was lobbying for the association—"

"And probably himself, since he's now the minister of tourism."

"And probably himself, since he's now the minister of tourism," Mello echoed.

"And in the case of Orlando?"

Mello referred again to the page he'd been reading.

"He was going to open a branch office up there. That's what he said, anyway. Claimed that Brazil had a lot to learn from the Americans in the hospitality area. He also just happens to own a home there."

"Coincidence, eh?"

"Amazing, isn't it?"

"And the branch office? Did it ever happen?"

"Nope."

"But on the surface, he's pretty clean?"

"Cleaner than many others in this town."

Silva snorted, frustrated. "Nothing else?"

Tarcisio leafed through the remaining pages of the document. Silva would have liked to do that himself, but he didn't want to ask. His friend had already bent confidentiality agreements to the limit.

"His other daughter, the one that doesn't work for the association, is a Wiccan."

"A Wiccan? What the hell is that?"

Tarcisio scratched his head. "I haven't the faintest idea," he said.

Chapter Fourteen

THE MANSION STOOD ATOP one of the high hills in the posh neighborhood of Morumbi. It had once been a wealthy family's home, and the properties on either side of it still were. The building had come into being with a French name, a French architect, and a front gate designed by Eiffel himself.

Back then, in the closing years of the nineteenth century, it had been called Sans Souci, French for carefree. The name might have been an apt description of the original owner's state of spirit, and even of that of his son and grandson, but it had no longer applied to his great-grandson, who entered his adult life with many cares indeed, all of them rooted in a lack of money.

The family's coffee plantations had been sold when the boy was still an infant. They'd brought in millions at the time, but it took his father less than twenty years to drink and gamble most of it away. By the time the young man achieved his majority, the only thing remaining of a once-great fortune was the house.

It was, therefore, no surprise that the great-grandson of the builder had been mightily pleased when his father took a tumble down the main staircase one evening and wound up at the bottom with a broken neck. There were those who said he might have been given a push, but after a zealous beginning to a short investigation, the delegado in charge took a sudden disinterest in the case and bought himself a new car.

The building was imposing, with a mansard roof and a

smaller building, originally the servant's quarters, at the rear. What had once been a vast front lawn had been reduced by half to make a parking lot. At first, this had disturbed the neighbors who felt that it took away from the residential nature of the street, but the new owner had been able to pacify them by planting shrubs against the cast-iron fence and having Eiffel's masterpiece lined with sheet metal painted in the same black as the gate itself. From the street, the only indication that anything other than a mansion occupied the two-acre lot was a discreet bronze plaque to the left of the entrance. Above it was a small aperture and, beyond that, a television camera. Twenty-four hours a day, a security guard monitored the images and appeared, unbidden, when anyone stopped their car in front of the gate.

Yoshiro Tanaka rolled down his window, identified himself to the guard, and was admitted to the grounds. Before he'd even parked his car, a woman was waiting for him at the front door. She led him through a warren of corridors and showed him into a room that overlooked a rose garden.

The man he'd come to see was dressed entirely in white: white suit, shirt, tie, socks, and even (Tanaka noted as the man crossed the room to shake his hand) white shoes. His outfit made him look like a high priest of Candomblé with only one false note: *babalorixás*, or *pais de santo* as they were sometimes called, were invariably black or mulatto. This man was Caucasian with blond hair turning white and light-blue eyes behind gold-rimmed spectacles. His lips were pursed in an expression of what might have been disapproval and his head seemed too large for his thin neck.

Coffee was offered.

Tanaka accepted.

A silver service was brought.

The host poured.

"Excellent coffee," Tanaka observed after he'd savored his first sip.

"Export quality, Delegado. I buy it at the port, in Santos. There's a little shop among the warehouses. Do you know it?"

"Regretfully, no."

Tanaka ran his fingertips along the polished surface of the desk that separated them. "Impressive place," he said, looking around, taking in the deep-blue carpeting, the marble fireplace, the little ormolu clock on the mantelpiece, the bookcases of solid jacaranda.

"Thank you," his host said.

Strict observance of Brazilian protocol would have dictated that pleasantries continue, at least for another few minutes, but the man in white couldn't contain himself. Tanaka's call, his request for an urgent meeting, his unwillingness to discuss the subject of that meeting over the telephone, had made him too curious.

He had to ask.

"How can I help you, Delegado?"

Tanaka put down his cup, a delicate affair in the willow pattern.

"It's not so much a question of *you* helping *me*, as it is of *me* helping *you*. Let me see, how shall I begin?"

The host slid forward in his chair, undoubtedly wishing the cop would get to the point. And then the cop did. With unsettling suddenness.

"I'm carrying out an investigation concerning the disappearance of the Lisboa family: a stonemason, his wife, and their two adolescent daughters."

"What's that got to do with me?"

Tanaka continued as if he hadn't heard the interjection.

"They lived in Jardim Tonato, a favela, and were ostensibly moving to a fazenda in the interior of the state. They never got there. In fact, there is no such fazenda. Their furniture, furniture that should have been transported to their new home, was sold to a shop."

"Sold?"

It came out as a croak.

"Sold," Tanaka repeated. "The seller accepted a check and deposited it in his personal account. He told the buyer that he'd acquired the furniture as an investment, acquired it from one of those trucks that sells merchandise along the highways. That would make it untraceable, of course."

While Tanaka was delivering this information, the man in white swallowed twice. Each time, his prominent Adam's apple bounced up and down on his thin neck. Tanaka paused for a few seconds and then drove in the final nail: "The seller's name is Roberto Ribeiro."

Tanaka's host reached for his coffee, but before he could grasp it his hand began to tremble. In an attempt to conceal his original intention, he began to tap his fingers on the desk.

"You know this Ribeiro, do you not?" Tanaka said.

Silence.

"He told me he works for you," the cop insisted.

More silence.

"He also claims he knows nothing about the Lisboa family. I don't believe him. Shall I tell you why?"

The man in white was looking at him like a cobra looks at a mongoose.

"It's because Ribeiro flaunts a medallion from Flamengo," Tanaka said, "and the man who took the Lisboa family away also wore just such a medallion. It's rare here in São Paulo to find a man who demonstrates his support for Flamengo like that. Coincidence, do you think? Or is he the same man?"

"I deny any—"

Tanaka cut him off. "Don't waste your breath. You've got

yourself a nice little racket going," he said. "A man could live well off the proceeds, couldn't he?"

His host blinked. It took him less than another second to recognize where Tanaka was going.

"Very well indeed," he said. "And not that man alone. Others could benefit as well. Others have."

The cop smiled. "I can see we understand each other," he said, lifting the delicate cup from its saucer. "I have my suspicions, of course, but I can honestly claim to be ignorant of what you're up to here. I didn't press Ribeiro for a complete confession, and I don't intend to, as long as we come to . . . an arrangement. Your business need not necessarily be my business. I'm sure you'd prefer I keep it that way."

"I would."

"Good." Tanaka drained the coffee and picked up his briefcase. "I have here," he continued, "the recordings of the interrogation of Ribeiro, the *only* recordings of that interrogation. If you look at the video, you'll note that I was the only one present." He slid two tapes across the desk, one a VHS video, the other an audiocassette. "They're for sale. The release of Ribeiro, my silence, and my promise not to pursue the investigation, are included in the package. It will cost you one hundred thousand American dollars. The price is not negotiable."

"And if I refuse?"

Tanaka lifted his eyebrows, feigning surprise.

"Refuse? I suggest you take a moment to consider the consequences."

"One hundred thousand dollars is a great deal of money."

"Yes, it is. Nonnegotiable."

When his host failed to respond, Tanaka stood, crossed to the mantelpiece, admired the ormolu clock, and idly picked up a photo in a silver frame. It showed his host as a much younger man, arm in arm with an older gentleman. They were standing on the lawn in front of the building, the part that had later been transformed into a parking lot.

"Your father?" he asked.

"No."

When no further information appeared to be forthcoming, Tanaka put the photo down. "Well?" he said. "Do we have an arrangement?"

In lieu of an answer, the man in white gathered the tapes and put them into the top drawer of his desk. Tanaka smiled and returned to his seat.

"When will Ribeiro be released?"

"This very afternoon," Tanaka said. "Now, before I leave, I must caution you. The federal police are also involved in this investigation. They've become very curious about a certain clandestine cemetery in the Serra de Cantareira, a cemetery about which I'm sure you know nothing."

"Absolutely nothing."

"No. That's what I thought. Well, there's nothing to prevent them from stumbling across Ribeiro, just like I did. That being the case, it might be best if he . . . disappeared."

"I understand."

"As to the payment, I'll give you three business days to get it together. I want cash, and I want American dollars. Once I've received the money, there'll be no need for either of us to see the other ever again."

"Nothing would please me more," the man in white said.

HE WAITED until the guard watching the front gate assured him that Tanaka was gone. Then he summoned Claudia Andrade. She entered the room frowning. She was almost always frowning, and her frown deepened when he told her about the policeman's visit.

"Are we going to pay him?" she asked when he'd finished.

"We are. To gain time. It's only a hundred thousand dollars, after all. A trifle."

"And take his advice? About Ribeiro?"

"Certainly not."

She walked to the window, turning her back to him, concealing her expression. When she spoke again, her posture hadn't altered, but her tone of voice had.

"I most emphatically disagree. The man's an idiot. He had strict instructions to destroy that furniture. Instead, he sold it, and for the sake of a few reais he's put us in jeopardy. We should get rid of him immediately."

"Perhaps you didn't hear me. I said no."

"Why not?"

"Because he continues to be useful."

"Useful?" She snorted. "He's dangerous, that's what he is. If that cop wasn't venal, where would we be then? Tell me that."

"Ah, but the cop *is* venal, which means there's no serious harm done."

"No? What makes you think we've seen the last of him? I've heard blackmailers always come back for another bite of the apple."

"They do. And that's the problem we should be concentrating our energies on, not Ribeiro. What's the name of that police official we have on the payroll?"

"Soares. Lieutenant Soares. Why?"

"Sit down and I'll tell you."

Chapter Fifteen

"IT'S ANOTHER ONE OF those crummy undercover jobs, isn't it?" Babyface Gonçalves said, looking back and forth between Hector Costa and the device on the table in front of him.

They were in the conference room of the federal police field office in São Paulo. The device was one of the latest-generation speakerphones. It looked like a little, gray pyramid.

Gonçalves was one of the principal participants in the conversation that was taking place, Hector a mere bystander.

"It is," Silva said, his voice emanating from the instrument.

"What are you guys gonna do when my face catches up with my age, huh?" Gonçalves said.

Agent Heraldo "Babyface" Gonçalves was going on thirty-five, but he looked to be in his early twenties, hence the nickname.

"Plastic surgery." Now it was Arnaldo's voice. "We figure you'll be able to go on forever."

"You read the report?" Silva asked, addressing Gonçalves, ignoring the exchange.

"Boceta's? About cults? Yeah. You told me to read it, and I read it."

"Good. Now, pay attention. The rest is confidential. You know Cavalcante, the minister of tourism?"

"We've got a minister of tourism? What the hell for?"

"Shut up and listen."

Silva related his conversation with Sampaio and Cavalcante.

"What's with him?" Gonçalves said when Silva finished.

"Sticking his nose into an investigation like that? He's the minister of tourism, for Christ's sake, not the minister of justice."

"Thank you for your trenchant observation," Silva said. "The answer to your question is exactly what I want *you* to find out. We have two hypotheses at the moment: the first is that the minister is being absolutely straightforward when he says his concern is tourism—"

"Sounds like bullshit to me."

"The second is that he's protecting someone."

"Who?"

"His daughter."

"Why?"

"She's a Wiccan."

"What the hell is a Wiccan?"

"A witch."

"Huh?"

"A witch. You know, black cats, broomsticks, magic potions."

"You're putting me on, right?"

"I'm not."

"And how did you—"

"Tarcisio Mello."

"Ah. Him. And you think—"

"I don't *think* anything. I *know* the girl's a Wiccan. I *know* her father is aware of it. I *suspect* he believes that she and her coven—"

"Coven?"

"A group of witches, generally thirteen in number."

"Where are you getting this stuff?"

"The Internet. Now, as I was saying, I suspect that Cavalcante believes his daughter and her coven might be murdering people for ritual purposes."

"What do *you* think?"

"I have no opinion one way or another. I'm not even sure Boceta's right about a cult being responsible for the deaths. But we have to check it out. And that's where you come in. The girl's a contemporary of yours. She's twenty-six and—"

"She's not. She's not a contemporary. I'm almost thirty-five."

"And she works as a disc jockey in a club by the name of Banana Banana. You know it?"

"Everybody knows Banana Banana."

"Wrong," Arnaldo said. "I don't."

"Because you're a fucking dinosaur," Gonçalves said.

"And neither do I," Silva said.

"Probably because you live in Brasilia, Senhor," Gonçalves said, without missing a beat. "It's *the* place to see and be seen in this town. They say the decor alone cost a million reais. They've got a sound system with speakers even bigger than my dick."

"Tweeters?" Arnaldo said.

Gonçalves continued, undeterred: "The bouncers are all Neanderthal types with low foreheads like Arnaldo Nunes. Unlike him, they're smart enough to separate glitterati from riffraff, maybe because they're riffraff themselves, again like Nunes."

"But you," Silva said, "being a handsome and personable young man, should have no trouble getting past those bouncers and turning your considerable charms onto the minister's daughter."

"What if she's got a boyfriend?"

"She hasn't. Tarcisio checked. She's unattached and lives alone."

"What's wrong with her?"

"You don't think being a witch might be an impediment to forming relationships?"

"Not if she's hot."

"That's the trouble with kids," Arnaldo said. "Their dicks speak louder than their brains, even when the dicks have tiny, little voices."

"Hey," Gonçalves said, "at your age I wouldn't have expected you to remember. I'll bet your dick hasn't talked to you for forty years."

"The girl's name," Silva said, "is Randi Calvacante."

"Randi? What kind of a name is that?"

"Short for Miranda."

"Okay. Suppose I get in there and make her acquaintance. Then what?"

"Before you even approach her, you do what I did. You get on the Internet and learn all about Wicca. Then you strike up an acquaintance, find a way to steer the conversation around to religion and express an interest. If she bites, you get her to introduce you to her coreligionists, find out if there are any grounds for us to be concerned."

"In other words, I'm supposed to find out if these . . ."

"Wiccans."

" . . . these Wiccans are mass murderers?"

"Exactly."

"What if they are? What if they come after me?"

"You want to wear a wire?"

"Hell, no. What if she finds it?"

"How would she find it? What do you have in mind?"

"You want me to get close to her don't you?"

"See?" Arnaldo said. "What did I tell you? Kid's already thinking about how he can get her into her pants, and he hasn't even met her yet."

"It's purely professional," Gonçalves sniffed. "How else do you expect me to extract . . . uh, confidential information? How about expenses?"

"What about them?" Silva said.

"The girl's the daughter of a minister, right? So she must be accustomed to the good things in life. I might have to buy her champagne, treat her to dinner in a fancy restaurant, that kind of stuff."

"Shower her with presents," Arnaldo said, "take her on a cruise."

"No jewelry, no cruises," Silva said. "I'll be going through your expense reports with a magnifying glass. You'd better be able to justify every damned item."

"I look forward to the opportunity," Gonçalves said.

Chapter Sixteen

"LIEUTENANT SOARES," SERGEANT BLESSA said, approaching his side of the service window, "How's that CD player? Still working okay?"

"Working fine," Soares said.

"And what can I do for you this time?"

Soares rested his briefcase on the counter and regarded Blessa through vertical bars evocative of a theater's box office.

"You can start," he said, "by letting me in there."

Sergeant Blessa slipped him a clipboard. Soares signed in, picked up his briefcase, and walked over to the steel door. There was a rattling of keys and the door swung open, squeaking on hinges long devoid of oil. Blessa motioned Soares inside and locked the door behind him.

Directly ahead, a long, dimly lit corridor stretched into darkness. There were parallel corridors to the right and left. Lining them, up to ceiling height, were metal cupboards. Each cupboard bore a number, a heavy steel hasp, and a padlock. The two men were standing in the evidence locker, situated in the basement of the *delegacia central,* headquarters of São Paulo's policia civil.

Orestes Blessa, the man who ran the operation, had a skin bleached by the sunless light in which he spent his days. He had virtually no neck, a wide mouth, and bulbous eyes, all reminiscent of a toad, an albino toad in a police uniform.

With concrete walls, a steel door, and only one entrance, the evidence locker gave every appearance of being secure.

It wasn't.

Blessa had been working there for fifteen years and for most of that time he'd been running the place like a shop.

"What's your pleasure?" Blessa asked, sounding, as he usually did, more like a merchant than a cop.

"I want to be alone with that"—Soares pointed to Blessa's computer—"and I want access to the cupboards."

Blessa nodded agreeably.

"Okay, Lieutenant, but remember, if whatever you need is something that might attract attention—"

"It won't. You won't even miss it. And it's small. I'll be taking it away in this."

Soares hefted his briefcase.

"I run a special for cases that require, uh . . . a certain degree of discretion," Blessa said. "Five hundred reais and no questions asked."

"*Five* hundred?"

Five hundred was nothing. The deal Soares had negotiated with Claudia Andrade was for ten thousand, but it was against the lieutenant's principles to accept the first price he was offered. He lifted an eyebrow and waited for Blessa to crumble.

And after a few seconds, Blessa did. He was, after all, only a sergeant. Soares was a lieutenant and the brother-in-law of the secretary of public safety, to boot.

"Normally, yeah," Blessa said, "five hundred, but for you, being a special customer and all, four fifty. A twenty percent discount."

"I'll take it."

Blessa opened a drawer in his desk, took out a brass ring holding a single key, and went over to pull down a shade over the service window.

"Fifteen minutes?" he said, offering Soares the ring.

"Twenty," Soares said, taking it. "This is the master key?"

"Yeah," Blessa said. "Fits all the padlocks."

Blessa might have been a crook, but he was an efficient and extremely well-organized crook. Items in his cupboards were always in their proper place and meticulously listed in his database. The computer allowed searches by name (of both the victim and the accused), by case number, by date of entry into the locker, and by item. Soares started searching by item.

When he couldn't find the listing he was looking for, he opened his briefcase and took out the notes he'd made during his search of the archives. The man who styled himself Abdul Al Shakiri was a terrorist, arrested fifteen months earlier while in transit through Guarulhos airport.

International pressure, mostly from the Americans, had resulted in a speedy trial. An appeal was under way, but it wasn't likely that the exhibits used to convict Al Shakiri would be required any time soon, if at all. Soares typed in Al Shakiri's name and hit ENTER.

Nothing.

He referred back to his notes and tried the man's real name, Muhammad Wahabi.

And got a hit.

When he'd done the search by item, he'd tried "explosive," "plastic," "*plástico*," and "plastique." Now he could see why he'd been unsuccessful. The stuff Al Shakiri/Wahabi had been arrested with was listed under its brand name: Semtex. The detonators were in the same cupboard as the explosive. Both were securely stored away in his briefcase by the time Sergeant Blessa knocked on the door.

"Find everything you need?" Blessa asked.

"Four fifty, you said?"

Blessa nodded.

Soares fished out his wallet and counted out nine bank-notes of fifty reais each. Blessa put them into his hip pocket and smiled.

"A pleasure doing business with you," he said, looking very much like he'd just snapped up a fat and extremely tasty dragonfly.

"THREE FULL watts of power."

The owner of the model-aircraft shop said it with a touch of pride, as if he'd designed and built the thing all by himself.

"And that's the most powerful one you've got?" Claudia said.

The owner looked hurt.

"Well . . . sure," he said. "That's the maximum permitted by law. You don't need any more than that. By the time it gets out of range of this baby, you're gonna need binoculars to see whatever you're flying."

"That should do it then."

"Absolutely. Aileron control here, rudder control here, and elevator control here," he said, stabbing at the front panel of the remote control designed for model aircraft.

"Receiver and motors?"

"In the box. Everything you need is in the box. Instructions, too. What's the wingspan by the way?"

Claudia knew nothing of aircraft models. She gave him the first number that popped into her head.

"One meter sixty-two."

It was her height.

The owner whistled. "That big, huh? Jesus, you don't fool around, do you? I can see why you'd be afraid of losing it. You're gonna need a set of batteries. They're not included."

"Okay."

He selected some batteries from a shelf behind him, turned back to the register, and started hitting buttons.

"The whole business," he said, "comes to eight fifty seven and sixty centavos. Let's call it eight fifty seven even, okay?

"Fine."

Claudia opened her purse and took out her wallet.

"Cash or credit?"

"Cash."

"I don't get many women in here," the shop owner said, taking her money and giving her three reais in change.

"It was my uncle's hobby," Claudia lied. "He taught me."

In fact, the things her uncle Ugo had taught her were more in the nature of what an erect penis looked like, and how she'd better keep her mouth shut about what he did to her with it.

The shop owner closed the drawer of the register, brought out a plastic bag from under the counter, and filled it with her purchases.

"You got any questions, just call," he said.

Chapter Seventeen

BRAZIL ABOLISHED SLAVERY IN 1888.

The imperial family and the majority of the people were in favor of the act.

The great landowners were appalled. Who'd pick their cotton? Cut their sugarcane? Harvest their coffee?

In desperation, they turned from Africa to the Orient, solving their labor problem by importing tens of thousands of Japanese peasants to work as indentured servants. And work they did, for the five years it took them to fulfill their contractual obligations. Then they gravitated to the great cities, struck out on their own, and worked even harder. So hard, in fact, that many of the new immigrants made modest fortunes.

By the end of the twentieth century, Brazilians of Japanese descent were doctors, lawyers, politicians, and university professors. They were businessmen, firemen, and policemen like Yoshiro Tanaka. And they'd transformed São Paulo into a city that boasted more ethnic Japanese than any place outside of the home islands.

Liberdade, the heart of the Oriental district, had become fully as large, and equally as colorful, as San Francisco's Chinatown.

It was there, in Liberdade, under a red Shinto arch that marks the entrance to the neighborhood that Gilda and Hector agreed to meet. Hector arrived fifteen minutes early. Gilda was spot on time. He took her arm and led her to a little restaurant that was patronized almost exclusively by the locals. It was a narrow, but very deep establishment, wedged between a grocery smelling of dried seaweed and a shop displaying a

suit of samurai armor. They were guided to the sole unoccu-
pied table.

Two hours later, four customers remained: Gilda, Hector,
a man in a blue suit, and a woman in a kimono. The woman
was seated Japanese-fashion, perched high on her chair,
calves doubled under thighs, her white-crowned head only a
few centimeters from that of the man in the suit. He looked
to be less than half her age, possibly her son, perhaps her
grandson. They were murmuring softly in Japanese.

Gilda put down her chopsticks, picked up her rectangular
box of cold sake, and managed to sip from it without dribbling anything on her chin, a trick that Hector, for all the
time he'd spent in establishments like this one, had yet to
master.

The waiter came to take Gilda's plate, noticed there were
still two pieces of tuna on it, and asked if she was finished.
Gilda shook her head.

"Not quite," she said.

"I think he wants to close," Hector said, when the waiter
was gone.

"Close?" Gilda blinked and looked at her watch. "*Nossa*,"
she said. "Five to three already? I have to get back."

She popped another piece of *sashimi* into her mouth, put
down her chopsticks, and reached for her purse.

Hector realized, with something of a shock, that they
hadn't gotten around to discussing the findings of the medical examiner's office. And that, ostensibly, was the reason
for the lunch.

"I sent the report to your office," she said, as if she could
read his mind. "It'll probably be waiting for you when you
get back."

"It's finished?"

"It's finished."

"That was quick."

"I haven't slept much over the last couple of days."

That explained the dark circles under her eyes, circles that hadn't been there the first time he'd met her.

"When I was excavating the bodies," she said, "long before we had DNA results, I just *knew* I was looking at parents buried with their children. And I *knew* it was murder. It revolts me. I want to see whoever did this put into a cage."

"I sometimes wish we had a death penalty in this country."

"I don't."

He would have liked to debate that one. He picked up his box of sake, paused with it halfway to his lips, decided he'd done too much dribbling for one day, and put it down.

"So the DNA results are in?" he said.

She bobbed her head, fidgeted in her chair, looked again at her watch.

"All part of the report," she said. "The corpses interred in common graves were blood related: mothers or fathers, sometimes both, buried with their children."

Hector reflected on the many corpses she must have seen, thought again how it must take a strong stomach to be a medical examiner. He'd been exposed to no more than thirty murder victims in the course of his career, and the image of every one was burned into his brain. He could seldom face lunch or dinner after visiting a murder scene.

"Let me ask you something else," he said.

"Ask away, but be quick about it. I told Paulo we'd be lunching together. He says I'm allowed to answer all your questions."

"Including what you were starting to say when he cut you off?"

"Uh-huh."

"What was it?"

Gilda raised a hand, caught the waiter's attention, and made a gesture as if she were writing on a pad. He hurried over to their table.

"Coffee?" he said. "Dessert? I've got a nice sweet made from beans."

Both shook their heads.

"Just the check," Hector said.

The waiter smiled in satisfaction, gave a little bow, and hurried off. Gilda watched his retreating back for a moment, and then fixed her gray-green eyes on Hector.

"Every corpse had a split sternum," she said.

"A split what?"

"Sternum. Breastbone. Cut through from top to bottom. Like this."

She reached across the tiny table and traced a vertical line on his chest, dividing his ribs. It was a strangely intimate gesture. He had a sudden attack of gooseflesh and couldn't be sure what was causing it, her words or her touch.

"Paulo cut me off because we weren't sure, then, that the sternum-cutting applied to all of the corpses. It would have been premature to suggest that it did."

"What reason could anyone have for doing something like that?"

"Only one I can think of: to obtain access to something behind the ribs."

"The heart, maybe?"

"Maybe."

Hector recalled a woodcut he'd once seen of a victim bent backward over an altar while an Aztec priest ripped the heart out of his chest.

"Seems to reinforce the idea of ritual killing," he said.

She hesitated for a moment. "Possibly," she said. "But, if

you really want me to make a wild and unsubstantiated guess . . ."

"Live dangerously."

"A doctor did it."

"A doctor?"

"I'll rephrase that. Not just a doctor. A surgeon. He or she did a clean job of it, and he or she used a saw."

"A *saw?*"

"A sternal saw. It's a device with an electric motor and a blade that moves like this,"—she waved a finger up and down in the air—"a medical instrument that has only one purpose, to open the chest cavity."

"How can you be sure?"

"Sternal saws have a unique signature. Under a microscope, the serrations stick out like a Caucasian in this neighborhood. They're unmistakable."

The waiter appeared with the check. Hector took out a credit card and slipped it into the leather cover embossed with the name of the restaurant. "So, if it's not a cult thing," he said when the waiter was gone, "if it's not some kind of ritual murder, what else could it be?"

"We don't—"

"Speculate. Yeah, I know."

"How did you know what I was going to say?"

"You started with a *we*. That's the medical examiner's office talking."

She sighed.

"Look," she said, "you may not like it, but I think Paulo's right. We're supposed to deal in facts. If we start speculating, there'd be no end to it. Experience has taught us it's better if we just tell you guys what we know, and *you* come up with a hypothesis to explain it."

The waiter came back. Hector scrutinized the bill and the accompanying credit card slip.

"Service included?"

"*Sim*, Senhor."

Hector scrawled his signature. The waiter thanked him, detached the customer's copy of the slip, and wished them both a pleasant afternoon.

"Mind you," she said, when they were alone again, "I don't think you can rule out ritual murder just because the killers used a saw. The cult thing remains a distinct possibility; I'm not saying it isn't, but . . ."

"But you have another theory?"

"Yes."

"How about sharing? Not the cop and the medical examiner, just a young couple having a romantic lunch?"

"Romantic lunch, huh? What would your *namorada* have to say about that?"

"Was there a question behind that question?"

"Absolutely."

"If it was what I think it was, the answer is no. I haven't got a namorada."

"It was what you think it was. You're not gay?"

"No."

"So?" She made that writing gesture again.

He reached into his pocket, pulled out his notebook, and handed her a pen. She jotted down her address and telephone number.

"It's the building on the corner with Rua Aracajú," she said. "Fourth floor."

"Thursday night?"

"Friday's better."

"Eight o'clock?"

"Fine."

She'd released her purse, left it on her lap. Now, she picked it up again and stood.

He remained glued to his chair.

"You're not going to tell me, are you?" he said.

"Maybe on Friday. It will give you something to look forward to."

"I already have something to look forward to."

"Which is?"

"Seeing you."

"There. That wasn't so hard, was it? You *do* know how to flatter a girl. You were just holding it in."

"I wasn't holding it in."

"And you can wipe the hurt puppy expression off your face. It's not going to help. I'm not telling you what my theory is, not today at any rate."

"Why not?"

"I need a second opinion. I have a girlfriend, a specialist. She's in a position to give me one."

"What do you need a second opinion for?"

"Someone has to tell me I'm not crazy."

And before he could ask her what she meant by that, Gilda had turned her back on him and was heading for the door.

Chapter Eighteen

YOSHIRO TANAKA'S TELEPHONE RANG. He leaned to his left to look through the open door. Sergeant Lucas, who should have been screening incoming calls, wasn't at his desk. Tanaka cursed and grabbed the receiver.

"Tanaka," he said sharply.

"Delegado?"

"Who's this?"

"Sergeant Corvo."

Corvo was in charge of the police garage, the building the cops called the Beehive because of its tapering, circular shape.

"What is it, Sergeant?"

"Uh, Delegado, I think you'd better come over here."

"Why?"

"Well, uh . . . they broke into your car."

"Broke into my . . . right in the middle of your goddamned garage?"

"*Sim,* Senhor. Smashed the front window on the passenger's side. The radio and CD player are still there, though. Bastard must have gotten interrupted before he could get them out."

"Interrupted, but not caught, right?"

"Hey, Delegado, this is a big place, and I've only got three—"

"Save it for your annual evaluation meeting, Sergeant. You're going to need it. I'm on my way. Meet me out in front."

* * *

AN UNHAPPY-LOOKING Sergeant Corvo was waiting for Tanaka at the base of the ramp. They started climbing it together. A shift change was under way, and Corvo had to raise his voice to be heard over the sound of the ascending and descending vehicles.

"Detective Vieira came in a few minutes ago," he said. "His slot is right next to yours. He saw the damage and clued us in. It had to have happened here because there's broken glass all over the floor, not just on the front seat."

"Bastards," Tanaka said, wrinkling his nose, as he always did, at the smell of the place. Gasoline exhaust, he figured, was even more toxic than tobacco smoke. They reached the second floor and came in sight of his car. The front window on the passenger's side had been smashed.

"One thing I can't figure out," Sergeant Corvo said.

"What?"

"That package you left on the front seat? They didn't take it."

"Package?"

"And there's no glass on top of it. It's like someone brushed it off after they smashed the window. I mean, nobody would have broken the window and then put it there, right? People break into cars to take stuff out, not to put stuff in."

They were only a few meters away from Tanaka's four-year-old Volkswagen Gol. The delegado stopped dead in his tracks. Sergeant Corvo stopped, too, and studied Tanaka's face.

"Hey, Delegado, what's wrong with you? You look like you're gonna be sick."

"HERE HE comes," Roberto Ribeiro said.

Claudia Andrade tossed her newspaper into the backseat.

"Finally," she said.

There was a uniformed sergeant waiting for Tanaka at the base of the ramp.

"Now," Claudia said, as the two cops disappeared inside the oddly shaped building.

Ribeiro pushed the button on the stopwatch. Claudia had taken the same stopwatch onto the ramp and timed the walking distance to Tanaka's car. His legs were shorter than hers. She'd calculated it would take Tanaka twenty-two seconds to get there.

"They're not walking fast," Roberto said. "I think we should give it a couple of extra seconds."

"Oh, you do, do you?"

"I just—"

"Give me that," Claudia snapped.

She reached out and snatched the watch. Plastic explosive was powerful stuff. A small error either way wasn't going to make much of a difference. The stopwatch was a digital one, counting off the seconds in racing-red numbers. Twenty-one, two . . . Claudia pushed the spring-loaded switch, the one marked "rudder," on the radio-frequency transmitter. Above her, in the garage, the receiver picked up the signal and activated the solenoid. The contact points closed and electricity flowed from the battery to the detonator—all in a fraction of a second. A ball of flame spouted out of the open gallery on the second floor. The shock wave hit them a second later, rocking her car as if something heavy had bounced off the hood.

"Jesus Christ," Ribeiro said, scrubbing both ears. "I shoulda used earplugs."

Thick, black smoke roiled out of the building. There was a flash and a boom as a fuel tank exploded.

The place was an inferno.

Chapter Nineteen

IT MIGHT HAVE BEEN the personalities of the women he chose, or the fact that he liked them young, or the fact that he looked more like a sympathetic priest than a hard-nosed cop, thereby awakening in his partners a need for confession. But whatever it was, it had been Babyface Gonçalves's experience that many women did exactly the same thing after their first sexual encounter with him: they reached for a cigarette, propped themselves up in bed, and started bitching about their mothers.

Miranda Cavalcante was different.

She started bitching about her father.

"It was hell growing up with him," she said. "Sheer hell. He doesn't care about anybody below the age of twenty. He doesn't like babies, doesn't like young kids, doesn't even like dogs and cats. He only shows an interest in people who are capable of some kind of verbal exchange."

"Um-hm," Babyface said, hating the cigarette smoke, but not wanting to complain about it. Complaining might cause her to clam up.

"It's not like he's any kind of intellectual," she went on. "He doesn't care about art, or history, or any of that kind of stuff. He doesn't even care about *futebol*, unless it's the World Cup."

That went without saying. You couldn't be in Brazil during the World Cup and not care about soccer. Even the American tourists got caught up in it, and most of them didn't give a shit about the sport. Not caring about the World Cup, Gonçalves mused with the part of his mind that wasn't listening to Miranda's rant, was impossible. Like being in two places at the same time, like a serial killer being soft hearted.

"All he really cares about is himself, and politics."

Babyface thought that sounded like someone else he knew: Nelson Sampaio, the head of the federal police. "Sounds a little cold," he said.

What he almost said was, sounds like a cold-hearted bastard, but that was motivated more by thoughts of Sampaio than Randi Cavalcante's statements about her father.

"Cold is right," she said. "I doubt he ever talked to me for more than a minute at a time in all the years I was growing up. And when he did, it was to tell me to do this or that or *not* to do this or that. He never asked me to tell him what I thought, what I felt, anything like that. He likes bossing people around, but he hates listening to their problems."

Babyface made a noncommittal grunt.

"I had a baby brother," she said, stubbing her cigarette out in the big glass ashtray next to her bed and immediately lighting another. "He passed away when I was thirteen. He was only four months old when he died of SIDS. Ever heard of it?"

"Sudden infant death syndrome."

"Yeah, that's right," she said, sounding surprised that he knew. She exhaled another cloud of smoke, this time taking care to blow it toward the window and not at her latest lover. "My parents got up one morning and he was cold in his crib. He slept right there in the same room with them. My father hated that, him sleeping in the same room I mean, but my mother insisted. One of the only times I ever saw her put her foot down. Told my father that if he'd get up to feed him she'd move him into another room, but otherwise he was going to stay right there. The poor little tyke died and never made a sound. My mother was devastated. We all were, except for my father. I didn't see him shed a tear, not that morning, not at the funeral, not ever. The baby was named after him, too. Little Caio."

"Jesus," Babyface said.

"But now, now that he's getting old, and I'm not little anymore, and my mother is dead, he's changed. Now he's getting worried about who's going to take care of him when he gets frail and who's going to cry at his funeral. He's got the rest of my brothers and sisters under his thumb. At least he *thinks* he has them under his thumb. He has no idea what they really think about him, and they're all too shit scared to tell him. They all work at the same place, and his influence keeps them there, and that's one of the things they resent most of all, but he just doesn't get it."

She took another puff, let the smoke drift out of her mouth as she continued.

"Me? I wouldn't have it. I wouldn't take his fucking job. I never let him get his hooks into me. I went out and made it on my own. He respects that, in a way, but he hates it, too. Now he's on a whole campaign, sending me stuff I don't need or want, calling me almost every day. He's driving me nuts."

"About what?"

"Everything. My job, my love life, my friends, my religion."

"Religion? You're not Catholic?"

Smoke was making her eyes water. She waved her cigarette back and forth to disperse it.

"No," she said. "I'm not. I'm a Wiccan."

"No kidding?" Babyface said, propping himself up on his pillow.

She looked at him in surprise. "You know what a Wiccan is?"

"Sure," he said. "The Rede, the Ardanes, the Virtues, the Law of Threefold Return."

That was enough to set her off.

* * *

PLEADING AN early-morning staff meeting at the broker-
age house where he'd said he worked, Babyface left Miranda
Cavalcante's apartment at 6:30 am. He went home to his
place in Vila Madelena, showered, and set the alarm for nine
fifteen. After two hours' sleep, and two strong cups of coffee,
he called Silva at his office in Brasilia.

"We're barking up the wrong tree," he said.

"Tell me."

"She's not a bad-looking girl. Thin, with small tits, but she
has a nice—"

"I didn't ask you for a critique, I asked you to find out
about this Wicca business."

"Okay. Well, first of all, your hypothesis about her old
man is right. He *is* trying to protect her."

"How can you be sure?"

"Because she told me flat out, said her father called her up
and told her that if she and her friends were killing people
they had to stop it right away because the cops were on their
trail."

"Just like that?"

"Just like that. She treated it as a joke. Said that if her
father knew anything about her religion at all, he would
have known they weren't hurting anyone, much less killing
them. A couple of years ago, she tried to tell him about the
Wiccan Rede, but he obviously wasn't listening, so she
gave it up."

"Wiccan Rede?"

"I thought you said you looked all this up on the Internet."

"I did, but I must have missed that one. What is it?"

"It's a sort of maxim. The basic idea is that if you do no
harm to anyone, you can do anything else you damn well
please. When she was talking to her dad, she stressed the not

doing harm part. Wiccans, she told him, use magic for things
that are positive and good. She's a touchy-feely kind of person. Has four cats, a poodle, a cage full of birds, and a pair of
sugar gliders named Romeo and Juliet. We had to lock the
cats and the poodle outside of her bedroom so we could get
it on. The damn poodle kept scratching at the door and the
cats—"

"Get back to the point, Babyface."

"The point is, this girl isn't killing people. No way. And
the fact that her father thinks she'd be remotely capable of it
just goes to show what an unfeeling blowhard he is. He
apparently didn't listen to a word she said."

"Unfeeling blowhard?"

"Well . . . yeah, in a matter of speaking."

"You liked her, didn't you?"

A pause. Then Babyface said, "Yeah, I kinda did."

"Going to see her again?"

"Uh . . . maybe."

"Fine. Your private life is none of my business. But don't
let me catch you bitching the next time I need you for an
undercover assignment."

Silva had no sooner hung up with Gonçalves when
Sampaio stuck his head through the doorway to his office.

"Any news on the Pluma investigation?" he asked, completely ignoring the presence of Arnaldo.

"No, Director. Nothing yet."

"Stick with it, Mario. There's got to be something there.
There always is."

Sampaio wandered off.

Arnaldo lifted his eyebrows. "So now it's the Pluma
Investigation, is it? Makes it sound like something important. Who've you got working on it?"

"It's a highly confidential inquiry."

"Meaning you're supposed to be working on it yourself?"

"Exactly."

"And are you? Working on it, I mean?"

Silva shook his head. "Of course not. Pluma continues to bad-mouth Sampaio to the minister, and the way I figure it, that's God's work."

"Amen," Arnaldo said.

Less than ten minutes later, Hector called from São Paulo.

"You're not going to believe this," he said.

"I have seen many wonderful things in my long life, Nephew. You'd be surprised at what I'd believe. Try me."

"You're hanging around a lot with Arnaldo, aren't you?"

"As a matter of fact I am. Why?"

"Because you're beginning to sound like him, except you've got a bigger vocabulary."

"Fuck you, Hector," Arnaldo said.

"I neglected to mention," Silva said, "that you're on the speakerphone. So what did you think I'm going to have a hard time believing?"

"Fuck you, too, Arnaldo. Remember that Jap delegado, Tanaka?"

"What about him?"

"He's dead. Blown up by a bomb somebody put in his car. It could be entirely unrelated to our investigation, but . . ."

"You're going to check it out."

"His delegacia, first stop. I'll keep you posted."

Chapter Twenty

"UGLIEST DAMNED THING I ever saw," Hector said, speaking of the shocking-pink holding cell in Tanaka's delegacia.

"Uglier, even, than the director's wife?" Arnaldo said.

The director's wife, Neidy Sampaio, had been no beauty to begin with, but she'd let herself go after marriage. Her picture, the one in the center of the triptych on her husband's desk, was at least fifteen years old and bore no relationship to the current article. These days, Neidy had a problem with facial hair and was at least forty kilos heavier than when the photograph was taken.

And if her appearance fell short of attractive, her personality was worse. She was a surly woman who seldom had a good word for anyone, including her husband. Silva had often asked himself why his boss remained married to her until he found out she was the sole heiress to a considerable fortune.

So, although there was truth in Arnaldo's comparison between the holding cell and the wife of the head of the federal police, the bold comment still stopped Hector short. But only for one reason: "Didn't you guys tell me I was on the speakerphone?" he said.

"You are. But it's just the two of us here," Silva said. "Besides, the door is closed and our fearless leader is at lunch."

Silva and Arnaldo were in a conference room at federal police headquarters in Brasilia. Hector was calling from beyond closed doors in Tanaka's office.

"Okay, then," Hector said. "The answer is yes, even uglier than Senhora Sampaio. That cell is bizarre. I don't care if it's just for females. There are certain things that shouldn't be pink. What's next? Pink handcuffs? A pink pistol for female agents?"

"I take your point," Silva said.

"There's a sergeant here, a guy by the name of Lucas. He told me it was Tanaka's idea, some kind of publicity stunt. He let the prisoners choose the color. There's a clipping about it on the wall of his office, interviews with Tanaka's boss and the state secretary of security. Both of them loved it. Or said they did."

"No accounting for taste."

"Yeah," Arnaldo said. "Look at Sampaio."

"So what did you find out?" Silva said.

"I had a long chat with Sergeant Lucas. He didn't know, until I told him, any of the details about the cemetery in the Serra. Tanaka never bothered to fill him in. Or anybody else, as far as I can determine."

"And this guy Lucas doesn't read newspapers?"

"Sports pages, maybe. Probably not much more than that. When I mentioned there were cases of children buried with their parents, he put two and two together. He thinks he knows what Tanaka might have been up to."

Arnaldo leaned closer to the speakerphone. Silva sat up straighter in his chair.

"Tell me more," he said.

"There's this favela called Jardim Tonato. According to Lucas, Tanaka never gave much of a damn about what happened there. He used to say that if they wanted to kill each other, it was fine with him. The vast majority of the people who lived there were felons anyway, and he wasn't going to waste manpower trying to intervene, because most deaths went to reducing the number of crooks in his district. Then this family, some stonemason, his wife, and two daughters, goes missing. It's brought to his attention on the afternoon of the very day he promised to get back to us about entire families."

"And he took a sudden interest."

"Uh-huh. He insisted on interviewing the couple who made the complaint. He did it in his office, the one I'm calling from right now. And he did it from behind a closed door. Then he came out and told Lucas to get him a car. Usually, Tanaka wants to be driven and Lucas does the driving. Not that day. That day, he takes the couple with him and disappears. Lucas goes home, but later he finds out that Tanaka calls up and wants to talk to a detective named Danilo."

"That place is a hotbed of intrigue."

"Just like federal police headquarters," Hector agreed. "Anyway, Danilo meets Tanaka, and a while later they're back with some thug. Tanaka tells Danilo that he doesn't need him anymore and takes the thug into an interrogation room. They're in there for almost an hour. Then he has the thug thrown in a holding cell and takes off for places unknown."

"Did they make any tapes during the interrogation?"

"They did. And here's where it really gets interesting. Tanaka takes the tapes, both the video and the audio. He never brings them back and, get this, the arrest report and the original complaint are both missing."

"As is the thug?"

"Tanaka released him and there's no record, no record at all, of who he was."

"Tanaka was onto something," Arnaldo said.

"Impressive deduction," Hector said. "You ought to be a detective."

"I *am* a detective."

"Some people question that."

"Those that do had better be very big and very strong," Arnaldo said.

"Anyway," Hector said, "we did have one stroke of luck. Lucas took down the original complaint in longhand. He's still got it. The name of the missing couple is Lisboa, Edmar and Augusta. Two daughters, named Mariana and Julia."

"And the complainants?"

"Portella. Ernesto and Clarice. We've got their address, such as it is."

"What do you mean *such as it is?*

"Favela, *chefe*. No street signs, no numbers."

"But Lucas knows how to find their shack?"

"He does."

"Go for it. Call me when you know more."

HECTOR CALLED back three hours later. Silva told him to wait and went down the hall to where Arnaldo was working a telephone, calling cops at delegacias within a five-hundred-kilometer radius of the little town of Villasboas, trying to garner more information on anything that might remotely have been construed as ritual murder.

Before Silva could ask, he said, "Nothing about corpses with their sternums sawn through. Not yet, anyway."

"Hector's on the line," Silva said. "Come back and listen."

"Sergeant Lucas took me to the Portellas' house," Hector said a minute or two later. "No luck. Nobody home."

"The neighbors?"

"Here's how it works: you got people who're at home during the day and people who're at home during the night. Most of the people at home during the day are lowlifes who're sleeping off a drunk or a hard night of breaking and entering or drug dealing. The folks who are at home during the night are mostly hard-working types. The Portellas, by all accounts, are in that category."

"So somebody has to go back at night."

"Right."

"Not nice. Days are bad enough in those places, but nights. . . . Well, it can't be helped. Somebody has to do it. Send Babyface. And tell him to bring a gun."

"I don't think I'll have to tell him," Hector said.

Chapter Twenty-one

BABYFACE GONÇALVES LEARNED ABOUT the Portellas' whereabouts the hard way—by getting hit on the head. The wound was painful, but it could have been worse. If his assailants had found his credentials, they would have killed him, that being the protocol for handling cops who stick their noses into favelas after dark.

Fortunately, the two punks who came up behind Babyface simply mistook him for an easy mark. After they'd hit him behind the left ear with a lead pipe, they limited themselves to patting down the places where people normally carried their wallets. When they found his, they took it and made themselves scarce. They never discovered the special pocket he used for carrying his badge and police identification card. And they never found his Glock.

Unlike most cops, Babyface Gonçalves didn't carry his gun where people could see it. He carried it in a special holster in the small of his back, which is where the woman who found him put her hand when she helped him to his feet. She pulled back as if she'd been burned and took two steps away.

Babyface stood there, groggy, still tottering. For a minute, he thought she was going to run.

"I'm not one of the bad guys," he said, when he saw that her eyes had assumed the dimensions of saucers. "I'm a cop."

"Sweet Jesus," she said.

Other than the yellow glimmer of kerosene lamps shining through cracks around ill-fitting doors, the street seemed to be devoid of human presence. She sighed and seemed to come to a reluctant conclusion. "Alright, damn it. Come with me," she said, her voice angry now, but scarcely more than a whisper.

She led him through the mud and stopped at a hovel not twenty meters from where she'd found him. Like the other shacks lining the unpaved street, the place was built from scraps of wood and sheet metal. She reached into her purse, removed a key, and started fumbling with a padlock. A moment later, Babyface heard the squeak of rusty hinges. She pushed him ahead of her into the dark.

Inside, it smelled of lamp oil, excrement, and urine. It was Babyface's second visit to a favela and the first time he'd been under someone's roof. He'd been told they seldom had electricity, almost never had indoor plumbing. The smells confirmed it.

"Wait," the woman said.

He heard her strike a match. It flared, illuminating her face. She was black, white haired, appeared to be about sixty, not as tall as he was, but probably heavier. And she looked like she'd just taken a big swig of milk and found it sour. She lit the wick of a kerosene lantern and covered it with a glass chimney. Then she hung the smoking lamp from a hooked piece of wire suspended from the ceiling.

"Sit," she said, indicating a pile of coffee sacks.

Babyface sank down. The contents of the sacks squeaked. He put his hand onto the jute and squeezed broken pieces of foam plastic. The jute seemed sticky.

"Watch what you're doing with that hand," the woman said. "Get it off my bed."

He did as he was told and looked down. It wasn't the jute that was sticky; it was his hand, bloody from the wound behind his ear.

"You're one hell of a mess," she said.

"They hit me," he said. "Stole my wallet."

"If you really are a cop, you're lucky they didn't kill you."

She picked up a cloth, moistened it with water from a plastic jug, went around behind him, and started dabbing at his wound.

"Ouch," he said.

"Should have left you where you were," she said. She sounded less frightened, but no less angry.

"Why?"

She stopped her dabbing and walked around to look him in the eye.

"Who do you think you're fooling?"

"Senhora, I appreciate your helping me, I truly do, but you seem to be angry about something and honest to God, I've got no idea what it might—"

"No idea, huh?"

"No."

"And never heard of the Comando Vermelho either, right?"

"Comando Vermelho? Sure. They're a drug gang, in Rio."

"In Rio and right here in Jardim Tonato, Senhor Policeman, and don't tell me you didn't know that."

"But I *didn't* know that."

"And didn't know either, I suppose, that they kill people who help cops? That they'll kill me if they find out you're here?"

"No, I—"

"Should have left you right where you were. Stepped right in the shit this time, I did. Good and proper. Umm-hmm. Really put my foot in it. What's your name?"

"Gonçalves. Agente Gonçalves. Federal police. And, at this moment, I don't give a damn about the Comando Vermelho or their drug business. I'm not here because of them."

"No? Then why are you here?" she asked, curiosity getting the better of her.

"HE'S OKAY," Hector said, when he called his uncle at eleven the next morning to report on Babyface's condition, "but he came out of it with a bump on his head the size of a walnut. I made him go to the hospital to have it looked at. They wanted to keep him there under observation, but he wouldn't have it. Says he feels like a jerk for letting some lowlife punk get the drop on him like that."

"I guess they didn't find his badge."

"Nope. Nor his gun either. He had it in the small of his back."

"Babyface is one lucky boy. I expect he knows that."

"He does."

"Did we get anything out of it?"

"We did."

Hector told him about Babyface's benefactor, whose name was Samantha Cruzeiro, and how she'd turned out to be a friend of Clarice Portella, the woman they were looking for.

"Clarice," he said, "has a younger sister who's getting married. The two of them, Clarice and her husband, left yesterday for the wedding. It's way the hell up in Pernambuco. They're supposed to be gone for two weeks."

"Merda," Silva said.

"From what Samantha told Babyface, Ernesto—that's the husband—shares your sentiments. He can't stand his wife's family, and she had a hell of a time convincing him to shell out for the bus fare. Until the wedding came along—a somewhat hasty affair as I understand—he had the money earmarked for a down payment on a television set."

"What's he do for a living?"

"Works in construction."

"And the woman?"

"A faixineira in Fazendinha, a different lady for every day of the week."

"Fazendinha?"

"A luxury condominium right next to the favela."

"Charming."

"Big fence all around it, big houses on the inside. Babyface went there directly from the hospital."

"Boy deserves a raise. Too bad there's a salary freeze."

"A freeze that doesn't seem to apply to directors' salaries."

"Heard about that, did you?"

"It's all over the office."

"Here's something to add fuel to the fire: Sampaio got it in exchange for a promise not to give a raise to anyone else."

"Filho da puta."

"One hundred percent. What else did Babyface find out?"

"The guards at the gate are all moonlighting cops. They keep a list of day workers and the people who employ them. Turns out all of the ladies Clarice works for knew about the wedding, and all of them agreed to give her time off. None of them could give him a contact address or a telephone number."

"Not surprising. I can't imagine any of them would call her for a chat."

"Samantha didn't have any contact information either. It wouldn't have made any sense. She can't write, and she doesn't have a phone. You want us to keep asking around?"

"Probably a waste of time. Same thing applies to involving the cops in Pernambuco."

"Yeah. By the time you get anything out of those yokels, you'll be long retired," Hector said. "Hell, come to think of it, *I'll* be retired. We'll just have to wait until the Portellas get back."

"I don't think we have any choice. You left word for them to get in touch?"

"With Samantha, at the condominium gate, and with every woman Clarice works for. Babyface also slipped a note under the door of the Portellas' shack."

"How about that detective, Danilo? The guy who helped Tanaka bust the thug? You talk to him?"

"He's dead."

"He's what?"

"Dead. The PCC killed him the night before last."

The PCC, Primeiro Comando Capital, was another of São Paulo's gangs, one that had its roots in prisons. Originally, they'd dealt exclusively with the interests of prisoners, lobbying and threatening in an effort to get better food, more living space, less brutality from the guards.

They'd gone on to resolving grudges with the law.

There were now thousands of them, inside prisons and out. Over the past few years they'd killed almost a hundred cops and prison guards, shooting them down on the streets and even staging full-scale assaults on delegacias. Their weapons of choice were AK-47s and hand grenades, but they'd also been known to use light machine guns and rocket-propelled grenades. It was another step toward turning São Paulo into the most dangerous urban environment on Earth.

"The PCC, huh?" Silva said. "Are we sure?"

"We're sure. They got the guy who did it. Took him alive and he confessed. Seems Danilo killed his brother in a fire fight about a year and a half ago. I don't think there's any relationship between what happened to Danilo and what happened to Tanaka, unless someone in the PCC also had a grudge against Tanaka. But, if there was, the guy they nabbed doesn't know anything about it."

"Alright. So where are you going to take it from here?"

"I'm going to talk to Tanaka's wife. Sergeant Lucas said she's the one who wore the pants in the family. If that's the case, and if Tanaka was up to something—"

"Which it sure as hell looks like he was."

"Which it sure as hell looks like he was," Hector repeated, "then there's a good chance Senhora Tanaka knew about it. I figured I'd better bring a search warrant along just in case. I'd be over at her apartment right now if I wasn't waiting for it. Soon as I have it in hand, I'll be on my way."

Chapter Twenty-two

IN 1957, A YOUNG ARCHITECT named Lucio Costa was given the go-ahead to start constructing Brasilia. He projected his country's new capital as a metropolis for the automobile age, a place where roads and avenues flowed through tunnels and over viaducts, never once meeting at intersections. The way he imagined it, there'd be five hundred thousand inhabitants and not a single traffic light.

Half a century later, the population of Brasilia was two and a half million, there were traffic lights galore, and the dream of free-flowing traffic was dead, suffocated under a cloud of gasoline and diesel fumes.

It took Silva forty-two minutes to cover the eight kilometers from his office to his home, a two-bedroom affair in a government-owned building. The apartment had been part of Costa's original project and was considered ancient by Brasilia standards, but Silva liked the high ceilings and ample terrace.

His parking slot was close to the service elevator, so he went up that way, letting himself in by way of a laundry room that divided the kitchen from the maid's quarters. The quarters were entirely occupied by shelves lined with books. Silva and his wife, Irene, didn't maintain a full-time domestic servant.

They did, however, employ a faixineira. She invariably arrived after Silva had left for work, and left before he returned home. He was, therefore, surprised to find her sitting at the kitchen table.

He was even more surprised to find his wife completely

sober. It was almost ten minutes to eight, and if Irene had been running true to form, she would have downed enough *cachaça* by then to slur her speech. As it was, there was only an empty coffee cup in front of her.

Silva kissed his wife, smiled at the faixineira, walked to the stove, and sniffed at the coffeepot. The coffee smelled fresh, but the pot was only lukewarm. He lit the gas.

"Maria de Lourdes," Irene said to his back, "has a problem."

The faixineira was a small woman, perhaps in her fifties, perhaps younger, a native of one of those states to the south of São Paulo—Paraná or Santa Catarina. Silva couldn't remember which. Her full name was Maria de Lourdes Krups. If it had once been Krupps, which Silva suspected it had, the spelling had fallen victim to an ancestor's illiteracy or perhaps to the ministrations of some careless clerk in a public registry office.

And if her name-giving forebears had been Caucasian (like their illustrious namesakes, the armaments barons of Essen), Maria de Lourdes had lost that, too. She was a *mulata* with almond-shaped eyes.

Silva's coffee was now warm enough to drink. He shut off the gas, poured out a cupful, and took it to the table.

"How can I be of assistance?" he said, somewhat formally.

He'd been raised with servants and was comfortable with them as long as it didn't involve sitting down for a chat. On the rare occasions like this one, he found it difficult to bridge the social gap, especially with women. Gardeners and drivers were easier. With them, you could always talk about soccer.

Maria de Lourdes looked at her lap.

Silva drained his beverage, and waited.

"Go on," Irene said to her cleaning woman.

Maria de Lourdes looked at Irene and bit her lower lip.

"It's about her son," Irene said. "He's missing."

"That's a matter for—"

"No, it isn't, Mario. I know what you're going to say, and it's *not* a matter for the policia civil. Listen to her story." Irene turned to Maria de Lourdes. "Tell him," she said.

Maria de Lourdes took a deep breath, and then started talking in a rush.

"I didn't intend to trouble you, Senhor Mario, but I was talking to Dona Irene about it, and she said you might be able to help."

Irene reached out and offered Maria de Lourdes a supporting hand. Maria de Lourdes took it and squeezed. Unlike her husband, Irene had no problem befriending servants. Maria de Lourdes was squeezing hard. Silva could see his wife's knuckles going white.

"He always wanted to go to America," Maria de Lourdes continued, speaking more slowly now, her eyes still on her lap, "always been crazy about American things: American music, American movies, even that stupid game where they throw the ball with their hands and knock each other down."

She stopped talking, as if she'd lost the thread. After a few seconds of silence, Silva gave her a prompt.

"And?"

"And that's why he decided to sneak into the United States."

Silva got up from the table and went to the attaché case he'd left on the kitchen counter. Maria de Lourdes looked up when she heard the snap-snap of the latches, watched him as he took out a yellow legal pad, and followed him with her eyes as he returned to the table.

"What's his name?" he said when he'd resumed his seat.

"Norberto. Norberto Krups."

"No middle name?"

"No."

"Age?"

"Nineteen."

"Father's name?"

Maria de Lourdes drew her mouth into a thin line and shook her head.

"Unknown," Silva said, making a note, as he had when she'd responded to the other questions.

"I'll need a picture," he said.

She opened the hand that wasn't gripping Irene's and revealed a small photo, passport sized, the type that could be obtained from machines in bus stations. Damp with her perspiration, the paper had begun to curl. She offered it to him. He studied the image.

Norberto Krups's skin was lighter than his mother's, more milk than coffee in the *café com leite*. The kid's hair was so badly cut that, if there were penalties for such things, his barber would have been sitting in a cell somewhere. He was wearing a baseball cap with what Silva recognized as the logotype of the New York Yankees baseball team over his uneven shaggy hair. On his T-shirt a red heart acted as a substitute for the English word "love," and what Norberto Krups loved was New York.

"Can I keep this?" he asked.

Maria de Lourdes nodded.

"I brought it for you. Dona Irene said you'd need one."

That confirmed Silva's suspicion that the meeting with him had been some time in the making, but Irene hadn't said a word about it. He shot a glance at his wife. She appeared to be studying a defect on the stem of her coffee spoon.

He put the photo between two pages of his legal pad and waited for Maria de Lourdes to go on.

She didn't. She, too, seemed to have taken a sudden interest in Irene's coffee spoon.

Silva thought he knew why.

"What Norberto did," he said, "isn't a crime. We wouldn't put him in jail for trying to get into the United States. Your son has nothing to fear from Brazilian law."

That seemed to reassure her. She truly met his eyes for the first time and her voice became more confident.

"There's a travel agency in São Paulo," she said. "They charged him five thousand dollars. Dollars, not reais."

"Five thousand dollars? Where did your son get that kind of money?"

"He lived like a monk for over three years, saving every centavo, scraping it together. Worked seventeen, eighteen hours a day. Worked weekends and holidays. Never went to bars. Stopped buying cigarettes."

"I'm assuming the Americans refused him a visa?"

She nodded.

It was the usual story. The Americans *always* denied visas to Brazil's undereducated poor. They were convinced that, as soon as the Norberto Krupses of the world got over their border, they were going to stay. And the Americans didn't want any more people like Norberto Krups.

"This tourist agency," Silva asked, "they proposed to smuggle him through Mexico?"

It was the normal route: a flight to Mexico City, a truckload of immigrants up to the border to hide for a day, then a mad dash across in the wee hours of the morning.

"I don't know the details," she said, toying with her empty cup. "He wouldn't tell me, said he didn't want me to worry."

"What does he do for a living, this son of yours?"

She brightened. "Norberto's a carpenter," she said. "Everybody says he's very good and very fast. He said they need good carpenters in America. He said he could earn twenty dollars an hour."

The way she said it made twenty dollars an hour sound like a princely sum and as if she didn't quite believe it.

"You have an address for this travel agency?"

Maria de Lourdes bobbed her head and reached for her purse, old and showing signs of many repairs. Covered with all of those L's and V's that were the designer's trademark, it was an obvious castoff from one of her clients. She fumbled around inside the bag and removed a piece of paper.

"He left this," she said.

Silva unfolded it, found it to be a receipt from the travel agency. The address was on the Rua Sete de Abril, a busy shopping street in the heart of São Paulo.

"May I keep this?"

She nodded.

"Any news of him since he left? Anything at all?"

Again, she reached into her purse. This time she handed him a postcard.

"All going well," someone had written. "I'll call you soon."

An incomprehensible scrawl followed the short message. Silva put a finger on it.

"This is his signature?"

"Yes."

"You're sure?"

"I'm sure."

The photograph on the card showed three models in skimpy bathing suits. The legend above them informed the reader that they (and presumably the sender) were having "A Great Time on South Beach."

Silva was still wearing his jacket. He reached into his breast pocket, retrieved his reading glasses, and subjected both sides of the card to closer scrutiny. The stamp had been canceled in Miami.

"He was going to Miami?"

Maria de Lourdes shook her head.

"He never mentioned Miami," she said. "He was going to Boston. He has a friend there. Well, not really a friend, but someone he knew, someone he could stay with until he found a job."

"Do you have the man's address?"

"No." Then added quickly, "He said I wouldn't need it, that he wouldn't be staying long. He expected to be set up on his own in no time."

Silva waved the postcard as if he were fanning himself. "No other cards? No letters?"

"No."

"And the call he refers to?"

"Never came. But . . ."

"But what?"

"I don't have a telephone at home," she said, "only a cell phone, and it's new. Somebody stole my other one, took it out of my pocket in the bus. When I went to get a new one, I found a place that was cheaper, but I had to change the number."

"It's one of those prepaid things?"

"Yes."

"So your son would have nowhere to turn if he wanted to discover your new number."

"I didn't think about that at the time. But then, when he didn't write and he didn't call, I tried to get my old number back. They wouldn't give it to me."

"Why not?"

"Someone else had it."

"Have you tried calling that new number? Telling whoever answers that you're worried about your son? Telling them he might try to get in touch?"

"Yes."

"And?"

"The first few times the man was nice. Then he got impatient. Now he hangs up whenever he hears my voice."

Probably called him a hundred times, Silva thought, *probably drove the guy nuts.*

"He could have been picked up by the Americans," he said. "If that's the case, they'll hold him for a while and deport him. They never keep illegal aliens for long. If they did, they wouldn't have enough room in their detention centers. I suggest you give your son a couple of weeks, maybe a month, to reestablish contact. If he doesn't, we can talk again."

He made to rise from the table, but Irene put a hand on his arm, gently pulling him back into his seat.

"Tell him how long it's been since Norberto left," she said, looking at Maria de Lourdes.

Maria de Lourdes looked at her, then at Silva.

"Two months," she said. "It was two months last Tuesday."

Chapter Twenty-three

AS THE ORNATE FACADE suggested, the apartment block had once been in the heart of one of São Paulo's most prestigious neighborhoods. But those halcyon days were gone. Now, the area was a hangout for drug dealers and male prostitutes.

Tanaka's building faced a patch of withered grass and stunted trees called the Praça de República, Republic Square. On the far side, trembling under a flux of constant traffic, was Avenida Ipiranga, one of the busiest thoroughfares in the city. The honking of horns and the rumble of buses pursued Hector into the creaky, old elevator and followed him up to the second floor.

The elevator opened onto a dark corridor illuminated by low-wattage lamps and perfumed by frying garlic. Hector located the door for apartment 2F and looked for a bell. There wasn't one, so he knocked. A moment later, he saw movement beyond the peephole.

"Who's that?"

It was a deep voice that could have been male.

Hector held up his credentials.

"Federal police. I'm looking for Marcela Tanaka."

The door opened as far as a chain would permit. A suspicious and heavily shadowed eye stared through the crack, the brown pupil oscillating between Hector's face and the photo on the document he was holding.

"That's me. What do you want?"

"Senhora Tanaka, I'm sorry to intrude on your grief. I'm Delegado Costa of the federal police. May I come in?"

"Why?"

"I'm investigating your husband's murder."

"That's a job for the policia civil. How come you people are interested?"

"I'll be happy to explain."

At first, Hector thought she was going to tell him to do it from the corridor, but then she slipped the chain and revealed herself. She was a little shorter than Hector, but much heavier, wearing a loose-fitting dress in white linen that reminded him of a circus tent. She blocked the opening from side to side, and had to take two steps back to let him enter.

The front door opened directly onto a small living room. Heavy drapes framed French doors and a miniscule terrace, its white-painted metalwork blackened with grime. Through an open door to his left, Hector could see a hallway. There was another door to his right, but it was closed. The carpet was threadbare and the furniture had seen better days. Overall, the place was a dump. With one exception: a large-screen television, one of those plasma jobs. Hector had been pricing one just like it for a couple of months now and kept coming to the conclusion that he still couldn't afford it. This one looked brand-new.

Senhora Tanaka didn't offer refreshments, and she didn't suggest he sit down. She simply sank her considerable bulk into an armchair and stared at him. Hector picked a place on the sofa, facing her across a coffee table with a stained surface only partially concealed by a lace doily.

The doily was the only delicate thing in the room. Everything else looked massive, solid. And that included Marcela Tanaka. If she had Japanese blood, it wasn't evident. She was dark complexioned, had a slight mustache on her upper lip. And she seemed angry.

Hector had been prepared for grief, not rage. He considered

inquiring about the source of her irritation, but decided not to. He had a feeling she'd tell him soon enough. He did a mental shrug and got down to business.

"Can you think of anyone with a reason to murder your husband?"

"What kind of a stupid question is that? You got any idea how many pieces of trash my husband put away in his lifetime? Any one of them could have popped him."

She talked like a cop. There was nothing surprising in that. She'd been married to one for years.

"No one in particular comes to mind?"

"No."

"How about recent threats? Did your husband—"

"Look," she said, "I have nothing to add to what I already said. You want answers? Go over to the delegacia and talk to them."

"Senhora Tanaka," Hector said patiently, "I'm only trying to help."

"Help? You want to help? So go complain about the lousy pension they're giving me. You know how much it is? Eight hundred a month, that's how much. How am I supposed to live on eight hundred a month? The answer is I can't. I got two young daughters to raise. I got rent to pay. I need food for the table. I'm gonna have to go out and get a job. A *job*. Me. At my age."

"I'm sorry—"

"Sorry? *You're* sorry? *I'm* the one who's sorry. You know what? You can kiss my ass!"

Hector couldn't think of a less appealing prospect. Senhora Tanaka's ass was the size of a mule's and equally attractive. He made an attempt to get the conversation back on track.

"I'd like to have a look at any papers your husband might have left around the house," he said.

"What for?"

The answer should have been obvious, but Hector gave her the benefit of the doubt. "There might be some clue as to who killed him."

"There isn't. There are no papers here, no official papers anyway. He never brought anything home. Now, if you're done . . ."

She rose to her feet.

She hadn't repeated her question. She no longer seemed interested in why the federal police had taken an interest in her husband's murder. That was odd. And there was something else as well: Hector had the distinct impression she was trying to get rid of him. He decided to dig in his heels.

"I'm sorry, Senhora Tanaka," he said, not stirring from his seat, "but I must insist."

"You can fucking insist all you want. I don't want you sticking your nose into my bedroom."

"Your bedroom?"

She was already flushing, but now she turned an even darker shade of red. "My bedroom, my daughters' bedroom, anywhere in the house. Now, leave."

Hector pulled out the search warrant and dropped it on the table.

Marcela's mouth dropped open.

Less than ten minutes later he found the money. It was in a canvas bag, stuffed into the back of her bedroom closet, concealed under a pile of old sheets.

Chapter Twenty-four

"SHE SAID IT WAS their life's savings," Hector reported to his uncle two hours later.

"And pigs have wings," Silva said.

"When I asked her why she didn't keep the money in a bank, she said they didn't trust banks. Not after Collor."

"Oh, *please*," Silva said.

Fernando Collor had assumed the presidency of Brazil in 1989, a time of economic turmoil. His first significant act in office had been to freeze withdrawals from private bank accounts in an attempt to contain hyperinflation. People eventually got most of their money back, but it took a year. It took much longer for them to get over the fear of it happening again.

But hyperinflation was now a thing of the past. Faith in the fiscal responsibility of government had been restored. Anyone who could justify where their money came from, and who wasn't earning interest on it, was a fool. Tanaka hadn't struck Silva as a fool.

"She's a piece of work," Hector went on, still somewhat shaken by his confrontation with Tanaka's wife. "For a moment, I thought she was going to jump me. She outweighs me by God knows how many kilos. I started wishing I'd brought Arnaldo."

"I fail to understand why you went over there on your own. You know you're not supposed to do things like that."

"I had no idea of what I was getting into," Hector said, his tone defensive. "I'd pictured a visit to a bereaved widow, not an angry rhinoceros."

"You should have brought Babyface."

"If she'd wanted to, she could have snapped Babyface like a matchstick. Even Arnaldo would have had trouble if she'd decided to make a fight of it."

"But she didn't."

"In the end, she didn't. When I found the cash, she just collapsed. It was like letting air out of a balloon. But then she started thinking about how she's gonna get it back."

"And you know that because?"

"She started yelping about a receipt, made me count it twice, sat there watching me like a hawk while I did it. Before we even started, she called the office to verify my identity, make sure I was who I said I was. Then she put me on the line to talk to Babyface."

"Why Babyface?"

"He was the guy I told her to ask for. She got me to talk to him, and then she took the phone back so she could hear his reaction to my voice. She made him give her a question that only Hector Costa would know the answer to."

"What was the question?"

"That's not important."

"What was the question?"

"Okay, okay. The question was, what is the eye color of the assistant medical examiner who works with Dr. Couto?"

"I seem to recall that Babyface is the office expert on people's love lives. You think he was suggesting something?"

Hector didn't deign to respond to that. "Senhora Tanaka wouldn't take my word for the office's number, either. She looked it up in her telephone book."

"What kind of money are we talking about here?"

"Ninety-four thousand American dollars. Rosa and Danusa are ranking the serial numbers as I speak, but there doesn't appear to be any sequence. All the bills are old. Chances of tracing them are about nil."

"So there's no way we can prove ill-gotten gains? The lady is going to get it all back?"

"So it appears, deserving creature that she is. A hundred thousand dollars in the closet, and in the beginning of our conversation all she did was bitch about her paltry pension. You know what I think?"

"What?"

"Between being married to that woman, and being where he is now, Tanaka is better off dead."

Chapter Twenty-five

GRANT UNGER'S EYES WERE both gray, one a slightly darker shade of gray than the other. They were eyes that reminded Silva of those of his sister's cat. The cat, Diogenes by name, had been a huge tom, finally brought low by a summer downpour that swept him into a storm drain. Silva's sister, Clara, thought it was a tragedy and cried for a week. But the cat's demise had been a relief to the other cats in the neighborhood, some of the smaller dogs, and most of Clara's neighbors. To all of them, Diogenes had been a thoroughly disagreeable creature. And being disagreeable was another trait it shared with Grant Unger.

Unger had a habit of cupping a hand behind his ear when someone talked to him. A hearing aid might have caused him to change that habit, but Unger didn't use one. Knowing Unger, Silva thought he avoided the apparatus for vanity's sake. He also thought that Unger's use of a hearing aid would have been superfluous much of the time. Unger was one of those people who paid scant attention to what others said, especially if they weren't other Americans who were higher up in the pecking order. He never seemed entirely content unless he was doing the talking. And because he was hard of hearing, Unger seemed to think that everyone else was, too. He didn't talk to you, he shouted at you. The noise he was making at the moment evoked cold stares from neighboring tables. He and Silva were in the Belle Époque, a French restaurant that was one of Silva's favorites. Not Unger's, though. He'd just finished telling Silva how much he disliked all things French.

Unger was the FBI's LEGAT, the legal attaché, at the American Embassy in Brasilia. His job, among other things, was to liaise with the Brazilian federal police. He'd been in the country for two years, but his Portuguese was still halting, which put him at a definite disadvantage since most of the people he was supposed to be liaising with weren't fluent in anything but their native tongue. Unger's predecessor, Norton Wallace, had mastered the language in a little over a year. Silva sometimes wondered if Unger's superiors were aware of the lousy job he was doing.

Brasilia is a city of diplomats, so to hear English being spoken isn't unusual. But loud, American-accented English is another matter. The more sophisticated Americans are all too aware of how unpopular they'd become since the war with Iraq. Most of them took care to speak softly when in public.

Not Grant Unger.

"Jesus," the FBI agent said, picking at his *truite almondine*, "they call that a trout? That's not a trout. It's a minnow. I'll bet the damned thing doesn't weigh more than four ounces."

Silva didn't bother to make the conversion to grams.

"And the taste?" he asked.

"It tastes okay," Unger admitted grudgingly, "but they've got a lot of nerve charging thirty reais for it."

Silva had issued the invitation and was paying. He thought the trout was delicious and well worth the price, but in the interest of harmony, he chose not to pick up the gauntlet.

"So what do you want?" Unger said, breaking off a piece of bread and slathering it with butter.

On every previous occasion, it was Unger who'd wanted something and Unger who'd issued the luncheon invitation. Whatever else he was, the FBI agent wasn't stupid. When

Silva called *him*, he'd immediately recognized that the shoe was on the other foot.

"Some information about an illegal immigrant," Silva said.

"To my country?"

"Yes."

"A Brazilian?"

"Yes."

"What makes you think we've got a record of him?"

"I don't think you do, and I don't think you don't. I'm simply inquiring. If you do, it could have been as long ago as ten weeks."

"Christ, Silva, why don't you ask me something easy? Do you have any idea how many Brazilian illegals there are in the United States?"

"I—"

"Probably a million and a half and counting, that's how many. Pisses me off. Okay, I admit, I wouldn't want to stay in this dump myself if I was in their position, but why the fuck don't they try to sneak into Canada, or England, or some other civilized place? We've got too many of your people as it is."

"I understand your concerns," Silva said, straining to keep his temper.

Unger chose to take *understand* to mean *agree with*.

"Sure you do. Anybody who's got their head screwed on does. It's costing us a fortune. We've spent a bundle on fences, and electronic surveillance, and all that kind of shit. We've had to call in the National Guard to help patrol the Mexican border. So what are your Brazilians doing? They're using the sea route, that's what, going to Florida by boat. Some of them die of thirst. Some drown. Fortunately, the Gulf Stream runs a few miles offshore. If it didn't, their bodies would be washing up on Florida's beaches, scaring the shit out of legitimate tourists."

The American took a gulp of his wine. The first bottle was almost empty. From past experience, Silva knew he'd finish another before the lunch was over.

After a few seconds of silence, Silva said, "The illegal immigrant I'm interested in is the son of a woman who's worked in our home for years."

He knew Unger didn't gave a damn about the man or his mother, but he did think a small diversion would help the FBI agent to recover from his alcohol-induced flash of anger about illegal immigration.

Unger took the bait. "Worked in your home?" he said. "As what?"

"A faixineira."

"What's a faixineira?"

"She helps my wife clean. Not full time. Several days a week."

Unger poured himself more wine.

"Why the hell would you want to go out of your way to help a cleaning woman? They're supposed to serve *you*, not the other way around, right?"

Unger had a driver, a cook and a full-time maid, but like many foreigners he'd never learned how to deal with them. More than once, he'd complained to Silva about the constant turnover of his domestic staff. You only had to spend five minutes with the man to understand the reason.

Silva ignored the FBI agent's question. "According to his mother," he said, "the fellow booked a trip to Mexico. He planned to cross the border from there."

Unger drained the bottle and held it up to show the waiter. The waiter nodded and headed toward the bar.

"From Mexico, huh? Just like a million other wetbacks.

We gotta do something about that. Fucking liberals in Congress are still talking about offering amnesty to those people. They're criminals, for Christ's sake! Can you beat it? Criminals who hold parades and march around the country demanding their rights? Rights? Crap! They don't have any rights. They all broke the law to get there. Don't get me started on this. I could go on and on."

"I promise," Silva said, "that I won't get you started. That would be a waste of a perfectly beautiful afternoon."

"You're damned right it would."

"Returning to the boy, his mother hasn't heard from him in more than two months. She's very concerned."

"Two months? She *should* be concerned. The kid's body is probably lying under some cactus, shriveled like a prune."

Silva inhaled patiently. "She received a postcard," he said.

He opened the briefcase that he'd put on the vacant chair to his left, took out the postcard Maria de Lourdes had given him and handed it to Unger.

Unger gave the card a cursory glance. "You know I can't read Portuguese," he said.

"The boy wrote that he was fine and that he'd call his mother soon. But that's not why I showed you the card."

"Okay, I'll play. Why *did* you show me the card?"

"The kid told his mother he was going to Boston."

"So how come he sends her a card from Miami?"

"I, too, found that strange," Silva said. "I suppose he might have wound up in Miami, on his way to Boston, although I can't imagine why. Nevertheless, he might be in the custody of your immigration people."

"If he is, and if he's in Miami," Unger said, "he'd most likely be at a place called the Krome Detention Center." He rubbed the nonexistent stubble on his jaw. Like all of the other FBI agents Silva had known, he was clean shaven. "Did the kid ever call?"

"No. But there might be an explanation for that. His mother lost her prepaid cell phone. When she replaced it, she got a new number."

"So why didn't he send her something else by snail mail? He coulda done that even if he was in custody. How much cash was he carrying?"

"I don't know. Why?"

"You can't trust those fucking Mexicans. They find out that one of their clients is carrying a lot of cash, they're as likely to kill him and steal it as they are to bring him across the border. Maybe he never made it into the States. Any chance the postcard is bogus?"

Silva shrugged. "I can't discount the possibility, but his mother said she recognized his handwriting and his signature."

"They could have made him write it and then killed him. Then they send the postcard in an envelope to some relative of theirs in Miami, and he puts a stamp on it and mails it. That introduces a red herring, while the trail goes cold. Meanwhile, the kid is under the ground somewhere in Mexico."

"Certainly a possibility."

"More than a possibility. Look at it this way: if he croaked on our side of the border, and it was natural causes, and nobody tried to hide his body, the odds are we'd know about it by now. We regularly scour every inch of that desert. Not that we'd necessarily have the kid identified by name. We might have him listed as a John Doe."

"He would have been carrying a passport."

"Yeah, and the coyotes—the real coyotes I mean, not those fucking Mexican smugglers—could have torn his body apart and scattered his stuff, including his ID."

"The boy is an only child," Silva said. "His mother is frantic. I'd appreciate your help."

Unger took a bite of his fish and stuffed a piece of bread into his mouth. When he started to chew, some butter dribbled down his chin. He wiped it off with his napkin.

"You got a picture?" he said, through a mouthful of food.

"I do."

Silva took out an enlarged copy of the photo Maria de Lourdes had given him.

Unger looked at it.

"Fucking kid needs a decent barber," he said. "Look at that haircut."

The waiter was back with another bottle of wine. While he made a show of opening it, Unger finished the contents of his glass. The waiter offered him the cork to smell, but he didn't take it.

"Just pour it in there," he said, pointing to the glass he'd just emptied, "and then buzz off. I'll let you know if there's something wrong with it."

The waiter, who spoke only limited English, looked to Silva for an explanation.

"Thank you," Silva said, in Portuguese. "Just fill the same glass. No more for me."

The waiter smiled, did as he was bidden, and tried to pick up Unger's plate, which still contained a fragment of fish.

"Put that down," Unger snapped. "I'm not finished."

That much English the waiter understood. His face turned red. He put down the plate, mumbled excuses, and fled.

"Asshole," Unger mumbled. He took a pen out of the pocket of his jacket. "Name?"

"Norberto Krups." Silva spelled it for him. Unger wrote it on the back of the photograph.

"Age?"

"Nineteen."

Unger noted that, too.

"He could be calling himself something else," he said.

"He could," Silva admitted.

"Makes no fucking difference to us. We print them, so we don't give a shit what they call themselves. They show up again, we can ID them within fifteen minutes."

Silva produced a white sheet of paper with a single thumbprint.

"From his national identity card," he said.

"Something we've been trying to adopt for years," Unger said, "national identity cards. You know what passes for identification in most states?" He snorted and answered his own question: "Driver's licenses."

"I've heard they're easy to get," Silva said.

"You heard right."

Unger put his pen away, folded the fingerprint over the photo, slipped both into another pocket of his jacket, and picked up his fork.

"I gotta admit," he said, "that our relationship up to now, yours and mine, I mean, has been pretty much a one-way street. This is the first time you ever asked me for anything, and I figure I owe you. So I'm going to get on to this right away, even if it is for a fucking cleaning woman." He looked at his watch. "It's three hours earlier in Washington. I should have an answer for you by tomorrow."

"Thanks," Silva said.

"Thanks, nothing," Unger said, grinning, "just take off your panties."

Silva vaguely remembered the joke, something about an elephant doing a favor for a mouse and wanting sex in return. It seemed appropriate. America, the elephant, Brazil, the mouse. He forced a smile.

Unger shoveled up the last bit of fish and put it into his mouth. "How are the desserts in this place?" he asked, still chewing.

Chapter Twenty-six

"I'VE GOT SOME FOREIGNER ON the line," Camila said. "I think he wants to talk to you."

"You *think?*" Silva said.

She shrugged. "He doesn't speak Portuguese."

Camila apparently found it unnecessary to add that she didn't speak anything else.

Silva's new secretary was surly and inefficient, but firing her was out of the question. She'd been appointed by Sampaio as a favor to her father, a highly ranked bureaucrat in the federal accounting office.

"I'll take it," Silva said.

"Line two."

The foreigner turned out to be Grant Unger.

"We've got nothing on this guy Norberto," he began without preamble. "There's a Krupps with two p's, but his first name is Adolph. How's that for a Brazilian name, huh? Adolph Krupps. Sounds like some fucking Nazi. Border Patrol picked him up last March. I had them e-mail me his mug shot. He doesn't look anything like your guy."

"And he's the only one with a similar name?"

"The only one. I put the print through AFIS, our computerized system. No match. Son of a bitch could be working some unregistered shit job or using somebody else's social security number. We got a law that punishes people who employ illegals, but you know how it goes. Lots of cheaters slip through the cracks. I arranged to have his picture posted and I got his name and print into the computers. If they pick him up, I'll hear."

"I'll keep my fingers crossed."

"Okay, but don't hold your breath."

When Silva hung up, he unlocked the top drawer of his desk, took out a large, manila envelope, and went down the hall to Arnaldo's office. Arnaldo was still working the phones, calling the cops in city after city, trying to get a lead on cults that might be involved in ritual murder.

"Any luck?" Silva asked.

Arnaldo hung up and made a checkmark on his list to remind him where he'd left off. "Nothing that rings a bell."

"How would you like to get back to São Paulo for a while?"

"Who do I have to kill?"

Arnaldo, a Paulista, born and bred, hated his temporary assignment to the federal capital. He gave all sorts of reasons for his displeasure, everything from the quality of Brasilia's restaurants to daily exposure to the director, but Silva suspected that Arnaldo's major problem was that he missed his family. He'd never admit it, of course. Arnaldo enjoyed bitching about his wife and two teenage sons, and he downright gloried in excoriating his mother-in-law.

"You don't have to kill anybody," Silva said, "but the job may involve some travel."

"I knew there had to be a catch. Same case?"

"Something different. A nineteen-year-old carpenter was trying to get into the States. He disappeared."

"What's that got to do with us?"

"Officially? Nothing. He's my faixineira's son. I want to help her."

"What good is power if you can't abuse it, right?"

"My sentiments exactly. Do you want the job or not?"

"Yes, I want the job. What's the timing?"

"Immediate.

"Good. You know how much time I spent sleeping at home in the last thirty days? Two nights, that's how much, two lousy nights. My wife is starting to think I've got a mistress."

"Do you?"

"On my salary? Kindly outline what I have to do to escape from durance vile."

"Durance vile?"

"You think you're the only guy who reads books? Brief me."

Silva detailed his conversation with Maria de Lourdes and showed Arnaldo copies of the postcard and the photo.

"You try the Americans?" Arnaldo said when he'd finished.

"I cashed in a favor with Grant Unger."

Arnaldo did a mock shiver. "I can see you're willing to carry this to great lengths."

"I am. Unger already called me back. They have no record of the kid."

Arnaldo pointed at the list on his desk. "How about all these calls I haven't made?"

"I'll put Camila on it, move her in here. It'll make her feel important."

"And keep her out of your hair."

"I never thought of that."

"Like hell you didn't. You'll have to answer your own phone, you know."

"I do now."

"This Norberto kid was going to the States of his own volition. What's our mandate here?"

"None."

"So how are you going to account for my time? Sampaio goes over the time sheets like a fucking miser counting his money. He'll be onto us within two weeks."

"I'll sign off on the sheets. Besides, I don't think it's going to take two weeks. And, by that time, he'll be grateful. It'll be another solution he can take the credit for."

"And if we don't have a solution?"

"We'll have a solution. My faith in you is boundless."

"I'll bet you say that to all the girls. Where do you want me to start?"

"Go to the travel agency he used. Act like you're desperate to get into the States."

"And then?"

"Take a cell phone, conceal it on your person, do what they tell you to do, follow the trail to where it leads."

"Including creeping through the desert in Arizona, or Texas, or wherever?"

"If it comes to that, yes."

"And Sampaio, when he notices I'm not coming into the office? How are you going to handle him?"

"I'm going to tell him you're following up a rumor about Romeu Pluma."

"What rumor?"

"The one about Pluma molesting teenage boys."

"Such a rumor exists?"

"It does now. It will turn out to be unsubstantiated."

"How much longer do you think you can keep using Pluma to get away with stuff?"

"He shows no sign of backing off, so Sampaio won't either. It could go on forever."

"We should give Pluma a citation for meritorious service. Alright, getting back to the Americans, if I wind up crossing their border, they're not going to like it."

"The Americans aren't going to know about it. Not if you don't get caught."

"They've got cameras. They've got helicopters. They've got vigilantes. They catch a lot of people."

"So they catch you. No big deal. They'll send you back."

"They'll print me first, and they won't let me back in if I ask for a visa. What if I want to take my kids to Orlando to see Disney World? What do I do then?"

"You can't afford to take your kids to Orlando."

"You're right. I can't. But what if my rich uncle Uriel dies?"

"You haven't got a rich uncle Uriel. Do you want to get back to São Paulo or not?"

"I want."

"I can't ask Ana to do the paperwork. Sampaio would never sign it. I'm gonna have to advance the money myself. Here."

He held out the envelope he'd been carrying.

"What's this?" Arnaldo said, taking it.

"Seven thousand American dollars, a ticket to São Paulo, and a thousand reais. The so-called travel agent in São Paulo is probably going to ask you for five of the seven. The rest is for expenses if you get into the States. Don't forget to bring sunscreen. The thousand Reais is for expenses here."

Arnaldo drew the flap and looked inside the envelope. He let out a low whistle. "You're really taking this seriously, aren't you? Want me to count it?"

"No need. I already did. Twice. I don't have money coming out of my ears."

"Your own damned fault. You're too fucking honest. This travel agency, you got an address?"

"Also in the envelope. It's called Estrela Viagens and it's on that street they reserve for pedestrians, the one near the Praça da Republica."

"The Sete de Abril?"

"That's the one."

Arnaldo glanced at his watch. "There's a flight in about an hour. If I hurry, I can make it."

"So, hurry," Silva said.

Chapter Twenty-seven

ALONG THE BACK WALL, a glass-fronted case contained petit fours, biscuits, *rosquinhas*, cookies, Lebanese *esfihas*, German pretzels, and a variety of cakes. Two attendants, dressed identically in paper hats and starched, white blouses, were behind the counter. They had no more than a half dozen customers and were having an easy time of it.

Not so the six attendants to Arnaldo's right. Charged with dispensing the bread, they were beleaguered by a crowd that was elbow to elbow and three rows deep. Service seemed to be on the basis of push and shove. Every now and then an altercation would break out. But since most of the buyers were females, fights never seemed to escalate beyond an exchange of insults.

The loaves in contention were marvels of the baker's art. There were narrow loaves, thick loaves, short loaves, long loaves, loaves made out of barley, manioc, rye, and wheat. There were loaves with sausage, cheese, and onion baked into the dough. There were French baguettes, loaves of Jewish rye, Syrian pitas, and German black breads, all reflective of the multicultural nature of the neighborhood.

Arnaldo could have done without the noise, but he adored the mouth-watering smells and the jostling, rollicking atmosphere that was unique to a São Paulo *padaria*. Brasilia, too, had padarias, but they were nothing like this.

Every few minutes a guy in a white apron, rivulets of sweat running through a dusting of flour on his forehead, would come out of the back where the ovens were. He'd be carrying a wicker basket filled with something freshly baked, and he'd dump the contents into one of the unpainted wooden boxes reserved for that kind of bread. The effect on the women was immediate. They couldn't wait to get at it. It reminded Arnaldo of the time he'd been in the Mato Grosso and had tossed the remainder of a ham sandwich into a pool of piranhas.

Most of the men, Arnaldo included, were gathered around the bar on the other side of the shop. São Paulo bakers sold sandwiches, fresh coffee, and alcoholic beverages, too. This particular baker seemed to be conveniently situated on the way home from work of many of his clients, and those clients appeared to be the kind of people who needed a drink to get their evenings under way.

The bar formed a perfect square. Arnaldo, with no little difficulty, had been able to belly up to a spot on the far side that had a view of the street.

He took another bite of his *Americano*, a grilled ham-and-cheese sandwich with a fried egg on a crusty French roll, and masticated slowly. The men around him were a diverse group that seemed to share only one characteristic: a taste for their cachaça straight up.

There were laborers and office workers; there were men in T-shirts and men in ties; there were kids barely out of their teens; and there was one gaffer who'd never see the shy side of eighty again. They were all making so much noise, and having such a good time, and demanding so much attention from the two men and a woman who were serving them, that no one bothered to ask Arnaldo if he wanted another beer, which was fine with him, because he wasn't there for the drink or the food. He was there to check out the travel agency directly across the street.

Estrela Viagens, Star Travel, the place was called, but if the proprietors were trying to suggest that their clients included the noteworthy of Brazilian media or sports, they were liars. Arnaldo had been in place for almost two hours, and the only people he'd seen go through the glass door and climb the stairs had been simple working men. The agency had a discreet sign at street level and a bigger sign in the window one floor up, directly above a shop that sold all sorts of imported junk from cheap perfumes to radios the size of a box of matches.

Arnaldo glanced at his watch. It was eight minutes to six.

According to the information stenciled on the door, business hours at the agency were almost at an end. Things were likely to go more smoothly if the people waiting on him had their minds on closing the shop. That way there'd be less time for chit chat, less conversation that could lead to a mistake.

Arnaldo had never thought of emigrating, never would, and he wasn't sure he could sustain the role of an emigrant for an extended period of time. He had an idea of what he was going to say, and how he was going to say it, but he wasn't sure he had it right. How did emigrants talk about the place they were leaving behind? And how did they talk about the country they were going to? And how did they come to make the decision to sneak into a place that didn't want them? It was all a mystery to him. And it was one of the things wrong with Brazil that more than a few of its citizens were so exasperated by the high crime rate and the lack of opportunity that they were willing to pay dearly to get out of their country.

Time to go. Arnaldo stood up. He'd left his gun at home and traded his jacket and tie for a faded, blue shirt. He put enough money to cover the bill under his beer glass, and moved toward the door. The space he'd occupied was immediately filled by patrons to his left and right.

He crossed the narrow street (closed to vehicular traffic

during business hours), pushed through the glass door, and climbed stairs that ended in a little alcove. The alcove terminated in a counter strewn with airline brochures. Beyond the counter, a girl was perched on a high stool reading a *fotonovela*.

She looked up, moved her chewing gum to one side of her mouth, and said, "Help you?"

"Yeah," Arnaldo said. "I'm interested in a trip to the United States."

"Sure," she said. "Where to? New York? Miami?"

"It's a little more complicated than that," he said.

"Oh." She winked. "You better talk to Juan. Hey, Juan."

The only other person in the office, a man in his midthirties with his hair parted in the middle, looked up from a desk by the window.

"Somebody for you," the girl said, and glanced at her watch. "Hey. Quitting time. See you tomorrow."

She retrieved a cheap, plastic purse, ducked under the counter, and clattered off down the stairwell. The guy with his hair parted in the middle strolled over, an insincere smile plastered below his sparse mustache. He extended a hand. Arnaldo took it.

"Name's Juan," he said in a singsong accent that couldn't be anything else but Argentinian.

"Arnaldo," Arnaldo said, trying not to screw up his nose at the guy's choice of cologne.

"What's your pleasure?"

"I want to go to the States," Arnaldo said.

"And?" Juan raised an eyebrow.

"And I can't get a visa. Got turned down."

"Why?"

"I worked there for years, overstayed my welcome, came home for my mother's funeral. They stamped my passport on the way out, and now they won't let me back in."

"Sad," the Argentinian said, but he didn't sound as if he meant it. "So what makes you think we can help you?"

"I heard you guys organize trips. Through Mexico."

"And where did you hear a thing like that?"

"Some guy I met."

"Who?"

"I don't remember his name. Just some guy."

"Where?"

"In Pompano."

Illegal Brazilian immigrants live all over the United States, but there are particularly large communities in Astoria, New York, near Boston, Massachusetts, and Pompano Beach, Florida. The locals drop Beach. They call it Pompano.

"Pompano, huh?"

The Argentinian looked Arnaldo up and down. Arnaldo did his best to look guileless.

"You're a pretty old guy for that sort of thing, aren't you? Sneaking across borders, I mean."

Arnaldo hated references to his age. It took a conscious effort for him not to tell the *Porteño* to go fuck himself.

"Not that it's any of your business," he said, "but I got family there. A wife and two kids."

"Guy's got a family, he should be more careful. Maybe you shoulda stayed where you were."

This time, Arnaldo almost lost it.

"I didn't ask for your fucking opinion, I just want to know if you can help."

"Hey, no need to get touchy. Travel is our business. We just got to be careful, you understand. You aren't breaking any Brazilian laws by trying to get into the States, but if we help you, we are."

"You want my business or not?"

The Argentinian seemed to come to a sudden decision.

"Cost you five thousand dollars American," he said.

"And what do I get for my five?"

"Here's how it works: you give me the five in cash, dollars, not reais. We put you up for a couple of days, room and board included, until we get a group of ten."

"Put me up where?"

"A place we got. We don't tell anyone where it is, and you don't contact anyone while you're there. No telephone, no letters, no nothing. Once we get a group together, we send everybody to Mexico. These days, the Mexicans are asking for visas from Brazilians. The Americans pressured them into that, but we have contacts. A little money changes hands and the visas get issued like that." The Argentinian snapped his fingers.

"The visa's extra?"

The Argentinian shook his head. "Included. Everything's included. When you get to Mexico City, our group leader puts you in touch with one of our associates. The associate brings you and the others across the border. Once he does, you're on your own. No guarantees."

"What do you mean, no guarantees?"

"We provide board and lodging along the way, the ticket to Mexico, the visa, and the services of reliable guides, people who've done this kind of thing hundreds of times. Every now and then, one of them gets caught, which could mean *you* get caught. It doesn't happen often, but it happens. The Yankees deport you, you come back here, and you try again. No discounts. If you want to try again, we charge you another five thousand dollars."

"What kind of a deal is that?"

"It's the deal we offer. It's the deal everybody offers. You can try it on your own, of course. Some people do. Most of them don't get very far. Aside from the fact that you probably haven't got contacts at the Mexican consulate, your chances of getting across the border without help are pretty low. That's what we charge for. Not the plane fare. Take it or leave it."

Arnaldo nodded. "I'll take it."

"Good. When do you want to leave?"

"As soon as possible."

"Then say your good-byes tonight. Come here tomorrow morning at eleven. Bring your luggage, one carry-on only, and my five thousand in cash. We'll have you on your way to the land of margaritas and mariachis in a few days. You'll be in the States within a week. Now, if you'll excuse me, it's closing time."

Less than a minute later, Arnaldo was back on the street.

Chapter Twenty-eight

SYLVIE CHARMET BLEW INTO the restaurant like a squall off the South Atlantic, bussed Gilda once on each cheek, and slipped into the chair the waiter had hastened to pull out. Gilda waited until she had Sylvie's full attention before pointedly looking at her watch. Then she lifted her eyes and stared at her friend.

"Once, just once, Sylvie, it would be nice if you'd show up for lunch on time."

Sylvie made a dismissive gesture. She was big on dismissive gestures. "I've got a new shrink," she said.

Sylvie was a cardiovascular surgeon, a lithe brunette in her early thirties and, like Gilda, still unmarried. When it came to her work, Sylvie was meticulous, but the rest of her life was a mess. Only the attentions of a full-time faixineira could keep her small apartment in order. The inside of her car looked like a teenager's room. She couldn't seem to find a new boyfriend and was flitting from psychiatrist to psychiatrist, trying to figure out why her fiancé of four years, another doctor, had abandoned her for a medical secretary with wide hips and thick glasses.

"What's a new shrink got to do with anything?"

"She's got man trouble, too. I got her to talk about it."

Gilda rolled her eyes at the breach of professionalism. "The halt leading the blind. Are you helping each other?"

"Too early to tell." Sylvie settled back in her chair and studied Gilda's face. "What's the matter with you?"

"Nothing," Gilda said, and buried her nose in the menu.

"Oh, come on. You can't honestly be in a tiff just because I'm a few minutes late."

"It's not that."

"But it's something. Man trouble?"

Sylvie was also big on projecting. If she had a problem, she was prone to believe that others had the same problem.

"I wish," Gilda said. "My boss is sixty-five if he's a day, happily married with grandchildren. The only young bachelor in the medical examiner's office is gay, and my patients are all dead."

Sylvie didn't bother to grin. She'd heard the crack about dead patients before.

"Prospects?" she said.

"Maybe one," Gilda admitted.

Sylvie wriggled in her seat. "Tell," she said.

"He's a federal cop, and he's cute."

"A federal cop?"

"Not just a cop. A delegado. You have to be a lawyer to be a delegado."

"Yeah. I know. But Gilda, a *cop?*"

"You think I should hold out for another doctor?"

"Touché. You have a picture?"

"Not yet."

"How'd you meet him?"

"I'll get to that later. And Sylvie . . ."

"Yes?"

"I don't want you shooting your mouth off about this. It's in the early stages yet."

"Your secrets are safe with me, querida. I don't even know any cops. Yet."

"Alright then. I'll trust your discretion. How's it going with you?"

"In the man department?"

Gilda nodded.

"The usual," Sylvie said.

"A complete disaster?"

"I work with an anesthesiologist who's interested, but he's a creep. I met a guy at a party who wasn't wearing a wedding ring, and I thought he was a legitimate target, but then his namorada showed up and dragged him off to her lair. My boss is unmarried, but he's even older than yours, and for all the attention he pays to women, he must have shelved his sexuality. Sometimes I think I should have dropped all the medical-school crap and become a secretary. Secretaries find men and get married."

"So do doctors."

"Yeah, but most of them marry nurses. Can you see me with a male nurse?"

"Frankly? No."

"Me neither." Sylvie picked up the menu and perused it. "What are you going to have?"

"While I was waiting for you, I had a long talk with the waiter. About half an hour's worth. I know his life story."

"Married?"

"Yes. Happily."

"And your point?"

"He said the snapper in lemon butter is good."

Actually the conversation with the waiter had taken all of thirty seconds, Gilda had no idea whether he was married or not, and he hadn't said a word about the snapper in lemon butter. It was just that the snapper was the cheapest thing on the menu. The waiter had nodded in a superior fashion when she'd asked him if he could recommend it. Compared to what Sylvie earned, Gilda's salary was paltry, and she was still reeling in shock over the prices on the menu.

"And it's your turn to pay, right?" Sylvie said, as if she could read Gilda's thoughts.

Gilda nodded.

Sylvie perused her menu, then looked Gilda straight in the eye and said, "I'm going to have lobster Thermidor and a split of Cordon Rouge."

"Sylvie—"

"On the other hand, I might have the snapper, but only if you come clean and you do it right now. What's bugging you?"

Gilda rested her forearms on the white damask and leaned forward.

"Let's order and I'll tell you."

Sylvie snapped her menu shut.

"Snapper it is, then," she said, "but you've got to promise you'll brief me on the cop before I leave this table."

Gilda raised her hand and crossed her fingers as children do when they're making solemn promises.

The waiter thought she was signaling him, and promptly came to the table. They ordered the snapper and compromised on a bottle of Chilean white.

When he was gone, Sylvie gestured with her hands, as if she were presenting the place.

"Well?" she said with a proprietary air.

"Very nice, but expensive."

"Worth every centavo. You're going to love it."

Gilda wasn't sure about that. Even the snapper in lemon butter was a strain on her budget. The waiter came back with the wine and let Gilda taste it. She nodded. He half-filled each of their glasses and went away again.

"So out with it," Sylvie prompted. "You pregnant? Been fired? Have a particularly bad morning cutting up one of your patients?"

"None of that," Gilda said.

"Then what?"

"I want you to tell me how you source human hearts."

Chapter Twenty-nine

Silvie had been leaning forward, resting her chin on the heel of one hand. She put her hand on the table and sat up straight in her chair.

"What?"

"Hearts. Hearts from people recently dead. The ones you use for transplants. Where do you source them from?"

Sylvie frowned. "From donors, of course. Why?"

"I'm paying. I get to ask my questions first. Where else do you get hearts from?"

"Nowhere else. That's it. Donors."

"And these . . . donors? They make that decision, to *be* donors, before they die?"

Sylvie shook her head. "Mostly not. Consent from their next of kin is what we usually get. And that consent has to be quick. If we don't get a heart into refrigeration within three hours after death, my boss won't use it. He won't use it, either, if the person died from any one of a number of diseases, and he won't use a heart from anyone over fifty, no matter what shape it appears to be in."

"And lots of people do it?"

"Do what?"

"Agree to donate their next of kin's hearts."

"Not enough. It's the biggest problem we have."

"So how do you go about it?"

The waiter was back with their fish. Sylvie put down her wine glass, picked up a fork, cut off a small piece of snapper, popped it into her mouth, and savored it.

"Delicious," she said. "You know something? I don't like lobster anyway."

"How do you go about it?" Gilda insisted. "The sourcing, I mean."

"I *don't* go about it," Sylvie said. "I just implant them."

"But you must have some idea."

"Some idea, yes. Basically, it works like this: a good prospect comes into a public hospital; maybe some kid shot to death in a favela, maybe a young woman run over by a car. Anyway, somebody who didn't die of a debilitating disease, someone who met a sudden, usually violent, end. If the upper torso doesn't seem to have sustained any major damage, if the area around the heart seems to be in good shape, somebody at the hospital tips off my boss and—"

"Why would somebody at the hospital do that?" Gilda interrupted. "Tip off your boss?"

Sylvie took a sip of wine.

"Good stuff, this," she said.

"Sylvie . . ."

Sylvie glanced at the neighboring tables and lowered her voice.

"There's this woman we have on staff," she said. "Once he gets the tip, she goes over there, has a chat with the family, tells them how much good they can do by helping someone else, and gets them to release the heart to us."

"Why don't they release it to the hospital?"

"Get real, Gilda. You have any idea how much my boss charges for a heart transplant?"

"What's that got to do with it?"

"It's got everything to do with it. He pegs his fees to the American dollar, and he gets the whole sum in advance. There's nothing unusual in that. All the private clinics do it. The current price is four hundred thousand dollars."

"*Dollars?*" Gilda did a quick calculation. Four hundred thousand dollars was only a little less than eight hundred thousand reais.

"God," she said. "I had no idea. Are you suggesting that he uses part of that to pay for tips from hospital staff and part to pay survivors? That he *buys* hearts?"

"I'm not suggesting anything," Sylvie said.

But both of them knew she was. And both of them knew it was illegal. In Brazil, as in most countries, the law proscribes trafficking in human organs.

"Four hundred thousand dollars," Gilda repeated, still trying to come to terms with the enormity of the sum. "How can he get away with charging so much?"

Sylvie continued to dissect her fish. "He not only gets away with it, he has patients standing in line to pay. If shelling out the money is the only thing that's going to save your life, you shell out the money. And, if you don't have it, you beg, borrow, or steal. You know where I worked before?"

"You worked in a number of places. You mean where you first started doing transplants? The Hospital das Clinicas?"

The Hospital das Clinicas was owned and run by the state of São Paulo. Most of the patients were people who received free treatment under the government health scheme.

"Uh-huh," Silvie said. She put a morsel of fish into her mouth, chewed, and swallowed. "Any idea what their official charge is for a heart transplant?"

"Why 'official?'"

"They have to put a number on it. Some people fall outside the government health scheme, and that's what they'd charge, *if* they charged, but they never do. Guess. Guess how much it is."

"I haven't the slightest idea."

"Twenty thousand reais."

"So why doesn't everyone elect to do their procedure there?"

"Because, querida, the Clinicas, like every other public hospital, has a hell of a time getting healthy hearts. They source only one or two a month on average. And if you want one, there's a waiting list as long as my ex-fiancé's penis—which is very long indeed, believe you me."

"How does one—"

Sylvie anticipated her question. "Get to the top of the list?"

Gilda nodded.

"You make sure you're young, suffering exclusively from heart failure, and just about to die. And you make sure you've been on that list for at least six months, because, all other considerations being equal, hearts are doled out on a first-come, first-served basis."

While Gilda digested that, Sylvie ingested the rest of her snapper. She left the vegetables and potatoes on the plate and poured herself another glass of white wine.

"So," Gilda said, "Many patients at the Clinicas die while they're waiting for a heart?"

Sylvie nodded.

"If you're over sixty, or if you suffer from a life-threatening disease in addition to your heart problem, your chances of getting an organ through the Clinicas are nil."

"So that's the patient profile at your boss's clinic? The old? The people who suffer from other diseases?"

"Our patients aren't *all* old, and they don't *all* suffer from other diseases, but they're *all* people that can scratch up four hundred thousand dollars. Mind you, even with us there's no guarantee. We still have more patients than we can find hearts for. The money buys you a better chance, but it doesn't give you a guarantee. If we could guarantee a heart to any-one who asked, we'd probably be able to charge twice as much. But one thing's for sure: if you're poor, you can't afford us. You have to take your chances with a public hospital."

"Where the likelihood of someone getting a heart is akin to one's chances of winning the national lottery?"

"Exactly."

"And you think that's right?"

"I'm not a jurist, Gilda. I'm a surgeon. I don't dictate how the system works. I'm just telling you how it is. Besides, rich people have as much right to life as poor people, wouldn't you say?"

"But—"

"It's all regulated, Gilda. The survivors can donate the heart to whomever they want."

"But not for gain."

"Not legally, no. But who's to say it's for gain?"

"You just implied that—"

Sylvie waved a finger in front of Gilda's nose.

"No audit by health or tax authorities has ever detected an irregularity in my clinic's paperwork. I made sure of that before I took the job. I want to earn money, that's only natural, but not if it involves a risk of losing my license to practice medicine. What with my love life being the way it is, my profession might be the only thing I'll have to sustain me in my old age."

Gilda shook her head, more in condemnation of the practice than denial at Sylvie's prospects. Sylvie reached out and put a hand over one of hers. "Gilda, Gilda, you're always painting things in black-and-white. The world doesn't work that way. You have to see the other side of things."

"Other side?"

Gilda tried to withdraw her hand, but Sylvie held on to it and leaned forward in her chair.

"Look," she said, "if I'd stayed at the Hospital das Clinicas,

I might have done a heart transplant every six months. These days, on the average, I do three times as many. I save more lives and I make more money. What's wrong with that? Everybody wins. Not only me. The patients win, too."

"But the public hospitals—"

"Forget the public hospitals. They can't compete. Stop looking at me like that and eat your fish."

"I lost my appetite."

Sylvie shrugged and released Gilda's hand. "Suit yourself. But now it's your turn. I've been doing all the talking, and you haven't told me a damn thing. What sparked all this curiosity about heart transplants, and what's it to you?"

Gilda thought for a moment about how to begin. Finally, she just plunged in. "Have you seen the press coverage on that clandestine cemetery?"

"The one up in the Serra da Cantareira? All those desaparecidos?"

"They weren't desaparecidos. They couldn't have been killed by the military government. The corpses hadn't been in the ground long enough."

"Okay. So *when* were they killed? And *why* were they killed? And who killed them?"

"That's what I'm struggling with. The cop I'm seeing tonight is assigned to the case. That's how I met him. He came to the morgue to view the bodies."

"How romantic. What a great story to tell your grandchildren. How grandpa and I met one morning over the—"

"Not funny, Sylvie."

"No? I thought it was. Maybe you should lighten up."

"And maybe you should pay attention to what I'm saying. The cops seem to think that some cult is responsible for the murders."

"Some cult?"

"People performing ritual murders. It's happened before, apparently."

"But you—"

"Have another idea. And it seems crazy, even to me. I don't know whether I should tell him about it or not. I need a second opinion. You're a cardiovascular surgeon; you're the ideal person to ask."

"Gilda, what the hell are you getting at?"

Gilda leaned across the table. "Sylvie, in every case, *in every single case,* the sternums of the victims had been sawn through. Not hacked, not chopped, *sawn.*"

Sylvie paused with her wine glass halfway to her lips. "With a sternal saw?"

"Yes. With a sternal saw."

Sylvie put down her glass, pursed her lips, took in a deep breath, let it out slowly.

"Look, I wouldn't tell you that organ theft doesn't happen—"

"So it *does* happen?"

"Let me finish, okay? I'm attuned to all of this stuff because it directly affects what I do. There was a case a few months ago in one of the municipal mortuaries. A university student slit his wrists and died. His family sent clothes to dress him for his funeral. This is pretty macabre stuff. You sure you want to discuss it over lunch?"

"Have you forgotten what I do all day? Do you think I could do it if I had a weak stomach?"

"Okay, okay, take it easy."

Gilda sniffed. "Yes, I want to discuss it."

Sylvie took a hefty swallow of wine before she continued. "The student's mother got it into her head that she didn't like the choice of clothing, that she wanted to dress him herself. Last thing she could do for her son and all that. She goes to the mortuary, strips off his shirt, and finds stitches right down the middle of his chest. She goes ballistic and calls the cops. It turns out that one of the attendants had a nice little business going for himself, selling organs to a research lab."

"Not for transplant?"

"No. They were no good for that. He wasn't getting them out quickly enough. Then there was this ex-Israeli defense forces colonel up in Recife. You heard about him?"

"No."

"I'm surprised. It was in all the papers." Sylvie reached for the bottle of wine, refilled her glass, and made to top up Gilda's. Gilda put her hand over the mouth of the glass.

"I must have missed it," she said.

Sylvie shrugged and put down the bottle.

"It wasn't a case of theft per se. The colonel wasn't stealing, he was buying. Kidneys to be precise."

"Kidneys?"

"Yeah. It's damned near impossible to get kidney donors in Israel because there's something in their religion about the body being buried intact. The colonel was recruiting poor people who were willing to sell one of their kidneys. He had a deal going with a hospital in Johannesburg. The recipients would fly from Israel, the donors from Recife. They'd do the operation there, and the donors would come back without one of their kidneys. It took awhile for the federal cops to catch on. The colonel's partner was the local police chief."

"Jesus."

"Yeah. And then there was a couple who were willing to sell their kid."

"Sell their kid? So somebody could extract his organs?"

"Uh-huh. How sick is that? They were Albanians, living in Italy. They held an auction. Infant hearts are extremely rare, so they figured they could get a good price. The cops heard about it, mounted a sting operation, and nailed them."

Sylvie speared her last piece of fish and popped it into her mouth.

"So the baby survived?" Gilda asked.

Sylvie, still chewing, nodded. Then she swallowed and said, "In that case, yes."

"A couple of years ago," Gilda said, "I had a maid who told me foreigners were coming into the country, adopting kids out of favelas, taking them home, and cutting them up for their organs."

"The consensus on that one," Sylvie said, "is that it's an urban legend, but the rumor was widespread enough for the government to tighten adoption regulations."

"What about the regulations pertaining to transplants? Why don't they do something about that?"

"They already have. Clinics like mine are very strict about the paperwork. The origin of any organ we receive has to be proven beyond a shadow of a doubt."

"'Clinics like mine,' you said. Are there other kinds of clinics?"

Sylvie put down her fork and wiped her mouth with her napkin.

"At the Hospital das Clinicas," she said, "we had an average of six young men die of gunshot wounds every single day. Most of them, the ones who weren't shot in the chest, would have made pretty good donors. Those victims, alone, would have generated over two thousand hearts a year. You know how many hearts were donated last year?"

"No idea."

"One hundred and forty-seven. I'm not talking about the city of São Paulo, Gilda, or even the state. I'm talking nationally. One hundred forty-seven hearts donated in the whole damned country. You know how many people are on the waiting list as of this morning? Three thousand two hundred and twelve."

"Most of those people are going to die?"

"Yes."

"Because they can't get a heart?"

"Yes. So that brings me back to your question. There *have to be* other kinds of clinics. Personally, I don't know of any, but I know this country. I know you can pay to have someone killed. It happens all the time. And, if you can buy death . . ."

"What if a clinic was doing both the implants and the . . . harvesting?"

"Killing people to get at their hearts? It wouldn't surprise me at all. Someone could earn a bundle of money. Someone probably is. Hey, are you going to eat your fish?"

Chapter Thirty

"ABOUT TIME," SILVA SAID. "Where are you?"

Arnaldo mumbled something. Silva stuck a finger in the ear that wasn't covered by his cell phone.

"Speak up. I can hardly hear you."

"I said God knows where I am." Arnaldo raised his voice only a little. "Can you hear me now?"

"Yes," Silva said. "Go ahead."

"The Argentinian handed me over to some guy with a van. He made me sit in the back on the floor. No windows. After about an hour, the van stops and we're in a garage. The driver takes me to a bedroom. No, not a bedroom, more like a dormitory. It's full of other people. They assign me a mattress on the floor. I sit around for a while making small talk with my fellow emigrants, or maybe it's immigrants, I always get those two words mixed up. And then the driver comes back. He wants a blood sample."

"A *blood* sample?"

"Claims it's for the Mexican visa. All the other guys nod. He's done it to them, too, so I decide not to make a fuss."

"It's crap. The Mexicans don't ask for a blood samples."

"You know that, and I know that, but the other guys don't. They're simple people by and large, laborers mostly. When the driver leaves, I ask if anybody tried to make any calls, and they look at me like I'm some kind of nut. They all paid five thousand American dollars to get into the States, and that's a fortune for them. They're gonna follow the rules. They'd finger me in an instant if I pulled this cell phone out of my sock and started to use it. You see why I didn't call?"

"Who's that talking in the background?"

"Television set. I turned it on to cover the sound of my voice."

"How come you can get away with calling now? What happened to the others?"

"The driver came back this morning and picked them up. They're on their way."

"How come you're not?"

"They said there wasn't time to get the visa."

"You believe it?"

"Why not? I can't think of any other reason to send them on and keep me here. One other thing: remember that post-card of South Beach? The one you showed me? The one Maria de Lourdes got from her son?"

"I remember."

"That guy from the agency was here, the Argentinian. He gave me one just like it."

"Uh-oh."

"Yeah, uh-oh, is right. He told me it was part of the service."

"Part of the service?"

"He said that family members tend to get worried, and that they'd come up with this system to put their minds at rest. I could fill it out as if I'd already arrived, address it to anyone I liked. They Fedex all the cards to Miami, mail them as soon as they get word their customers are safely across the border."

"I don't like the sound of this at all."

"Me neither. Still, you told me the card Maria de Lourdes got was mailed from Miami, right?"

"Right."

"So maybe he told the truth. Maybe it is part of the service."

"How many other people got cards?"

"I don't know. By the time they gave me mine, everybody else had been cleared out of here."

"And you have no idea where you are?"

"None."

"No windows in that room?"

"Boarded up. Same thing goes for the bathroom down the hall. There's a space between the boards and I looked out, but all I can see is a row of houses on the other side of the street. Looks like we might be in Vila Madelena or someplace like that, but there's no way I can say for sure."

"You locked in?"

"No. But I'm supposed to confine myself to the dormitory, the bathroom, and the hall. They told me I can back out any time, but if I did, I wouldn't get my five thousand back."

"How about we triangulate the location of your phone?"

"Why bother? If I discover anything, it's not gonna be here; it's gonna be further down the road. Might as well leave it off and conserve the battery. Gotta go. Footsteps in the hall."

ARNALDO BARELY had time to get the telephone back into his sock before the door opened.

"Your visa came through after all," the driver said. "Get your stuff together. You're gonna be able to go with the group."

"I fly out tonight?"

"I don't know that. It's not my department. What I do know is that your guide called from the Mexican consulate. He's on his way over here to pick you up."

"Guide?"

"Your guide goes along on the trip to Mexico, makes sure you guys don't get into trouble along the way."

"And then?"

"He puts you in touch with the coyote. The coyote brings everybody across the border."

"This guide, he's a Mexican?"

The driver shook his head. "A carioca."

ARNALDO HAD the back of the van all to himself, windowless like the first one. The carioca handed him a bag of sandwiches and a thermos of lemonade.

"Better eat now," he said. "It's all you're gonna get until much later. And you don't want the bread to get soggy."

Once the doors were closed and the vehicle was rolling, Arnaldo took the cell phone out of his sock, turned it on, and punched the speed dial. Silva picked up on the second ring.

"I'm on my way," Arnaldo said.

"Tell me."

Arnaldo did, finishing with a description of the carioca: "Big as I am, but fat."

"Fatter than you? Man must be a hippo."

"I think you must have me confused with someone else. Maybe you're thinking of that lardass Silva. He's a federal cop, too."

"No, I know Silva. Nobody would ever confuse you with him. Silva is smart."

"Enough of this badinage, this carioca—"

"Badinage?"

"Badinage. Look it up. This carioca has the accent of others of his ilk—"

"Ilk?"

"You want a description or not?"

"I want."

"Like I said, about my height, one meter ninety or thereabouts; maybe a hundred twenty, a hundred thirty kilos; dark complexion; oily, black hair; dark-brown eyes; big, bushy mustache like a Mexican bandit. No tattoos that I could see, no scars. But he's wearing a gold chain with a big, fucking medallion from Flamengo."

"Flamengo? Did you remind the asshole where he was?"

"I didn't have to. I did a double take on it and he just smiled. I think he likes to fight. Probably pretty good at it, too."

"You got a name for this character?"

"I got one, but I don't know whether it's his or not. He introduced himself as Roberto Ribeiro."

ROBERTO RIBEIRO watched Arnaldo stuff the cell phone back into his sock. Then he fished his own phone out of his pocket and called Claudia.

"Filho da puta has a cell phone with him," he said, "one of those ultrathin numbers. He's carrying it in his sock."

"Has he used it?"

"Just now."

"Where the hell did he get a phone?" she said, sounding particularly bitchy, like it was his fault that the guy had a phone.

"How the fuck should I know?" he said, irritated. "I just picked him up."

"Who did he call?"

"What am I, psychic? I couldn't hear a word he said. There's no microphone back there, just the TV camera."

"Why didn't you take it away from him?"

"No place to stop. I can only get in there through the rear doors."

"I don't like it. I don't like it at all. God knows who he was talking to. As soon as you get back here, give that Argentinian at the travel agency a call and tell him to lie low for a while."

"Hey, I think you're overreacting. This guy—"

"I don't give a damn what you think. Just do what you're told. What's he doing now?"

Ribeiro looked down at the little black-and-white monitor suspended under the dashboard.

"Eating the sandwiches. And, yup, there he goes, pouring himself a drink of the lemonade. He's a big one. Gonna be a lot of dead weight. I'm gonna need help to unload him."

Chapter Thirty-one

THE WAITER ARRIVED WITH two little glasses of sambuca, the surface burning with a blue flame, coffee beans floating on the top.

"Courtesy of the house," he said.

When he was gone, Hector picked up Gilda's glass by the stem and blew out the flame, and then did the same to his. He'd chosen the Due Cuochi Cucina, debatably the best Italian restaurant in São Paulo; he'd splurged on a ten-year-old bottle of Barolo; and here they were, talking about murder rather than whispering sweet nothings to each other. The evening was definitely going down as one of his most unusual dates.

"Of course, I could be wrong," Gilda said, as she finished explaining her organ theft theory. "I wasn't always a suspicious person, but I seem to be getting that way as I get older. Sylvie says I spend too much of my time with cops."

"And she's an expert?"

"She claims she doesn't know any cops. But I know Sylvie. She's looking."

"I meant on transplants. Is she an expert on transplants?"

"Yes, she is."

"I've seen experts proven wrong before. Tell me more about this whole transplant business. I recall reading about the guy who performed the first one—but he died awhile back."

"Christiaan Barnard? The South African?"

"Yeah, him."

"Barnard didn't perform the first transplant. He performed the first *heart* transplant. And his patient died within a month. The first *successful* transplant was years before that, in Boston. The surgeon was Joseph Murray. Barnard didn't come along until the late sixties."

"So how come Barnard is famous and Murray isn't?"

"Because Murray's work didn't capture the public's imagination the way Barnard's did. Murray was working with identical twins. What he transplanted was a kidney. Both brothers lived on for years, but what Murray did was only applicable to twins, so the procedure didn't have much personal or emotional significance for the great majority of the population. Barnard, now, he did something entirely different. He took a heart, matched it for compatibility—blood type and so on—and got it to work in another human being totally unrelated to the donor. And it wasn't heart failure that ultimately killed the recipient. It was something else, a lung infection as I recall. Am I talking too much?"

"Not at all. I'm fascinated. Go on."

Gilda took a sip of her sambuca.

"Delicious," she said. "Okay, it's like this: the body's immune system normally attacks foreign organisms, which is mostly good, as in the case of a virus or a bacterial infection. But in the case of an organ transplant, it's a problem. The body wants to reject a new organ, tries to kill it."

Hector picked up his own glass of sambuca and cautiously touched his lips to the rim. It was cool enough to sip, and he did, the liqueur sweet on his tongue.

"So to make a transplant work," he said, "they had to find a way to get around the body's natural response."

"Uh-huh. And they did. They invented drugs that suppress the immune system. The first was cyclosporine. It was a breakthrough."

"But if you suppress the immune system—"

"You leave the body open to infection. Yes, that's true. It's a tricky thing, has to be carefully controlled. But when you consider the alternative . . ."

"I take your point. Alright, so now we've got . . . what did you call it?"

"Cyclosporine."

"Cyclosporine—and transplants are possible. But does it always have to be a human organ? What about other sources, other animals?"

"That's called xenotransplantation. Xeno from the Greek, meaning foreign."

"Got it. Like xenophobia."

"Exactly. Well, the name exists, but the procedure isn't feasible yet and probably won't be for decades, if ever. The same is true for genetically manufactured organs."

Gilda took another sip and ran her tongue around her lips licking off the sticky sugar. Hector watched the tip of her tongue and felt a tingling in his groin.

"So what you're saying," he went on hurriedly, "is that the only source of human organs is other humans."

"That's what I'm saying."

Hector put down his glass and drummed his fingers on the linen tablecloth.

"Alright, let's suppose for a moment that you're right. Suppose somebody is killing people to steal their organs. It seems to me that people who'd be doing what you suggest would have two principal problems."

"Yes," she said, and counted them off on her index and middle fingers. "Sourcing victims and disposing of their bodies."

Hector raised an eyebrow. "You've thought this through, haven't you?"

"If I was looking for people who I could make disappear without causing a stir," she said, "I'd probably look in the favelas."

Hector immediately thought of the Lisboas and their friends, the Portellas.

"Why the favelas?" he asked.

"No offense, but most of the cops I know, and I know a lot of them, don't even want to stick their noses into such places, much less investigate complaints."

"With good reason. The city administration doesn't run the favelas, the drug gangs run the favelas. And drug gangs kill cops."

"And drug gangs kill cops," she agreed. "I know. Who do you think gets their bodies for autopsy? But that's exactly my point, you see. Life in the favelas is cheap. Drug gangs kill cops, cops kill dealers, and lots of perfectly innocent people get caught in the crossfire. People die and disappear all the time. Favelas would be perfect hunting grounds for organ thieves."

"Okay, suppose you're right, suppose that's what those graves were about. That brings up another question."

"Which is?"

"You've established that none of the corpses were recently deceased. So why are the people who were killing them then not killing them now? Why should they kill thirty-seven men, women, and children and then simply stop?"

"Maybe they didn't."

"Stop you mean?"

"Uh-huh."

"You think we should be combing the Serra da Cantareira for more burial grounds?"

"Maybe. But even if there aren't any, it doesn't necessarily follow that the killer or killers suspended activities. They could simply be destroying the evidence."

"Burning the corpses?"

"Dissolving them in acid might work, but it would be a long and messy process."

"I can't believe we're having this conversation."

"I know. Bizarre, isn't it?"

"Yeah. Burning the corpses. You know what? I'm *warming* to the idea."

"Oh, *please*. Was that meant to be a joke?"

"Not funny, huh?"

She shook her head.

"If they're medical people," he said, "and they're burning the corpses, would they use a crematory oven?"

"I doubt it. Have you ever seen one of those things?"

"No."

"They're called retorts and they burn at a little over eleven hundred degrees Celsius, which means they have to be heavily insulated and need a substantial chimney. They're huge, costly to buy and install."

"How do you happen to know all of that?"

"I had a *namorado* who used to install those things."

"I don't think I want to hear about it."

"About what? The retorts or the boyfriend?"

"The boyfriend."

"Good. I don't like talking about him. He was a creep. They also have to be licensed, retorts that is, not boyfriends, although come to think of it, that might have been a good idea in his case."

"A namorado's license?"

"Uh-huh. To get the license you'd have to pass a test. There'd be sections on sensitivity, reliability, honesty, and all that kind of stuff. You'd have to show a girl your license before you asked her out. My ex would have failed on all counts, particularly the fidelity part, the *canalha*."

"These retort things," he said, as if the conversation hadn't taken a detour, "if they didn't have one, how would they go about cremating a body?"

"There are other devices, ovens designed for the disposal of medical waste. They don't burn as hot as retorts, so the process would take a lot longer, but they'd do the job. The advantages would be that they're much smaller, cheaper, and more common. They wouldn't attract attention if they were installed in a clinic, and although they require licenses, the licensing procedure is much simpler. The downside is that adult bodies wouldn't fit inside. They'd have to be dismembered before cremation, and once the burning is complete, the bones would still have to be reduced to powder. That's not a problem. There's a machine that crematories use for grinding bone. It's commercially available and quite small."

Hector sat back in his chair and looked at her.

"What a mind," he said. "We could make a good team. Professionally, I mean."

"Sure," she said, "professionally."

"And, professionally, would you suggest I start checking out all the clinics that have ovens for the disposal of medical waste?"

"No, I wouldn't. You might get lucky, but I doubt it. Unless you catch them in the act, all you're going to do is to put them on their guard."

"Hmm. You have another suggestion about where we go from here?"

"Let's just get together and see how it plays out."

"It's a deal. Tomorrow night?"

"Eight o'clock. My place. Do you cook?"

"Not well."

"Okay. It will be spaghetti with a meat sauce and salad. You buy the wine."

"Chilean? A Carmeniere?"

"Too heavy."

"A Cabernet Sauvignon?"

"Fine."

"Getting back to the case . . ."

"How about this: transplants, legal or illegal, are the last stop, the end of the line. They're what you do when the diagnosis is certain, when there's no other way to save a patient's life."

"So?"

"So you go back to the beginning. The path leading to a transplant begins with someone getting sick, going to a doctor, and having tests or treatment done. When it's a heart problem, there's going to be a cardiocath, or a radioactive stress test, probably both. The gear to do that kind of stuff is expensive. Only major hospitals have it."

"So we find people whose tests—"

"And/or treatments."

"—and/or treatments indicate they wouldn't survive without a heart transplant."

"Yes. And you cross-reference to the waiting lists for heart recipients. Anybody who didn't put themselves on the list must have had access to an alternative source. Anybody who did, and is no longer there, has gotten a legal organ, or died or—"

"Has gotten one illegally?"

"You catch on fast," she said.

Chapter Thirty-two

ON THE FOLLOWING MORNING, Hector called his uncle in Brasilia and told him whom he'd had dinner with and what she'd had to say.

"Your namorada may be onto something," Silva said when he'd finished.

"She's not my namorada, just a friend."

"And even if she isn't onto something," Silva continued as if he hadn't heard Hector's interjection, "it's a line of investigation we should have been exploring from the very beginning. Godo suggested it."

"Transplants? Godo suggested transplants?"

"No. He just said the motive might be rooted in what he called a 'utilitarian purpose.' We went from there to cults without considering the more obvious alternative."

"Are you going to tell Godo he might have been right after all?"

Silva sighed. "I suppose it's the correct thing to do. And if your namorada is right—"

"She's not my namorada."

"—Godo will wind up finding out about it anyway. It's going to make him even more insufferable."

"I'm not sure that's possible."

"I'm not sure you're wrong."

"What do you want me to do?"

"Put Danusa and Rosa on it."

DANUSA MARCUS and Rosa Amorim were a study in contrasts.

Danusa was in her early thirties, shapely, and darkly beautiful, the only child of a rabbi, a woman who'd spent all of her teenage vacations working on a kibbutz. After graduation, she'd returned to Israel and become an officer in the defense forces. She'd been happy there, might never have come home, if a group of Muslim terrorists hadn't bombed her father's synagogue. Both of her parents had perished in the explosion, as had thirty-four other people from São Paulo's Jewish community.

Danusa was what her father had once referred to as an *eye-for-an-eye person*, a believer in a vengeful God of many rules and little mercy. She'd joined the federal police in the expectation that the techniques she'd learn, and the contacts she'd make, would lead her to the murderers of her parents. She still hoped to find them, and if she did, she intended to kill them.

In the meantime, she fervently believed she was doing God's work by cutting a broad swath through Brazil's criminal underworld. She had an extensive private collection of automatic and semiautomatic weapons and didn't hesitate to use them when circumstances demanded—and sometimes when they didn't.

Rosa Amorim, on the other hand, was an agent in her midforties and the mother of three, two teenage boys and a daughter of nine. People meeting her for the first time often took her for an innocuous housewife. She was anything but.

Rosa had black belts in three martial arts and a degree in criminal justice from the University of São Paulo. For years, Silva had been trying to get her to stand for the examination for delegado, and for years she'd been refusing. Her husband was a successful businessman. Money wasn't an object for Rosa. Putting bad guys behind bars was. She kept telling Silva she wasn't "management material."

Rosa and Danusa were specialists in "street work," the canvassing process that most agents found tedious, but at which both of them excelled.

Hector briefed them at ten o'clock in the morning. They were already waiting, with a preliminary report, when he got back from lunch.

Danusa kicked it off: "It seems logical that if there's any substance to the theory of that namorada of yours—"

"She's not my namorada, just a friend."

"—we can limit our search to just a few hospitals and private clinics, all of them within a radius of about fifty kilometers from the Praça da Sé."

The Praça da Sé is a square in the heart of São Paulo. The zero kilometer post, from which distances on all of the state's highways are measured, stands in the center of that square.

"What if this place is completely clandestine?" Hector said. "What if it's not registered as a hospital or clinic?"

"Possible," Danusa said.

"But not probable," Rosa said. "Concealing the fact that it's a medical facility would be counterproductive, likely to attract even more attention. Better, we think, to admit to being a hospital or clinic and simply conceal the sort of thing that goes on inside. Fifty kilometers, because we're assuming the killer—"

"Or killers," Danusa put in.

"—or killers wouldn't run the risk of transporting the bodies for any great distance before disposing of them."

"Okay," Hector said, "but why only a few hospitals?"

"Or clinics." Danusa again.

"Or clinics," Hector dutifully repeated. "There must be hundreds of them in this town."

"There are," Danusa said, "but well-to-do people wouldn't be caught dead in most of them and when they are, they are."

"Huh?"

"Dead. Anybody who's alive, and possesses any money at all, is going to insist on the quality of care and treatment that can only be bought in a private hospital, someplace like the Albert Einstein or the Sirio Libanes. If they were, God forbid, to wind up in a public hospital like the Clinicas, they'd be in there with the poor, getting poor people's treatment."

"And the well-to-do don't want to put up with that," Rosa said. "They tend to frequent very few institutions, places where they'll be cosseted in accordance with their wealth and station."

"Cosseted?"

"Look it up. Anyway, our point"—Danusa cast a glance at her partner, extracted a nod and turned back to Hector—"is that it's only the well-to-do who could afford the kind of operation your namorada is talking about."

"She's not my namorada."

"Babyface says otherwise. Babyface says—"

"I don't care what Babyface says. Babyface doesn't know squat. How do these rumors get started anyway?"

"Babyface started dating a doctor by the name of Sylvie Charmet. Sylvie's a friend of your—"

"Enough about Babyface."

Danusa looked hurt. "You did ask. You wanted to know how rumors get—"

"How many of these hospitals and clinics are there?"

"Eleven."

"Only eleven in the whole city?"

"Only eleven in the whole city *and* in Guarulhos, Cotia, and the ABCD. Like I said, we're going out to fifty kilometers from the Praça da Sé."

The ABCD, as it was called, was composed of the adjoining cities of Santo André, São Bernardo, São Caetano, and

Diadema. All of them abutted the city of São Paulo on its southern border.

"Seems like damned few hospitals to me," Hector said, dubiously.

"Taken as a percentage of the whole," Danusa said, "there are damned few rich people in this city."

Chapter Thirty-three

THEY WERE ALONE NOW, alone for the first time, the mother, the father, and their baby.

A light pulsed on the heart monitor next to the baby's crib, every pulse accompanied by a high-pitched beep. His lips, rose-colored in the first few hours after birth, had taken on a bluish tinge. Sweat soaked his hair. His breathing was labored.

Clovis Oliveira flinched when the readout jumped from 136 to 137 beats a minute. He half expected to hear commotion in the hall, someone rushing toward him from the nurses' station. They had some kind of alarm down there, an alarm to warn them if Baby Raul's vital signs turned critical.

But there was no commotion in the hall, only the normal sounds of the hospital: a muted conversation, the buzzing of a fluorescent light, the distant ping of an elevator.

Clovis put out a hand. His son's forehead, barely two fingers in breadth, was moist and hot to the touch. Clovis tried to focus his mind as he'd seen the tribal healers do, tried to send energy from his body into Raul's, tried to slow his baby's heartbeat.

It didn't work. The readout didn't budge. Withdrawing his hand didn't make any difference either. The monitor remained constant at 137.

Raul had fallen asleep again. He slept almost all the time. He had to. He needed all of his strength just to stay alive.

Clovis couldn't bear to watch him anymore. He turned his back on his son, walked to the window, and leaned his forehead against glass cooled by rainfall lashing the other side of the panes. It was coming down hard, the kind of rain that drenched São Paulo almost every day in summer, but rare in this month of June.

Morumbi Stadium, the skyscrapers of Avenida Paulista, the blue-gray bulk of the Serra da Cantareira, all were gone, vanished behind a veil of falling water. On the street below, cars were creeping by, immersed to their hubcaps by the sudden flood. A long roll of thunder momentarily overpowered Ana Carmen's voice. Then the thunder was gone, and he could hear her saying the same words over and over again as she fingered the beads of her rosary. She lay on the bed, covers tossed aside, her hair in disarray, staring at the ceiling. The grief on her face made her look far older than her twenty-eight years.

Clovis leaned back from the glass, took out the paper Dr. Levy had given him, and stared at it. There was a telephone number, nothing more. No name, no address. He took his cell phone from his pocket and walked out into the hallway to make the call.

BY THAT time, the nightmare was sixty-two hours old. A nightmare that weakened when he snatched a few hours of sleep, returned with renewed force when he awoke. It had begun in the delivery room, just after Ana Carmen had given birth. It had begun, more properly, with the arrival of Dr. Dirceu Amaral, one of the house pediatricians.

Amaral, an outgoing fellow in his early forties, had arrived to examine the new baby, Clovis and Ana Carmen's first. He gave Clovis a firm handshake and smiled at a weakened but beaming Ana Carmen. He was still smiling when he applied his stethoscope to the baby's chest, the disk huge against Raul's tiny rib cage.

But then the smile disappeared. He whipped the earpieces from his head, ordered an immediate electrocardiogram, and paged Dr. Jacob Levy, a cardiovascular specialist.

Levy arrived within three minutes, even before they had the electrodes in place. He hung over the machine, analyzing the results as the paper emerged. Then he and the pediatrician went into a corner and started conferring in low tones.

After that, things happened fast. Raul was carried off. Ana Carmen was given a sedative and wheeled to her room. Clovis was shown to Dr. Levy's office and asked to wait. He took a seat on a couch between two end tables. Ten minutes later, a middle-aged woman in a blue pants suit came in with a stack of forms.

"What's this?" Clovis said.

"Just some authorizations," she said. "You sign here, here, and here."

Clovis read the paper on the top of the stack and balked.

"You're asking me to authorize you to cut his chest open?" he asked in disbelief.

The woman shook her head and put a motherly hand on his shoulder. "Only a precaution," she said. "In very rare cases, something goes wrong. And if it does, we have to get at the heart quickly. There's little chance of that. Dr. Levy's the best, but the insurance people insist—"

"What's going on? What's wrong with him?"

She extended a pen. "Dr. Levy will come and talk to you as soon as he's finished."

"No. Now. I want to talk to him now."

"You can't. He's with your son. Please, sign the papers."

Clovis shook his head.

The edges of the woman's mouth took on a stubborn set.

"We have no time for this," she said.

"But—"

"Doctor has to do a cardiocath, and he has to do it now."

"What's a cardiocath?"

"It's no big deal. We do it all the time. Now if you'll just—"

"What is it? I have a right to know."

She gave an exasperated sigh. "It's a procedure," she said. "Doctor makes a small incision in his leg, then slides a tiny tube, called a catheter, through his veins until it reaches his heart."

"Through his *veins?*"

"Through his veins. That way it isn't necessary to open his chest to have a look."

"A look at what?"

"After the catheter is in place, doctor injects a dye. He uses the catheter to take samples and blood pressure measurements and uses a fluoroscope to photograph the dye as it moves through your baby's circulatory system. The sooner he has the results, the sooner he'll be able to come back here and give you his diagnosis."

"But he must already have some idea. What does he think the problem is?"

"I couldn't say."

"Can't or won't?"

Again, she shook her head. Again, she held out the pen. This time, Clovis took it.

"Here, here, and here," she said.

When he'd finished scrawling his signatures, she gathered up the papers and hurried away without another word.

THERE WERE magazines on the end tables. One of them was *Gente*, a magazine that Ana Carmen never admitted to buying, but always seemed to be lying around the house. He picked it up and leafed through weddings, divorces, betrayals, and scandals until he came to an article about the bourgeoning love affair between a starlet in the current hit *novela* and a rapper.

He moved closer to the light and read the first paragraph without absorbing a thing.

He started again at the beginning and finished with the same result.

After that, he just sat there, the magazine on his lap. He wasn't a religious man, but once or twice in the course of the next two hours he prayed.

When the door finally opened again, he sprang to his feet. It wasn't Dr. Levy. It was the same middle-aged woman.

"He's with your wife," she said. "You're to go upstairs and meet him there."

Clovis brushed past her, hurried to the elevator, pushed the button, got tired of waiting, bolted up the stairs.

DR. LEVY'S diagnosis was dilated cardiomyopathy.

When he gave it to them, Ana Carmen, despite the fact that she'd been mellowed by the sedative, bit her lip so hard it turned white.

Clovis asked the question, "Dilated cardio what?"

"Myopathy," Levy said. "The myocardium is the heart muscle. Cardiomyopathy is when the actual muscle cells are sick."

Ana Carmen clenched a hand in front of her mouth, as if she were about to stifle a cough.

"Is it . . . life threatening?" Clovis asked, glancing at his wife, then back at Levy.

"I'm sorry," Levy said.

Ana Carmen started to cry. She'd apparently been doing a lot of that in the course of the last two hours. The area around her nostrils was red and raw. She snatched up a crumpled paper handkerchief from the bedside table, gently blotted her nose, and studied the tissue for signs of blood as the tears rolled down her cheeks.

"I have him on four medications," Levy said. "Captopril, digoxin, Lasix, and atenolol. The captopril will dilate his arteries and reduce the strain on his heart. The digoxin will improve the pumping function and combat arrhythmia. Lasix is a diuretic, to reduce fluid buildup in his lungs. The atenolol will help to control his blood pressure."

Clovis didn't care about any of the medical mumbo jumbo. He cut to the chase. "Will any of that stuff cure him?"

Levy took a deep breath. "No," he said, "but it will help to keep him alive." He didn't add the words *for a while*. He didn't have to. "There's no repair. Raul's heart just isn't strong enough. The only way to save him is with a heart transplant."

In the silence that followed, Levy opened a file he'd been balancing on his lap. Clovis suspected that consulting whatever was in there was pure theater, that the doctor was only doing it to avoid their eyes.

"That having been said," Levy went on, "the rest of my news isn't bad. There are no other complications. It's just the heart itself. The five-year survival rate for transplant patients is over 75 percent. It's true he'd have a lifelong dependency on certain drugs, but if he had a transplant—"

"What do you mean, if?" Clovis interrupted. "Didn't you just say there's only one option? Of course, he has to have a transplant. No ifs about it."

Dr. Levy raised his eyes and looked at Clovis.

"It's not that simple. Finding a heart is . . ." He sought for a suitable word and finally settled on "difficult."

"Difficult?"

Dr. Levy nodded.

"He needs a heart from a healthy baby. They're very rare. Raul will have to go on a waiting list, first come, first served. It takes . . . time."

Time.

Dr. Levy paused to let the word sink in.

Time was running short for Raul; he'd as much as told them that.

"We'll take him abroad," Ana Carmen said, speaking quickly, her voice sliding up the scale toward hysteria.

Dr. Levy shook his head.

"The shortage is universal. All countries give preference to their own citizens."

"Are you telling me," Ana Carmen said, "that, with all the infants who die in this country, every single day, my son could still lose his life because there are no available hearts? Are you telling me those hearts are just cast away, disposed of as if they were garbage?"

There were still tears on her cheeks, but she wasn't crying anymore. Now, she was angry.

Her husband reached out and put his hand on her forearm. She pulled it away and sat glaring at the doctor.

Clovis intervened. "And there's no way we could obtain preference? No way we could move him to the top of the list?"

Dr. Levy shook his head.

Clovis looked at his wife.

Ana Carmen was staring at the wall, her shoulders slumped, her anger suddenly dissipated.

The doctor studied her, ran a hand through his thinning hair, and then used the same hand to rub his chin. Then he nodded, as if he'd made a decision. He put a hand into the pocket of his green medical scrubs and took out a single slip of paper.

"This . . ."—he swallowed and began again—"This will put you in contact with a man who might be able to help."

Clovis studied the paper: eight digits in black ballpoint; typed not written, no city code; a São Paulo telephone number. He opened his mouth to say something, but Levy held up a hand to silence him.

"I had a patient once," he said, "a friend of my mother's. Like your son's condition, hers was critical. Unlike him, she was too old, and too sick with other maladies, to get an organ through conventional means. She was also a very wealthy woman."

"What are you telling me?"

"I'm telling you that she couldn't possibly have survived for more than six months with her heart in the condition it was. But then she went away for a while, and when she came back, she was . . . much healthier. She stopped consulting with me after that. We'd had an excellent relationship, but I couldn't get her to come in for an examination. It made me curious. She lived on for almost five years, and when she died it was cancer that killed her, not heart failure. I went to her funeral. I spoke to her son."

"I don't understand—"

"That's all I'm going to tell you, except for this: the man whose telephone number is on that piece of paper runs a private clinic. As a doctor, it would be unethical of me if I were to suggest that you explore . . . other sources. But, if Raul were my son, I'd call that man. His name is Bittler, Dr. Horst Bittler."

Chapter Thirty-four

"REMEMBER THAT COUPLE, THE Portellas?" Hector asked.

The telephone connection was, for once, a good one. Silva could even hear the rumble of traffic on the street in front of Hector's office.

"The ones who turned in that complaint about a missing family," he said. "You bet I do."

"We got a call from a lady by the name of Alcione Camargo. Clarice Portella cleans for her on Tuesdays."

"And?"

"And Clarice is on her way back from Pernambuco."

"Wasn't she supposed to stay two weeks?"

"She was. But no more. According to what she told Dona Alcione by telephone, there's a family feud going on up there. It seems that Ernesto, that's Clarice's husband, fancies himself a member of the oppressed masses. His brother-in-law, the guy they were staying with, owns a shop and has a couple of employees. The two of them, Ernesto and the brother-in-law, downed a bottle of cachaça the night before last. The brother-in-law was opening another one when Ernesto accused him of being one of the oppressors. The brother-in-law told Ernesto that if he felt that way he could buy his own damned cachaça. By that time it was well past midnight and all the shops and bars in town were closed, so Ernesto made a grab for the bottle. It isn't clear who hit whom first, but Clarice and her sister had to break it up. And now the Portellas can't stay there anymore, and none of their other relatives have any room for them, and they can't afford a hotel, so they're coming back."

"And Dona Alcione told you all this?"

"No. She told Babyface."

"Babyface, huh? And he managed to extract all this information in a simple telephone call?"

"He did. His charm continues to amaze."

"Why would Clarice go into the ugly details with someone she works for?"

"Babyface says Dona Alcione and Clarice have one of those relationships where they bitch to each other about their husbands."

"Dona Alcione told him that, too?"

"Uh-huh. Babyface ought to be wearing a warning label. He's a danger to women, that's what he is. They pour their hearts out to him. If he wasn't working for us, we'd have to consider arresting him."

"You sound jealous."

"I am."

"When are the Portellas due back?"

"The day after tomorrow, sometime in the afternoon. Babyface will be waiting. He'll bring them here."

"Don't start questioning them without me. I'll be there by four."

"Understood. Heard anything from Arnaldo?"

"Not a word."

"Merda. Did he bring a gun?"

"No. Only a telephone. I had the service provider check. It's switched off. I'm beginning to get a bad feeling. He's been out of touch too long."

"Anything I can do?"

"Check out that travel agency on the Rua Sete de Abril. See what other information you can dig up. Make sure they're doing business as usual."

"Will do. How are things in Brasilia? Have you dug up any dirt on that fellow Pluma?"

"Not a thing."

"You're not even trying, are you?"

"And thereby ignore a direct order from my superior? Perish the thought."

"Isn't that superior's nose going to go out of joint if you get on an airplane and come here?"

"It most definitely is."

"He won't bankroll the trip. He won't sign the forms."

"That's what credit cards are for. I'll find some way to recover the money later."

"And you can't be here before four because you'll be leaving at lunchtime when he'll be ingratiating himself with some politician in an expensive restaurant."

"Exactly right, my boy. Your powers of deduction are excellent. They must be genetic."

THREE HOURS later, Hector placed another call to his uncle.

"Turns out that travel agency was doing most of its bookings with an airline called Mexicana."

"So?"

"So we're doing a computer run, crossing the names on Mexicana's reservations database with recent missing persons' reports from Brasilia, Rio de Janeiro, and São Paulo. Guess what?"

"A correlation?"

"Five hits so far, all within the last six months. Seems a bit excessive, don't you think? Especially when you consider that not one of those five people actually made the flight."

"It sure as hell does. Pick up that Argentinian."

"I'll have to find him first. The place has a big sign on the door: closed for vacation. We have no name for the guy other than Juan, which at least one out of every five *Argentinos* calls himself."

"I would have said one out of four."

"The office space is rented in the name of Gabriel Larenas, but it turns out Larenas died in 2005. The owner of the building didn't give a damn whose name was on the lease as long as he kept getting his check every month. The telephones and other utilities are in Larenas's name as well. Babyface had a look through the glass and he says the place has an empty feel to it. His guess is that the bird has flown. We're getting a search warrant. I'll keep you posted."

Chapter Thirty-five

BEYOND THE OPEN WINDOW of Dr. Horst Bittler's office, a bright sun shone out of a cloudless sky. Birds twittered. A cicada sang in the rosebushes.

In sharp contrast to the cheerful day, Clovis Oliveira sat like a man condemned.

Bittler, his eyes enlarged by gold-rimmed spectacles, studied his visitor as if he were a scientific specimen. Clovis was dressed in a cheap suit that hung on his frame like it was two sizes too big for him. His hair was disheveled. There were dark pouches under his bloodshot eyes. He was still young, probably in his early thirties, but his shoulders were stooped like those of an old man.

Bittler filled the younger man's demitasse, replaced the pot on its silver tray, and continued with the small talk that, like the coffee, opens every business meeting in Brazil.

"The FUNAI, eh?" he said, tapping a manicured finger on the open file that lay on the desk before him.

The FUNAI, Fundação Nacional do Índio, was Brazil's Federal Bureau of Indian Affairs. Clovis had listed them as his employer.

"The FUNAI, yes," Clovis said.

"And what, may I ask, is the nature of your work?"

"I'm an anthropologist. I work in the Xingu."

Clovis picked up his cup with a thumb and forefinger.

Bittler took a moment to absorb the stroke of good luck.

The Xingu was the name of a river, but also of Brazil's largest Indian reservation. Founded in 1961, home to many different tribes, it occupied a tract of rain forest about the size of the American States of New Jersey and Delaware combined.

"You work with the Indians?" Bittler cloaked his eagerness, made his question sound casual.

"That's right," Clovis said, taking another sip. The coffee was excellent, export quality, but the anthropologist showed no sign of appreciation. On the contrary, he was drinking it as if he wanted to get through the ritual as quickly as possible.

"You speak their languages?" Bittler persisted.

"Not all of their languages, no. No one does. There are tribes that speak languages that are unique, languages unlike any other. Some are spoken by a dozen people, or less. They're no longer of any practical value, only worth learning if you have an academic interest."

"Remarkable."

"I even know of a language," Clovis went on, warming to his subject in spite of himself, "spoken exclusively by a single old woman, the last of her tribe. She no longer has anyone to talk to in her native tongue. When she dies, the tribe will be extinct, and the language along with it."

"Astonishing," Bittler said. He removed a handkerchief from his breast pocket, took off his glasses, and set to polishing the lenses. The handkerchief was snowy white, whiter, even, than the suit he was wearing. "And have you worked in the area of establishing initial contact with these tribes?" he asked. "Contact with people who haven't previously been exposed to our civilization?"

"I have, yes," Clovis said, "but we don't make it a policy. We bring them no benefits, no benefits at all, only sickness and death. Our value system is very different, and who's to say which is better? They don't use money or anything that takes the place of money. Personal possessions are of little value. Food is communal, everyone sharing rights to what everyone else hunts or gathers. They're not resistant to our sicknesses. They know that now. They've seen contacted tribes decimated by diseases like simple colds. Now, they avoid us, run the other way when they see us coming."

"How many of them are there, would you say?"

"Uncontacted people?"

"Yes."

"No one knows," Clovis said. "Some estimates run as high as forty thousand."

Bittler smiled a genuine smile, rare for him. "As many as that?"

"I think it's probably a gross overestimation," Clovis said, "but, despite all of the pillaging and the burning, despite the landgrabs by predatory ranchers, and the lumber companies, and the prospectors, we're still lucky enough to have more than four million square kilometers of rain forest. Much of it is still unexplored. It makes sense to assume that a good deal of it is populated."

Bittler put his glasses back on. Clovis was talking about an area well over half the size of the continental United States.

"I've heard," he said, "that the Indians in the Xingu are permitted to live the lives they've always led, warring among each other, stealing their wives from other tribes, that sort of thing."

"That's not strictly true," Clovis said. "We do what we can to prevent bloodshed. It is true, however, that many of them resist any kind of integration into modern society."

Bittler leaned forward in his chair. "No integration, eh? So would it be right to say they have no birth certificates, no death certificates, no national identity cards?"

Clovis nodded his head. "Exactly," he said. "They have nothing like that. They're not required to."

His enthusiasm was fading as quickly as it had come. Impatience was beginning to show.

"But of course you didn't come here to talk about Indians," Bittler said smoothly. "We have something far more important to discuss." He mopped his brow with the handkerchief he'd used to polish his glasses, folded it, and put it back into his pocket. "I've read Raul's medical records," he went on, pointing at the file in front of him, being careful to use the boy's name. The parents liked it when he did that. It gave them the impression that he actually cared about their offspring. "But I'd like you to tell me more about him. What kind of a baby is he?"

Clovis beamed and his words began to flow. The child had been born with a full head of hair. You could see he was intelligent just from the way he moved his little arms and legs. His wife assured him that Raul resembled both his father and himself, although he definitely had his mother's . . .

Bittler kept his eyes fixed on Clovis and maintained a half smile. But he didn't pay any more attention to what the anthropologist was saying than he did to the singing of the cicada in the garden. He had weightier issues to consider than a father's twaddle about a dying baby. That, too, was a song he'd heard tens of times before.

But an anthropologist with access to the Indians of the Xingu? Now, that was entirely new, and it had set him to thinking.

" . . . I'm not wealthy," Clovis was saying as Bittler focused anew on the conversation. "I know operations of this kind are terribly expensive. I don't even know how I'll be able to pay you. Perhaps a little bit each month, with interest, of course. I'd be perfectly willing to sign any kind of a contract. I'd trust you to—"

"Don't worry about the money," Bittler said.

Clovis's mouth opened in surprise. "I beg your pardon?" he said.

"The money. Don't worry about it. It's not our major concern."

Bittler's use of the word *our* was intentional. He wanted the anthropologist to believe that it was *their* problem, that they were going to have to work *together* to solve it.

"What is it then? Our major concern, I mean," Clovis asked, grasping at the straw.

"Obtaining the organ," Bittler said.

Clovis sank back in his chair. "Yes," he said. "Dr. Levy explained the difficulty, but he also said you might . . ."

Bittler let the silence go on for a while before he said, "Might what?"

A sparkle appeared in Clovis's left eye, built to a droplet, started to roll down his cheek. He reached for his handkerchief.

Bittler continued to stare at him, making silence his ally.

"My son can't wait, Doctor Bittler," Clovis finally said. "We could . . . lose him. He could die waiting for a new heart."

"But surely, Dr. Oliveira, it *is* doctor isn't it?"

Clovis nodded and swallowed.

"Surely, Dr. Oliveira, you know about the lists? Surely, you're also aware that it's illegal to remove an organ from a cadaver without the express consent of the deceased or the deceased's immediate family?"

Clovis waved an impatient hand.

"I think it's a stupid law. What harm can it do if someone's already dead?"

Bittler nodded in agreement, but lifted his palms in a gesture of helplessness.

"A law, nonetheless."

Clovis bit his lower lip and stared at the floor. Now there were tears running down both cheeks. He was a picture of misery.

Bittler, on the other hand, had seldom been happier. He was careful, however, to keep his features immobile.

"Perhaps . . ." he said.

Clovis looked up.

Bittler pursed his lips, tried to appear as if he were giving the problem serious thought. " . . . there is something that might be done." But then he shook his head, as if he were rejecting the idea. "No, no, I couldn't do it. It would involve breaking the law."

"But you just agreed with me," Clovis said. "Some laws are stupid."

"Stupid, yes. But the penalties for breaking them are severe."

"Tell me what you were thinking. Maybe there's some way—"

Bittler waved a dismissive hand. "I'll have to give it more thought. Can you come back on Thursday at the same time?"

Of course Clovis could.

"Couldn't you give me some inkling," he said, "of what you're considering?"

Bittler shook his head. "That would be . . . precipitate," he said. "But keep your spirits up. By Thursday, I may have found a solution."

Clovis's eyes brightened. His shoulders straightened, as if some terrible burden had been removed.

"I don't know how to thank you," he said.

Of course you don't, Bittler thought, *but I do*.

Chapter Thirty-six

HORST BITTLER'S FATHER, OTTO, was a schoolteacher before the Second World War and the deputy head of an extermination camp by the end of it. A man much sought after by the Allied powers, he'd been wounded by the explosion of a mortar shell while fleeing from the Russian advance. The incident had left him with the use of only one eye, but that turned out to be a blessing in disguise. The wound had so distorted his features that his face no longer bore any resemblance to photos that had been taken of it.

It helped, too, that prior to the collapse, Otto had ordered one of his prisoners, an engraver from Krakow, to prepare a set of identity papers. The papers identified Sturmbannfuehrer Bittler as August Schultz, a Wehrmacht corporal and former farm laborer. Otto had rewarded the engraver by putting a bullet in his head.

The papers were good, but not perfect, so once he'd gotten away from the Russians, Otto had gone to ground in Munich, taking refuge at the home of an old classmate. The classmate was not pleased to have Otto show up on his doorstep, but he was hardly in a position to refuse shelter. He had a past of his own to hide—and Otto knew it.

Eight months later, Odessa, the organization of former SS members, was finally able to smuggle Otto, his wife, Erika, and their two-year-old son, Horst, out of the country.

In Brazil, Otto reverted to his original name and managed to get a job in a factory that built refrigerators. He died in 1956, when Horst was twelve. Whatever else he'd been, Otto was a devoted father and the only person Horst Bittler had ever truly loved. His son was devastated by his passing.

Horst's surviving parent was another case altogether. She was a shrew of a woman, obsessed with cleanliness and instilled with the conviction that no culture was superior to German culture.

Horst hated her to the very fiber of his being.

Along with his potato dumplings and cabbage, she dosed him with Schiller and Goethe, tapping her foot impatiently while he absorbed each morsel, forcing him to recite it aloud before ladling out the next one. He acquired, in the process, such distaste for literature that he read only scientific works ever afterward.

For her, there were no accidents and no excuses. Showing emotion was contemptible. Warmth was weakness. Non-Aryans were inferior. The sex act was necessary for reproduction, but to take pleasure in it was filthy. Most people were not to be trusted. The old Germany, the Great Germany, was gone. Only cowards and weaklings were left. No one who survived was deserving of loyalty or support. It was wasted effort ever to help anyone with anything.

In later years, it often gave her son pleasure to reflect upon how wrong she'd been. The fugitive he'd met in the winter of 1977 turned out to be neither a coward nor a weakling, and helping him was anything but wasted effort. Had it not been for his pains in shielding the man's true identity, and the financial reward that followed, Bittler might well have spent the rest of his life in a modest practice, eking out a living by treating patients on the national health scheme and being badly paid for it.

But fate had smiled on him, and here he was, three decades later, with a successful clinic that bore his name.

* * *

DOCTOR HORST Bittler rose weekdays punctually at seven and on weekends punctually at eight. He retired punctually at ten thirty, read professional journals for half an hour, and switched off the bedside lamp punctually at eleven, whether he'd finished the article or not. If he hadn't, he'd make a tiny dot in the margin with a pencil, always with a pencil, never with a pen. He abhorred physical exercise, practiced no sports, took no vacations, and had an aversion to the *kultur* that his mother had spent years drumming into him.

Except for opera.

Horst Bittler adored the opera, especially Wagner, especially Tannhäuser, which he always referred to by its full title: *Tannhäuser und der Sängerkrieg auf Wartburg.*

He'd never married, not because he was a misogynist, or because he had no interest in the other sex, but simply because he was uncomfortable when anyone, man or woman, sought intimacy with him. In his younger days, when his hormones were still raging, he'd made occasional use of the prostitutes on the Rua Aurora, or in the neighborhood of the Jockey Club, but with the appearance of AIDS and advancing age, he'd taken to satisfying himself with masturbation. That, too, had a time allotted to it: before breakfast on Mondays, Wednesdays, and Fridays. Like regular bowel movements, Bittler considered masturbation important to his health.

When he harvested an organ, he began the procedure promptly at midnight, always with his beloved Wagner playing over the loudspeaker system he'd installed in both of his operating rooms.

His lunch was served promptly at one and his dinner promptly at eight. He had seven luncheon menus and seven dinner menus, one for each day of the week, and they never varied.

All of his employees were well aware of his regular schedule, and if they suffered a lapse of memory about where he was or what he was doing at any given moment, they could find that schedule clearly posted in his outer office. His secretary, Gretchen, screened all of his calls. One of her principal duties was to assure he was never interrupted.

AFTER CLOVIS Oliveira left, Horst Bittler made a note in his agenda, registering the date and time of their next meeting. Then he called Gretchen and told her to summon Roberto Ribeiro. For the plan taking place in his mind, he was going to need a pilot, a very special kind of pilot, and Ribeiro was just the man to find him.

Chapter Thirty-seven

CLOVIS OLIVEIRA SAT BACK in his chair, his features contorted in disbelief.

"You can't be serious," he said.

"Oh, but I am," Doctor Bittler said, "I'm absolutely serious."

"It's . . ." Clovis fumbled for a word. Preposterous? Outrageous? Immoral? What Bittler was proposing was all of those things.

" . . . something you should have thought of as soon as you were informed that your son was going to need a new heart," Bittler said. "And you needn't look so shocked. There's nothing new about it. It's been going on for more than five hundred years, ever since white men first set foot in this country."

Clovis's head started to throb.

"Just because people have been preying on Indians for five hundred years doesn't make it right."

"I wasn't initiating a discussion on ethics, I was citing a precedent. More coffee?"

Clovis shook his head.

Bittler served himself from the pot, selected a single cube of sugar with a pair of silver tongs, and dropped it into his cup.

"Right or wrong isn't the issue here," Bittler said. "Practicality is. I've offered you an option to save Raul's life." He took a long sip of his coffee and stared at Clovis over the rim of his cup. "The choice is yours. It's that simple."

"It's *not* simple. Not for me. They're *people*, Dr. Bittler, people like you and me."

Bittler's eyes narrowed in exasperation.

"To compare Indians with you and me," he said, "is ludicrous. You and I, Dr. Oliveira, contribute to society. I'm a doctor of medicine. I do transplants. I save lives. You're a doctor of anthropology. You teach, you write, you add to the world's general knowledge. Indians, on the other hand, are useless. Of our species, yes, but otherwise creatures living lives unworthy of being lived. What do Indians do for anyone? People like you and me, indeed!"

The throbbing in Clovis's head turned to a steady ache.

"You're talking about murder," he said.

Bittler waved his hand in a dismissive gesture.

"Do you call slaughtering lambs for their meat murder? Cattle for their hides? Nonsense! Inferior creatures have been put on this earth to serve superior ones."

"Indians aren't inferior creatures."

Bittler snorted.

"Of course they are. They live, today, much as the superior races lived six thousand years ago. In all that time, they've made no progress in anything of note. Not in science, not in technology, not in medicine, not in philosophy, or art or literature or music."

"They have other values, other knowledge. If I were to put you down into the heart of the Amazon without any of your modern devices, you wouldn't last a week."

"I'm not talking about survival. I'm talking about the higher things in life."

Clovis ran a hand through his hair, as if he could wipe away the confusion inside his head. The hand came away wet with perspiration. Bittler sensed his desperation, pressed his point.

"Reflect upon this," the surgeon said. "Indians have no birth certificates, no death certificates. As far as the bureaucracy of this country is concerned, they're nonentities. Who would know, when they're gone, if they ever existed at all? We'll cremate their bodies, leave no remains. You have nothing to fear from the authorities. The risk of discovery is so small it's virtually nonexistent."

Clovis put his fingertips on his temples, pressed hard. Bittler didn't give him time to think, kept pouring on the arguments.

"And then there's your wife to consider. If your son were to die, and your actions could have prevented it, what do you think it would do to your relationship? Could you look her in the face again? Would she ever forgive you?"

Clovis closed his eyes.

"There must be another solution," he said. "Perhaps if an Indian child died of natural causes . . ."

"You're deluding yourself. There are certain requirements that have to be met. Allow me to enumerate them." Bittler waited a beat and then continued. "First, the heart has to be the right size, which means it has to be removed from another infant. Second, it must conform to Raul's blood and tissue type. Last, it has to be freshly removed from a living donor."

"Donor, you call him a donor?"

"It's the terminology we use, Dr. Oliveira. And it doesn't matter if the child is a him, or a her, as long as the other conditions have been met. Now, when I say 'freshly removed,' I mean it ideally should have been pumping away merrily no more than three hours prior to popping it into refrigeration. And it mustn't be allowed to remain there long. It would be best if we could initiate the implantation no longer than two hours later."

Clovis tried to interrupt.

"I—"

Bittler held up a hand to silence him. "After having chosen an infant of suitable size, we'll have to run some tests. It isn't just any heart that will do. A negative result would mean we'd have to move on."

"To another baby? You'd kill a second baby?"

"There'd be no need to euthanize anyone other than the donor. The tests can be run while the children are still alive. The medical records you've supplied indicate that your son is what we call a universal recipient, so it shouldn't be difficult to match him up, but a choice of hearts is essential if we're to be guaranteed of success. Initially, I suggest that we procure two infants."

"Two?"

"Initially, yes."

"The . . . euthanasia, when it comes, it would be . . ."

"Entirely painless. I can assure you of that."

"And if I help . . ."

"The odds are extremely good that your son will soon be on his way to recovery."

Clovis took a deep breath and met Dr. Bittler's eyes.

"God forgive me," he said.

Chapter Thirty-eight

"YOUR CONCERNS ARE UTTERLY without foundation," Bittler said.

Claudia sat back in her chair and glared at him across the expanse of his desk. The man had always been arrogant, often insufferably so, but this newfound conviction in his own infallibility was a dangerous development.

"I'm only suggesting that we proceed—"

He didn't let her get any further than that.

"You're not suggesting that we proceed at all. You're suggesting that we do exactly the opposite. And that, my dear Claudia, is an excess of caution."

"With respect," she said, her tone belying her words, "until the whole business with Tanaka blows over, I strongly advise that we—"

"If Tanaka had told anyone about our arrangement, his colleagues would have been at our throats by now."

"I give you that. But what if someone else delves into Tanaka"s recent investigations and comes to the same conclusions as he did?"

"Impossible. He destroyed all the records."

"He *told* you he destroyed all the records. The man was a blackmailer, for God's sake. Do you think you can take the word of a man like that at face value? How about that swine, Ribeiro? Didn't he tell you he'd destroyed that family's furniture? Let's kill him. Kill him now."

"In good time, Claudia. Not now. Now, we need him."

"We only need him if you persist in implementing this

scheme of yours. He's dangerous. Your plan is dangerous. That anthropologist is dangerous."

"No no no, you have it all wrong. Can't you see that using Oliveira will lead to less risk, not more?"

She crossed her arms, raised an eyebrow, and stared at him.

"You have no need to worry about Oliveira," he said irritably. "He's firmly within our camp."

"That may be true at the moment. But what about after we've saved his brat? What then?"

"After we've saved his brat, Oliveira will have become our accomplice. If he opens his mouth to the authorities, he'll have as much to lose as we do. Then, we'll start offering him financial incentives. Soon, we'll have him in a position where he'll be supplying us with untraceable organs forever."

"Some people aren't moved by money."

"In all my life, Claudia, I've only known one man who wasn't."

"And who was that?"

"The man whose picture is on the mantelpiece over there."

"You've promised to tell me about him someday."

"And someday I will. Not now. Do you want to hear the details of my plan or not?"

"Of course I do. It's my career, my future that you're playing with."

"I'm not playing. Stop being petulant."

"Petulant? Me?"

"And spare me your sarcasm."

Bittler took out a handkerchief and started polishing his glasses.

"Tell me," she said.

Bittler smiled and sat up straighter in his chair. He loved to talk, loved to impress people with his brilliance.

Claudia, on the other hand, wasn't much for talk, never had been, not even as a little girl, not even before the accident.

THE FUNERAL seven-year-old Claudia Andrade's parents had planned to attend was that of her maternal grandmother.

En route, their car was broadsided by a truck. Both were killed. It drew newspaper headlines at the time, the irony of their being on the way to a funeral and winding up at their own.

Claudia's brother, Omar, two years younger, was a mama's boy, deemed too young to attend the double burial, so Claudia, the one who'd always avoided her mother's embraces, was the one who got lifted up over the coffin.

"Kiss your mother good-bye," her uncle Ugo told her.

Claudia did as she was told, dutifully pressing her lips against the dead woman's cheek. Her mother's flesh was cold. Claudia reacted by making spitting noises and rubbing her mouth. Everybody knew that Claudia was a strange little girl. They didn't blame her. They blamed Ugo. *He* was the one responsible for causing a scene, and the Andrade family hated scenes.

Claudia's next brush with death occurred two weeks before her thirteenth birthday. She'd been living, then, with her great-aunt Tamara and had been walking home from school.

Omar was running half a block ahead, his pencil case in one hand, constricting his penis with the other. He was desperate to get to a bathroom before he peed in his pants. He crossed the street in front of the house, flung open the gate, and ran up the steps, ignoring the family dog, a little dachshund named Gretel.

The dog dashed out of the open gate and ran to greet Claudia.

Happy barks were cut off by a loud thump and a wail of pain. The car that struck her, a black Ford LTD with tinted windows, never slowed down. Whether the driver was a man or a woman would remain a mystery. The cops weren't about to waste their time trying to hunt down someone who'd done a hit-and-run on a dog.

Gretel's battered body came to rest in the gutter at Claudia's feet. The dachshund was still alive—barely—bleeding from the mouth and panting for breath.

Claudia put a hand on the soft, reddish-brown fur. She could feel Gretel's heart, fluttering, fluttering, and then, suddenly, it stopped. Claudia shuddered. Her head began to spin. She sensed a shortness of breath, an increase in her heartbeat, a sharpening of her senses.

It was . . . wonderful.

THEY BURIED Gretel in a corner of the backyard. Omar cried at the funeral and planted a cross of two sticks bound together with kite string. Claudia squeezed out a tear or two, more to make Omar feel guilty than from any sense of loss. Head down, hands over her eyes, she found herself thinking . . . thinking.

Would they catch me if I killed the neighbor's dog? How about our cat?

It was then and there, standing over that little mound of earth, that Claudia Andrade decided what she was going to do with her life: she was going to become a doctor. No one got closer to death than a doctor did. No one had a more continuous and intimate look into last moments.

And last moments, for thirteen-year-old Claudia Andrade, were profoundly exciting, more than boys, more than parties, more than clothes, more than jewelry, more than anything. She bought a box of razor blades and started experimenting with small creatures, seeing just how much she could lop off without causing immediate death. Sometimes she'd bind up the stump of a leg, or sew an incision after removing something from inside one of the little bodies. She'd stuff cotton into their mouths and bind it in place with adhesive tape to stifle their screams. One time she cut into a pregnant guinea pig and the babies came pouring out, six in all, almost at term.

Almost wasn't good enough. They were dead within a matter of minutes. All of her other subjects died, too, but few of them so quickly. One brown hamster with a white belly suffered the loss of all four legs, but kept eating and drinking, and lingered for eleven days.

Finding subjects to experiment upon wasn't difficult. After the owner of the local pet shop started getting suspicious, and refused to sell her any more hamsters or guinea pigs, she'd hang around outside of supermarkets, looking for families who were giving away kittens, or she'd pick up small dogs on the street, luring them into the toolshed when her great-aunt was out shopping.

After sustaining a number of bites and scratches, she took to wearing heavy workman's gloves to protect her from the animals' teeth and claws. She kept them, and the instruments she called her "surgical tools," under a pile of firewood stacked up against the back wall of the shed.

When it came to somewhat larger animals, and the cotton and adhesive tape didn't keep the victims quiet enough, she started cutting out their tongues. And when that proved insufficient, she went to the library, got out a book on veterinary science and learned how to cut vocal cords. Fortunately, Tamara was more than a little hard of hearing.

She only once happened upon her great-niece while she was at work, and that was when she came into the shed to look for a pair of gardening shears. Claudia was busy with a six-week-old kitten at the time.

She blocked what she was doing with her body, folded the razor she was using as a scalpel, slipped it into her pocket, and claimed she'd found the mutilated animal on the street. She was successful in convincing the old lady that she was attempting to save its life, mostly because Tamara didn't want to believe otherwise.

Six years later, Claudia was cutting into her first corpse at medical school. Shortly after becoming a surgeon, she met Dr. Bittler. Their relationship had been going on for almost five years, and in that time Claudia had been content.

Her employer didn't care how she harvested organs, and as long as she did it cleanly and efficiently, he left things like the choice (or even the use) of an anesthetic to her. They'd seldom had occasion for conflict.

Until now.

BITTLER PUT his glasses back on his nose and began outlining the details of his plan.

"Are you familiar with the FARC?" he asked.

"They're a gang of Colombian rebels and drug lords trying to overthrow the legitimate government in Bogota. What have they got to do with anything?"

"Roberto has found us a pilot. This pilot has his own aircraft and makes his living by supplying the rebels with arms. They pay him in cocaine. He brings it back here and sells it to the major drug dealers. According to Roberto, the man sells himself extremely cheaply and has no morals at all."

"Two peas from the same pod, eh?"

"Exactly. Now, this pilot, whose name is Manolo Something,

and Roberto, will fly into the airstrip at Posto Leonardo, the administrative center for the Xingu reservation. The pilot will be posing as a reporter and Roberto as his photographer. The two of them will ostensibly be preparing an article for the *Estado de São Paulo* on the tribes of the Xingu."

"No one will believe that idiot Roberto is a photog—"

"I agree. No one will. But no one except Oliveira is going to have any contact with him. All flights into or out of the Xingu reservation have to be authorized by an official of the FUNAI. Oliveira has that power. He'll meet the aircraft and immediately guide Ribeiro into the forest."

"And then?"

"Oliveira claims there's a river where the Indian women from various tribes come to bathe in the cool of the night. No warriors accompany them, but they bring their infants. Ribeiro waits for the right moment and—"

"When is all of this supposed to happen? The Oliveira boy's heart—"

"—could give out at any time, I know. There is need for haste."

"And how about the other Indians? The relatives of the children you're planning to snatch? Doesn't Oliveira expect them to kick up a fuss?"

"He believes they'll blame another tribe. Apparently, it's not uncommon to steal women and children. The Indians do it all the time when they feel their numbers are getting too small. More children and more women lead to more warriors, and more warriors lead to greater success in their little conflicts. Anyway, that's how Oliveira explained it."

"And suppose they don't blame another tribe? Suppose they play by white men's rules and file a complaint with the authorities? What then?"

"I asked the same question. Oliveira says he'll promise

them an investigation and then destroy the paperwork. He'll also say, if anyone asks, that the journalist and the photographer couldn't have had anything to do with it. He'll swear he was with them all the time."

"What happens if they're seen boarding the aircraft with the infants?"

"Oliveira will accompany them back to São Paulo. If they happen to be spotted, he'll claim the children have been exposed to a contagious disease, one that Roberto was suffering from, but failed to inform him about. He'll say he has to take the children for urgent medical treatment. Then he'll hold them for a week, return them, and try again."

"By which time it might be too late for his son."

"True. But it's unlikely that anyone will see them. They're bringing lights to illuminate the runway, and they'll take off in the dead of night."

"And no one will find *that* suspicious?"

Bittler smiled a smile so superior that Claudia wanted to lash out and slap him across the face. "Newspapers have deadlines. They wait for no man. Such is the life of journalists and photographers."

"What happens if we don't have compatibility between Oliveira's son and one of the infants?"

"Bad luck for the Oliveira family, but not a problem for us. As a matter of fact, I rather hope we *don't* get a suitable heart on the first try. Then we'll have to go back again and maybe again. The more Indians we take in the first round, the better, the more committed Oliveira becomes. You see? I've thought of everything."

Chapter Thirty-nine

MANOLO NABUCO DROPPED THE nose of his ancient Cessna 310B and leveled off at nine thousand feet. It was a moonless night, with an unlimited ceiling and thousands of stars above. Below, on the black mass of the firmament, there wasn't a single light. The pitch-blackness down there wouldn't last much longer. Once they'd cleared the reservation, there'd be the occasional glimmer of light from an isolated farm. And then the lights would multiply, and the illumination build, until they finally reached a crescendo. By then, they'd be on their final approach to Congonhas airport in São Paulo.

Manolo was anxious to roll into the hangar and cut the engines. He needed a snort. Not because of his nerves. His nerves were fine. Ask anybody. They'd tell you. Manolo Nabuco was a stand-up guy with nerves of steel. He wasn't like most of the other coke smugglers, the ones that only found their courage after they'd snorted a line or two.

Yeah, okay, he snorted. Maybe he snorted a lot. But who didn't these days? One thing about him, though: he never snorted when he was working, never got behind the controls when he was high on cocaine. Sometimes he did it when he was a little drunk, but high on the white stuff? Never.

Manolo Nabuco wasn't addicted. Not him. Ask anybody. They'd tell you. They'd tell you Manolo Nabuco just used it because he wanted to, not because he had to. There'd been times when he was alone, high above the pitch-blackness of the Amazon rain forest, heading south with a full cargo of snow on board. It would have been easy to put the Cessna on autopilot, climb back there, cut into one of the bundles, and help himself to a healthy snort. He'd been tempted, but he'd never done it. Not once.

Hell, who wouldn't have been tempted? Since the fucking air force got permission to shoot down unidentified aircraft, you never knew what might be coming at you. The radar coverage had gotten better, too, so no matter how low you were, there was always a chance you could show up on somebody's screen. It was scary. But despite all that, he'd always stayed in his seat, never once taken out his knife. Not once.

Sometimes he wondered, though, how much it could hurt if he—

"How much longer?" the little wimp in the backseat said, interrupting the pilot's musings.

Annoying little bastard! Manolo thought.

For some reason, he was on a short fuse. Funny, he'd always been kind of laid-back and good-tempered, but recently he'd been flying off the handle for no reason. What he wanted to do at the moment was to turn around and bust the little wimp in the mouth. But he didn't. He just gritted his teeth and suppressed a sigh.

The wimp must have thought he hadn't heard him, because he went and asked the same question again, using exactly the same words and in the same tone of voice. Merda! They hadn't been in the air for more than fifteen minutes, and the little prick was already asking when they were going to land.

"You mean, like, are we there yet?" Manolo said, raising the pitch of his voice on the last four words, doing what he thought was a pretty good imitation of a whiny kid.

Roberto Ribeiro, sitting next to Manolo in the copilot's seat, must have thought the imitation was pretty good as well. The big carioca's lips curled back in a smile.

Manolo turned his head and glanced into the rear of the aircraft. The wimp had been staring at the back of his head, but as soon as they locked eyes, he turned his gaze away, crossed his arms, and leaned his forehead against the window.

Manolo set the automatic pilot, let his eyes sweep over the instrument panel, and addressed Roberto. "Where did you get *him* from?" he asked, cocking a thumb over his shoulder.

"Friend of the boss," Roberto said.

"I'm not your boss's friend," the wimp said, "I'm not anybody's friend. I don't want to be. I don't even want to be here."

"Who the fuck was talking to you?" Roberto said.

"I'm only doing it for my son," the wimp persisted, "to save his life."

Manolo adjusted one of the trim tabs and studied the effect. He figured that by bringing up the subject of his sick kid, the nervous little asshole was going for sympathy.

But Manolo Nabuco didn't do sympathy, and he didn't give a shit about the wimp's kid, and he sure as hell wasn't going to give the wimp the satisfaction of asking him any questions.

But he did turn around.

The wimp's lower lip was trembling and he looked like he was going to burst into tears again. He'd actually been doing just that, bawling like a baby, when he and Roberto had broken out of the jungle, the carioca running ahead and carrying a bundle under each arm. When they mounted the wing to climb inside, Manolo had seen big, wet tears rolling down the wimp's face.

Roberto had handed in the bundles, which turned out to be babies, one after the other. The little bastards were also crying, squalling and red-faced, making a hell of a lot more noise than the wimp.

"Didn't you bring anything to shut 'em up?" he'd asked Roberto.

He'd been thinking of something in the nature of a gag, or maybe an injection. Roberto worked with doctors. They could have given him something to knock the little bastards out.

"I got something," Roberto said, and surprised Manolo by taking a couple of pacifiers out of the pocket of his bush shirt. He stuffed one into a baby's mouth, and the kid started sucking on it and immediately shut up. The other baby refused the rubber nipple, kept spitting it out, kept on howling.

"There's a roll of electrical tape in that locker," Manolo said, offering his knife. "Hack off a piece and tape his fucking little mouth shut."

Roberto shook his head. "Can't," he said.

He'd gone on to explain that taping their mouths shut could suffocate them and that he had strict instructions to deliver them alive. Now, almost twenty minutes later, the first kid had spit out his pacifier, and both of them were squalling again.

They were lying right next to each other, and next to the wimp, but he didn't reach out to try to shut them up, not once. It was like they were contaminated or something, like he was afraid of touching them. The constant bawling was starting to give Manolo a headache.

Other than that, it had been a pretty good night, profitable as hell, and with almost no risk. The Brazilian Air Force didn't give a shit about who flew in and out of the Xingu. They were only concerned about flights coming in from places like Colombia and Bolivia.

"How'd you manage to snatch them?" Nabuco asked Roberto. Not because he was interested, or because it was any of his business, but just to pass the time.

"You don't want to know," Roberto said.

"He killed their mothers," the wimp said, "He cut their throats and threw them in the river. He didn't have to do that.

He didn't have to kill them. He told me he was going to take the mothers along."

"Yeah, you asshole," Roberto said, "and you wanted to believe it, didn't you? You trying to tell me you're so stupid you didn't notice there's no goddamned room in this thing, no room for anybody besides us and those two brats?"

"I didn't. I didn't notice. I thought you were going to put them into the luggage compartment or something. And I'm not the one who's stupid. You're stupid."

"Me stupid? I should wring your fucking little neck. I would, too, if the boss hadn't told me to take care of you."

"You want to know why you're stupid? You didn't ask me before you did it! You didn't ask me about what to do with the bodies. You had me next to you all the time and you never asked."

"Why the fuck should I ask you anything?"

"Here's why: Indians never pollute a river. Never. They don't urinate in them, they don't defecate in them, and no Indian would ever use a river to dispose of a body. Once they find those women, and they will, they're going to know they weren't murdered by another tribe. They're going to know it was white men who did it. They'll complain for sure."

"Shut up," Roberto said, and made a gesture with his fist.

The wimp looked at the fist, almost half the size of his head, and did what Roberto had told him to do. He shut up.

The murders were news to Manolo, but the news didn't bother him. He'd done his share of killing. He waited until the wimp had lapsed into silence and nudged Roberto. "What's your boss gonna do with the little buggers?"

Roberto shook his head. "You wouldn't believe me if I told you."

"Try me."

"He's gonna cut out their hearts."

Manolo's only visible reaction was to raise his eyebrows slightly. The answer was a surprise, but he figured that playing it cool was what a guy like Roberto would expect from a guy like him.

"You're shitting me," he said.

Roberto waved a finger back and forth. "I shit you not. That's the boss's business, taking out hearts and giving them to people who can afford to pay for them."

"I'm not paying him," the little fairy in the backseat said. Both of them ignored him.

"So he does, what the fuck do you call it?" Manolo said.

"Heart transplants."

"Yeah, that's it. Heart transplants. What do you figure he gets for an operation like that?"

"Six hundred thousand," Roberto said.

"Reais?"

"Dollars."

Manolo whistled. "Fuck me," he said. "I shoulda asked for more money."

"You shoulda," Roberto agreed. Then he leaned in closer so that the wimp couldn't hear him above the sound of the engines. "Next time," he said, "you hold the old bastard up for another twenty grand. Half of it's mine, okay?"

"A quarter," the pilot said.

Roberto pursed his lips and thought about that for a moment. Then he extended a hand, and the pilot shook it. "Five grand," Manolo said, quantifying the deal, making sure there wouldn't be a misunderstanding later. "But what makes you think he'll agree?"

"You're on board now. You're part of the club. You know how he earns his money. Not many people do, and he wants to keep it that way. He'll take it."

"So you figure there'll be more jobs? Like this one?"

"I can virtually guarantee it."

"What are you guys talking about?" the wimp asked.

Manolo turned around and stared at him again. "Why don't you just shut up?" he said.

Roberto didn't even bother to turn his head. "Yeah," he said. "Shut the fuck up."

The wimp started crying again. And he kept on crying, all the way back to São Paulo.

Chapter Forty

"ANY NEWS?" THE DIRECTOR said, sticking his head into the doorway of Silva's office.

Silva could have told him about Tanaka, about the impending return of the Portellas, about Arnaldo's disappearance, about the minister of tourism's misplaced concerns about his daughter, but he knew there was only one kind of news that would truly interest Nelson Sampaio.

"You're talking about the Romeo Pluma investigation?"

"Of course I'm talking about the Romeo Pluma investigation."

Silva shook his head. "Nothing yet," he said.

Sampaio raised a suspicious eyebrow. "You *are* giving this case the importance it deserves?"

"Absolutely."

Silva didn't consider that a falsehood. In his opinion, he was giving the press secretary's background check *exactly* the importance it deserved.

"There's got to be something," Sampaio said, more to himself than to Silva. "Got to be. Let's discuss this further when I get back from my luncheon appointment. Perhaps I can suggest some new directions for the inquiry."

Sampaio's head disappeared. Silva waited until he heard the ping of the elevator, went to the window and peered through the blinds.

A minute or two later, the director came out of the building and entered a black BMW smack in the middle of the no-parking zone. The uniformed chauffeur closed the door, got behind the wheel, and drove off.

Silva left the window, took an overnight bag out of his closet, and headed for the airport.

THE PORTELLAS hailed from the city of Caruaru in the northeastern state of Pernambuco. By road, the distance from there to São Paulo is a little over two and a half thousand kilometers, a bus trip that's supposed to take forty-two and a half hours, but seldom does.

The roads in Pernambuco, and in the next three states to the south, Alagoas, Sergipe, and Bahia, are in a deplorable state of repair. The equipment used for public transport is sorely tried. Breakdowns are constant. Accidents are frequent. Even in the dry season, the traffic often slows to a crawl. Scheduled arrival times are more in the nature of an ideal than a reality.

Babyface Gonçalves knew all of this. Instead of subjecting himself to the discomforts of the bus terminal, with its noxious fumes and wall-to-wall people, he elected to await the Portellas arrival in a little bar across the street from their one-room shack.

There were hours to go before dark, and Babyface wasn't particularly concerned about being set upon in daytime, but he kept his Glock loose in its holster and had chosen a chair with his back to the wall.

"You want another coffee?" Bento asked.

Bento owned the place. The two of them were on first-name terms by now, Bento and Heraldo, Gonçalves being damned if he'd tell Bento that most people addressed him by the hated sobriquet of Babyface.

It was almost three hours after the scheduled arrival time of the Portellas' bus. The "lunchtime" crowd had cleared out, and the "dinner" crowd hadn't yet arrived. Lunch and dinner were relative terms at Bento's place, because most of the patrons never ate anything more than a *coxinha* or an *empada,* and most of them spent mealtimes drinking straight cachaça. Nonalcoholic beverages weren't in high demand, which made it all the more surprising that Bento's coffee was as good as it was. Babyface considered the offer before shaking his head.

"That's enough for one day," he said.

"You look young to be a cop," Bento said. "Anybody ever tell you that?"

Babyface sighed. "All the time," he said.

"I'm not surprised. When you walked in here, I would have taken you for . . . hey, look, that's them."

Bento pointed to a couple at the Portellas' front door. The man was a bit shorter than the woman, thin and wiry, wearing jeans and a sweat-stained yellow T-shirt with a hammer and sickle on the front. On his head, he had a black beret. The woman was as dark skinned as he was, with her hair gathered up into a serious bun. She was also wearing jeans and a T-shirt, but her T-shirt was black, except for some rings of dried perspiration around the armpits, rings that showed white against the fabric.

While she struggled with the padlock, the man was standing there holding the bags. He had to. The street was unpaved and covered with a thick layer of mud. He looked around, caught sight of Bento, and nodded his head.

Bento nodded back. The nods were perfunctory. Babyface didn't think there was any love lost between the guy wearing the beret and the owner of the bar.

"The Portellas?" he asked.

"Uh-huh."

"What's with the hammer and sickle?"

Bento grinned. "You'll find out soon enough," he said.

The couple disappeared inside. Babyface paid his bill,

squished his way down the narrow street, and knocked on the plywood door. Ernesto opened it. The black beret was still on his head, and now that Babyface was standing less than a meter away, he could see that the beret bore a little pin in the shape of a red star.

Ernesto took one look at Babyface's jacket and tie and turned belligerent.

"What?" he said.

Babyface held up his ID. "Federal Police."

"Oh, the federal police is it? Our very own Brazilian gestapo. Our very own Praetorian guard."

Babyface blinked. "Praetorian guard?"

Ernesto Portella was probably the only guy in the whole favela who'd ever even heard of the Praetorian guard.

"Don't give me that innocent look. You guys fool most people, but you don't fool me. I know what you are. You talk up a storm about maintaining law and order, existing to serve and protect the people, but it's all a big lie. The reality is you're the ones who shore up the bloodsuckers."

"Bloodsuckers? What bloodsuckers?"

"You know damned well who the bloodsuckers are. They're the ones who prey on the masses. If it wasn't for you and your cronies, capitalism would be a thing of the past."

Babyface recognized that the guy had just come off a long bus ride, and he was inclined to cut him some slack, but not too much. And he sure as hell wasn't about to be drawn into a political discussion. He opened his mouth to reply, but didn't get a chance. The man's wife appeared in the doorway and brushed her husband out of the way.

"Is this about the Lisboas?" she said. "The missing persons report we filed?"

"As a matter of fact, it is."

"Why didn't you say so? Come in."

"Actually," Babyface said, "I'd like you to come out. I'd like you to accompany me to our field office. I've got a car. I'll bring you home afterward. It shouldn't take more than an hour or so."

"Are you out of your mind?" Ernesto said. "We just got home from a trip to Pernambuco. I'm not going anywhere. I'm going to sleep."

"Shut up, Ernesto," Clarice said. And then, to Babyface, "*Federal* police, you said? Why are you people getting involved?"

"It might turn out to be a kidnapping," Babyface said. "It's part of our mandate to investigate kidnappings."

"Look, Agente . . ."

"Gonçalves."

"Agente Gonçalves, I'd like to help, I would. That's why I went to the police in the first place, but I've told them everything I know. Not once, but twice. Read the report, talk to Delegado Tanaka, he'll—"

"Delegado Tanaka's dead."

"What?"

"Delegado Tanaka is dead. Someone blew him up with a bomb. We think it might be related to what you told him."

"But, what . . . how?"

"Senhora Portella, I don't want to stand here in your doorway, trying to explain the whole thing. I want you to come with me and meet a gentleman who's flying in from Brasilia specifically to interview you and your husband."

"From Brasilia?"

Babyface nodded.

"And this gentleman thinks it's that important? To speak to us, I mean?"

"He does," Babyface said. "We all do."

Clarice turned and addressed her husband.

"Ernesto," she said, "splash some cold water on your face and change that damned shirt."

SILVA AND Hector were waiting for them in one of the conference rooms.

Ernesto had changed to a T-shirt that had Alberto Korda's famous portrait of Che Guevara on the front, the one where Che is wearing a beret. The beret was black, and it looked just like the one Ernesto had on his head, red star and all.

Silva took one look at Ernesto's shirt, and his eyes narrowed. It wasn't because of Che's politics. Silva felt politics were a man's own business, even if the man in question was a goddamned Communist. No, politics weren't the issue. Nationality was.

In 1978, an Argentinian tie with Brazil, and Argentinian victories over Poland and Peru, had knocked Brazil out of contention for the World Cup. Then, in 1990, Argentina had done it again, playing a defensive game and beating Brazil 1–0 in some of the least spectacular soccer ever.

Soccer in Brazil is a serious business, and World Cups are the most serious soccer of all. Silva knew his smoldering resentment of Argentinians and things Argentinian was bigoted, but he couldn't help himself. His dislike was visceral.

"Senhora," he said, taking Clarice's hand and giving her a little bow. To Ernesto, he said, "You *are* aware, are you not, that that man"—he pointed to the portrait on the front of the shirt—"was an Argentinian?"

Ernesto, who disliked Argentinians quite as much as Silva did, and for much the same reasons, raised a belligerent jaw.

"He was not," he said. "He was a Cuban and a hero of the revolution."

"Argentinian," Hector said.

"Argentinian," Babyface said.

"Argentinian," his wife said, "who went to Cuba to help Castro. Now shut up, Ernesto."

Ernesto mumbled something about lies spread by capitalist lackeys and lapsed into a sullen silence. It was with no input from him that Clarice recounted, at Silva's request and for the third time in succession, the circumstances of the Lisboa family's departure. Then she went on to tell them about her experience in the secondhand furniture shop. She didn't go into detail, just glossed over everything to finish the story as soon as possible.

"And you told all of this to both Sergeant Lucas and Delegado Tanaka, is that right?" Silva said.

Clarice nodded.

"And I showed him the envelope, the one with the money."

"By him, you mean Delegado Tanaka?"

"Yes, Delegado Tanaka."

"And what did he do then?"

"He told us to bring him to the shop. He wanted to talk to the owner and see the furniture."

"No goddamned consideration for the working man," Ernesto said, speaking for the first time in about ten minutes, "none at all. It was a workday, we earn by the hour and we—"

"Shut up, Ernesto," Clarice said.

If she hadn't said it, Silva would have.

"So the three of you went to the shop?" he said.

"Yes, and Augusta's armario was still there, and so were the table and chairs. The bedside tables, the ones with the Formica tops, had already been sold."

"Do you recall the address of the shop?"

"I don't think I ever knew it. But I can show you where it is."

"For the second damned time," Ernesto said.

Everyone ignored him.

"And the name of the owner?" Silva asked. "Do you remember that?"

She thought about that for a moment before shaking her head.

"Sorry," she said.

"Alright, what did Delegado Tanaka do next?"

"He sent us away. It was almost as if . . . as if . . ."

"As if what, Senhora Portella?"

"Well," she said, "I know this is going to sound silly, but . . . as if he were trying to get rid of us."

"And I had to take three buses to get to work instead of two, and when I got there the foreman told me it was too damned late, and that I could turn around and go home," Ernesto said.

This time, Clarice paid some attention to her husband.

"Delegado Tanaka knew we were going to be late, but he didn't offer to pay for the bus, or anything. Not like this young man here"—she pointed to Babyface—"who says he's going to take us home after we're done."

"And he will," Silva said. "Now, answer me this, and it's very important. Do you recall anything about Delegado Tanaka's conversation with the shop's owner?"

"Everything," she said. "We were right there. Until he sent us away, that is."

"Tell me."

"Delegado Tanaka asked the owner about the furniture, how he got it, and the owner said he bought it, and Delegado Tanaka asked him if he could prove it, and the owner said he could, that he paid by check and he got the canceled check back, and he even had a copy of a paper he'd given to the carioca."

"Carioca? What carioca?"

"Didn't I mention that? The man was a carioca."

"How did you know?"

"If it talks like a carioca," Ernesto said, "and if it has a big, fucking medallion from the Flamengo Futebol Club hanging from its neck on a gold chain, it *is* a carioca."

Silva felt his heart pounding in his chest. The hairs on the back of his neck were starting to stand up.

"You saw this man? You saw the man who sold the furniture?"

"Don't you get it?" Ernesto said. "He was the same guy who picked up the Lisboas, the same guy who offered Edmar the job. Jesus. You guys are slow on the uptake."

"It must have been the same man," Clarice said. "The shop owner said he had a mustache and black, oily hair, just like the man who came to fetch Edmar, Augusta, and their kids. Not only that, he gave the shop owner the same name he'd given us."

"The same name?" Silva said.

And I'll bet anything, he thought, *that it's the same name that Arnaldo gave me. Christ Jesus!*

"When we first spoke to Delegado Tanaka," Clarice went on, "he asked me what the man's name was, and I couldn't remember. Neither could Ernesto. But then the shop owner went and fetched the check, and he read it off. And I've been able to remember it ever since."

"Roberto Ribeiro," Silva said.

Hector and Babyface looked at Silva in surprise, but they knew better than to interrupt.

"Yes," Clarice said brightly. "That's the man. Roberto Ribeiro."

Chapter Forty-one

ERNESTO WAS PROVING TO be of no help at all. In fact, he was proving to be a downright pain in the ass. To everyone's relief, including Clarice's, Silva suggested Babyface take him home.

"Why?" Ernesto asked suspiciously.

"We're going to see that secondhand furniture dealer," Silva said. "There are three of us and your wife makes four. It's a small car."

"I'm not a big guy. You can pack me in. I know my rights."

"Rights? What rights?"

"My wife hasn't done anything. Me neither. You got nothing to arrest us for."

"We're not arresting you."

"No?"

"No."

"So you need my wife to go with you voluntarily?"

"Yes."

"But you don't need me?"

"No."

"Clarice, you want to go with these cops? You want to go back to that shop? Again?"

"I want to see the end of this, Ernesto. I want to find out what happened to Augusta and her family. I'm going."

"You see?" Silva said. "It's voluntary. She's simply agreeing to help us with our inquiries."

"Aha," Ernesto said, as if he'd caught Silva in an admission of wrongdoing.

"What do you mean, aha?"

"It's the duty of every citizen to help the cops with their inquiries, right?"

"Yes."

"So it's my duty to go along, too."

"But we don't need you," Silva said.

"Let me get this straight. Are you suggesting I don't do my duty as a citizen? What kind of cop are you, anyway?"

"You'd better let him come, too," Clarice said, putting a hand on Silva's arm. "Otherwise, I'll never hear the end of it."

"Gonna be a tight fit," Babyface said.

WHEN THEY entered his secondhand furniture shop, Goldman was standing at a counter near the door, reviewing some paperwork. He looked up when he heard the bell, but the budding smile vanished from his lips when he saw the Portellas and their companions.

"What, again?" he said.

"It's the federal police this time," Clarice said apologetically.

"Federal, schmederal," Goldman said, "the police are the police."

"I'm Chief Inspector Silva. This is Delegado Costa and that's Agente Gonçalves."

They all shook hands.

"No offense," Goldman said, "but I think your visit is a waste of time. I already told everything I know to that Japanese fellow."

"Delegado Tanaka," Silva said. "He's dead."

"Dead?"

"Somebody blew him up with a bomb. It happened before he filed his report of his conversation with you. We think it might have had something to do with what you told him."

"*Caralho*. A bomb, huh? He have kids?"

"Two. Both daughters."

Goldman shook his head.

"The violence in this town is beyond belief," he said. "I should move to Israel."

"Or maybe not," Silva said. "They've got bombs there, too."

"Yeah, I suppose you're right. Okay, how can I help?"

"What can you tell us about this guy Roberto Ribeiro?"

"She was here," Goldman said, pointing at Clarice. "She must have told you."

"We want to hear it from you," Hector said.

"Not much to tell. Ribeiro came in here with a load of furniture. I bought it off him, sold some of it. Then this lady and her husband—"

"Me," Ernesto said.

"Yeah, you," Goldman said, looking at Ernesto's T-shirt and beret with distaste, "came in and started looking at the merchandise."

"*Overpriced* merchandise," Ernesto said.

"You told me that the first time you were in here," Goldman said. "You don't like my prices, go buy from somebody else."

"I'll buy from anyone I like," Ernesto said. "Last I heard it's still a free country, although God knows for how—"

"Shut up, Ernesto," Clarice and Silva said in almost perfect unison.

"Just get on with the story," Silva said.

"Okay, so this lady here finds some furniture she thinks belongs to a friend of hers. I tell her I bought the stuff fair and square and that I've got a canceled check to prove it. She says her friend would never have sold it. I say she must have. She goes off and a couple of days later she comes back with the Jap . . . uh, I mean, Delegado Tanaka. He says he wants to see the canceled check. I give it to him. End of story."

"So Tanaka held on to the check?"

"And the receipt."

Silva had a sinking feeling in his chest, but he asked the question anyway: "And you didn't make a copy?"

Goldman's answer surprised him: "Of course I made a copy. You think I'm gonna send original checks and receipts to my accountant? What if he loses them? What then? How would I justify my expenses?"

"Senhor Goldman," Silva said, "I would be most grateful if you would give me those copies."

"No way," Goldman said.

Silva frowned.

"I'll make copies of the copies and give you those," Goldman said.

THE MAN they were steered to at Ribeiro's bank, the man who could have given them access to all his account information, was a vice president by the name of Bertoldo Perduzzi, and he was a stickler for details. Silva explained the situation with great patience. He wheedled. He cajoled. He came close to losing his temper. But Perduzzi wouldn't budge. He just kept shaking his head.

"It's not a question of not *wanting* to help you," he said. "I understand this guy might be some kind of dangerous felon, but what if he isn't?"

"He is," Silva said. "I can assure you, he is."

"Okay, he is. I'll take your word for it. But accounts in this bank are inviolable and the law's the law. You give me a warrant, and I'll be happy to give you whatever you need. But without a warrant, my hands are tied."

"There's a dead man, a delegado by the name of Tanaka,

who managed to get whatever the hell he needed out of you people. And he did it without a warrant. How come he could and we can't?"

"I have no knowledge of this man, Tanaka," Perduzzi sniffed, "but if he'd come to me I would have told him the same thing."

"I want to talk to your boss," Silva said.

And he did. And Perduzzi's boss backed him up.

The only recourse was the legal route, and Silva took it. There was a judge he knew who was friendly, accommodating, and willing to work from home. But by the time the paperwork was ready, all of the people who could have furnished him with the information he needed had left for the day.

Fuming, Silva was waiting on the doorstep when Perduzzi arrived for work on the following morning. The banker greeted the cop like a cherished customer, wished him a cheerful good morning, scrutinized the warrant, and turned to his computer.

Minutes later, Silva was out the door of the bank and into the waiting car.

"Where to?" Babyface said.

Silva looked at the printout in his hand and rattled off an address.

"Never heard of it," Babyface said.

"It's that street under the Minhocão," Hector said from the backseat. "Crime doesn't pay."

"I guess not," Babyface said, letting out the emergency brake. "Not in his case, anyway. Maybe he's got a habit, or maybe he gambles."

"Or maybe he just likes living like a pig," Hector said.

THE MINHOCÃO had an official name, but no Paulista ever used it; they just called it the Minhocão, the big worm.

It was a viaduct that curled between the city center and the *bairro* of Água Branca and had been designed to alleviate the traffic gridlock between the two. For a while, it had done just that, but then the growth of the city clogged that artery, just like it had already clogged most of the others. These days, both the viaduct and the street below were bumper to bumper from early morning to well past midnight seven days a week.

What had once been a middle-class bastion had become cheap and run-down. People chose the neighborhood only if they couldn't afford to live anywhere else.

There was no telling what color Ribeiro's building had originally been, or even if it had been built of blocks, stone, or concrete. Exhaust fumes, and time, had colored the facade a uniform, sooty black, just like the stanchions that supported the viaduct.

For want of a better option, Babyface pulled onto the sidewalk, the tires of the car crunching over broken concrete until they came to a stop. There was just enough room between the car and the front of the building to get the door open. While Silva struggled to work his fuller frame through the narrow space, Hector went in for a cursory reconnaissance of the target. He was back in less than thirty seconds.

"No rear entrance," he said. "No other way in or out."

Silva instructed Babyface to stay behind the wheel and to keep an eye on the door. Then he and Hector trudged up three flights of stairs and located Roberto Ribeiro's apartment. The doorbell didn't work, or perhaps it couldn't be heard over the rumble of traffic, so after three unsuccessful attempts, Hector pounded on the door with his fist.

There was no response. He tried it again, knocking even harder. If Ribeiro was in there, there was no way he wouldn't have heard it.

"Police," Silva said. "Open up."

Still no response. Both men took out their pistols. Silva tried the knob. It was locked. Hector examined the door and the frame.

"A cinch," he said, "unless he's in there and has it bolted from the inside."

"Do it," Silva said.

Hector was lifting his foot when a door across the hall opened.

"What's all this fuss?" a woman with a carioca accent said. She looked to be in her late sixties, was wearing a housecoat, and carrying a cat. The cat didn't take its eyes off Hector.

"Do you know the man who lives here?" Silva pointed at Ribeiro's door.

"Who the hell are you?"

"Federal Police." Silva produced his identification and held it up in front of her. She took a pair of reading glasses that were dangling from a chain around her neck, put them on the end of her nose, and leaned in for a closer look. Apparently satisfied, she stroked the cat and answered Silva's question.

"I know him. He's been here just about as long as I have. Three years. Seems like a nice boy. Polite."

"Name of Roberto Ribeiro? Carioca? Mustache?"

"Yes, all of that. What do you want with him?"

"Police business. Do you know where he is?"

The woman shook her head and transferred the cat to her other arm. The cat blinked and then went back to looking at Hector as if he were a bowl of cream.

"Any idea where he works?" Silva said.

Again, she shook her head, this time stroking the cat with her other hand. The feline began to purr.

"I hardly know him," she said. "Just, you know, to exchange a few words when we pass in the hall."

"He live alone?"

"Alone. Yes."

"Go inside, Senhora, and lock your door." Silva said.

For a moment, she looked as if she were going to ask another question, but in the end she didn't. She closed her door without another word. The cops heard her key turn in the lock.

"Remind me to call Dantas," Silva said.

Now that Ribeiro's neighbor had seen them, they could no longer claim they'd found the door already smashed. They were going to have to justify the break-in. That meant they'd have to get a predated search warrant, and *that* meant getting Dalton Dantas, that most accommodating of judges, to provide it.

RIBEIRO WASN'T there.

The place was surprisingly clean, even the curtains on the window that overlooked the Minhocão, even the windowsill. The curtains must have been washed, and the sill dusted, within the last few days. There was a vase of fresh flowers on the coffee table. The bed was made. There were no dishes in the sink. The place even smelled clean, with faint odors of furniture polish and pine-scented disinfectant.

Hector scratched his head. "Didn't that woman say he lives alone?"

"She did."

"Sure as hell doesn't look like it."

"No," Silva said, "it doesn't."

"A namorada, you figure?"

"Maybe. Or maybe he's gay, or maybe he's got the world's best faixineira, but this place doesn't look like your run-of-the-mill bachelor pad, that's for sure."

"If it's his faixineira," Hector said, "I'm going to fire mine and hire his. She'll be looking for a new employer when we put the bastard away."

The apartment consisted of a kitchen, a living room, a bedroom, and a bathroom. The interior of the kitchen cupboards was orderly, the rug in the living room was vacuumed, the sheets on the bed had recently been washed and even ironed, and the towels in the bathroom were neatly arranged on a rack.

A thorough search of the apartment turned up nothing of interest. No photos, no letters, no record of Roberto's workplace. The only papers they found were a stack of bills, some paid, some unpaid, and a checkbook from the Bradesco Bank.

After tossing the place, Silva and Hector canvassed the other apartments in the building. There were sixteen in all, four floors and four apartments on each. They'd already spoken to the woman with the cat. Seven of the other fourteen residents didn't answer their doors or weren't at home. They made a note of the apartment numbers for subsequent follow-up.

No one they questioned seemed to know anything about Roberto Ribeiro. He had no social relationship, as far as they could determine, with anyone else in the building. Finally convinced they'd done as much as they could, Silva called in a two-man team.

When the men arrived, he told them to keep the building under surveillance in the hope that Ribeiro would come home sometime soon. He and his nephew went back to Hector's office.

"Pictures," he said to Babyface when they got there. "Get me pictures. Ribeiro must have a national identity card, maybe he's got a record, maybe he's got a driver's license, maybe you can track down his family. Make up a circular and an e-mail. Get them to all the field offices, to local and state police, and to the border-crossing checkpoints, particularly the border-crossing checkpoints."

"Gonna cost a bundle to do all of that," Hector said. "Sampaio isn't going to like it."

"I don't care. Just do it."

Babyface nodded and left the office.

"You think he'll try to get out of the country?" Hector said.

"Pray that he does," Silva said. "And get the word out that I'll personally eat the liver of any agent who allows him to do it."

Chapter Forty-two

"WHY CAN'T I JUST go to Bahia or someplace?" Roberto asked.

He sounded like he was half in the bag.

One of Helena Ribeiro's hands whitened as she tightened her grip on the telephone. The other continued to stroke her cat. She'd called his cell phone while the federal cops were still tossing his apartment, reached him in the bar where he liked to drink his lunch.

He tried her patience, that son of hers did. He'd tried her patience ever since he was a little boy, always wanting to know why he had to do this, why he had to do that. Why he had to eat his rice and beans. Why he couldn't sleep in the same bed when she had a customer. There was a time when she'd thought he'd grow up, stop besieging her with questions, but, no, here he was, forty-one years old and still doing it.

She hovered over him too much. She knew it. She did his cooking, did his cleaning, made his decisions for him, treated him like a kid. So maybe she was at fault. Maybe the reason he'd never gotten married was because he'd never found a woman who would take care of him as well as she did. But it was too late now. He was grown. He'd never change.

"You can't go to Bahia or someplace," she said patiently, "because the men who're looking for you aren't the São Paulo cops. They're federal police and they're everywhere. They're in Bahia, and Rio Grande do Sul, and Rondonia, and Minas Gerais. Everywhere! If you want to avoid them, you have to do as I say."

There was silence on the other end of the line as he thought it through. She knew he didn't want to leave the country, didn't want to go anywhere they didn't speak Portuguese, anywhere he didn't know the ropes. But he'd wind up doing what she told him to do. He always did.

"How come you're so sure they're federal?" he finally said.

She took a deep breath.

"One of them waved his ID right in my face. And he wasn't just any federal cop, he was that Silva, the one who's on television every now and then. He's a big-shot chief inspector or some such. And, if he's on your case, it shows they're serious."

"I'm not scared of him. I've had trouble with cops before."

"It's not like the last time. Or any other time for that matter. You're not going to be able to bribe them like you do the locals. These people are relentless. If they catch you, they'll put you away for a long time. Is that what you want?"

"No, *mamãe*."

"Then for God's sake, stop arguing with me and do as I say."

It was hard for her to accept that she'd given birth to a dunce. Roberto's half brother, José Antonio, dead these five years after a drug-gang shoot-out, had inherited the brains in the family. Roberto was no more than a lout, but he was *her* lout, and she couldn't help loving him with a mother's love. That was the reason she'd moved into the apartment across the hall, to be close to her only surviving son.

"I have some money for you," she said.

"How much money?"

"After I pay for your passport, I should be able to give you five thousand American dollars."

"Only five? Caralho, mamãe, I'm going to need more than that. I'd better drop by the bank."

"Are you crazy? Remember how that Jap tracked you the last time? Who's to say the federals haven't done the same thing? No, Roberto, you stay away from that bank. Five thousand will keep you in food and lodging for five or six weeks at least. I'll send you more once you're settled. Now, listen carefully. I want you to go to one of those machines that make photos, you know the kind?"

"Where you put in some money and sit inside and—"

"Yes, yes, that's right. You have to get me a photo. There are different options you can choose from, but the one I want has to be passport sized. You're not allowed to wear any sunglasses, you have to look directly into the lens of the camera, and for God's sake, take that gold chain and that stupid medallion off your neck."

"It's not stupid, it's—"

"Don't argue with your mother, Roberto. If I say it's stupid, it's stupid."

"Alright. Alright. How long is it gonna take, this passport?"

"After I have a suitable photo, probably three or four days. I'll try to pay them extra for a rush job. We have to move quickly. They'll be circulating your photo before long, might even put it on television. Why, oh why, did you ever have to take up with those disgusting people? Now, see where it's brought you? You should have listened to me when I told you—"

"Okay, okay, you were right. Now, stop being a pain in the ass."

"Don't take that tone with me, Roberto Ribeiro. Apologize to your mother."

Silence.

"Tell me you're sorry."

"Alright, I'm sorry. But don't you think you're going overboard? All they got is a description. You know how those police artists are. They hardly ever get it right. I'll just shave off my mustache and cut my hair. It's not like they've got a photo of me or anything."

"Roberto, they *have* a picture of you."

"A picture? No way."

She sighed. José Antonio would have been one step ahead of her all the way. With Roberto, you had to explain every damned thing.

"They'll have gotten it from your national identity card."

"That one's no damned good. I was what? Fourteen? Fifteen?"

"They'll age it. We've wasted enough time in talking. Cut your hair, shave off the mustache, get the photograph, and then check into some cheap hotel downtown. Call me from there, and I'll come over and pick up the photo. Don't go back to that clinic. Don't even put your head out of the door of that hotel room until I come to you with the passport and an airline ticket."

"You mean I gotta sit around a fucking hotel room for three or four days?"

"Maybe longer."

"Goddamn it! Where am I going?"

"Paraguay."

"Paraguay? Fuck me."

SILVA LEANED over the photos on Hector's desk. The one from the national identity card showed Ribeiro as a teenager. The mug shot e-mailed by the police in Rio was more recent, only twelve years old. According to the paperwork, Ribeiro was now forty-one.

A police artist had taken the two photographs as a point of departure, spoken to the Portellas and Senhor Goldman, and done a likeness of how Ribeiro currently might look. He'd had to add a mustache and move Ribeiro's hairline up toward the top of his head. Then he'd made another version with shorter hair and without the mustache. Silva figured that the first thing Roberto would do was lose the mustache.

Just to be safe, the artist had also made a version with Roberto's hair tinged blond. They probably wouldn't need that one. The carioca's skin was swarthy. Blond hair would have made him more noticeable.

"What about his driver's license?" Silva asked.

Hector shook his head. "He's had it for years," he said. "It's like yours and mine. No photograph. The state of São Paulo didn't require them until 1998. He's kept renewing it without one."

"Alright," Silva said. "How soon can we get the flyer out?"

"You want to use this one?" He pointed at the version without a mustache and with the cropped hair.

"Hell, no. Use all of them. And add this headline: Wanted for the kidnapping and possible murder of one of our own. That should get everyone's attention. How soon?"

"We can distribute to the field offices, airports, seaports, and border crossings within an hour."

"Thank God for e-mail. How about the local cops?"

"Only sure way is to use paper flyers and distribute them by courier service. Two days, minimum."

"TV stations?"

"It'll be on the national news at eight tonight."

"Good. Okay, I think we're covered on Ribeiro. Let's get back to Arnaldo. What about that travel agency?"

"We tossed it. There's nothing useful in their paperwork. Rivas is looking at their computer as we speak. We still have the building covered."

"And Arnaldo's cell phone?"

"Hasn't been switched on since the last time you spoke to him."

PASSPORTS AND visas are not checked only upon arrival in Brazil, but also upon departure. The people who do the checking are the federal police, so Silva was in a position to exercise a certain degree of control.

He followed up the e-mails by initiating a series of telephone calls to the delegados responsible for monitoring Brazil's borders. He could have let Babyface, or Hector, or someone else do it, but he knew the personal touch, his own voice on the line, would have more impact.

He started with São Paulo's three international airports, moved on to the seaports of Santos and São Sebastião, and then continued the process in an ever-widening circle. He took a break, and caught five hours of sleep on the couch in the reception area, but he was up again at seven in the morning, calling people at home when he couldn't get them anywhere else.

By nine thirty, he'd gotten as far as Manaus, the self-styled capital of the Amazon and most definitely not one of his favorite places. Manaus was a cesspool, dirty, hot, foul smelling, with one of the highest indices of childhood prostitution in the country and administered by corrupt and indolent officials. Corruption and indolence had a way of affecting almost everyone transferred there, including members of the federal police.

"Who the hell is this?" the sleepy delegado said when Silva awoke him at home.

It was an hour earlier up there, but Silva still thought the lazy bastard should have been behind his desk, or at least on the way to the office.

"Chief Inspector Silva, calling from São Paulo."

"Oh." There was a rustle of bedclothes and a muffled complaint from a female somewhere in the background.

"What can I do for you, Chief Inspector?"

Silva explained the situation, told the delegado to check his e-mail, and moved on to the next number on his list.

Chapter Forty-three

WHILE SILVA WAS SPEAKING to the people in charge of border checkpoints, Denise Ramiro, a medical technician at Dr. Bittler's clinic, was gently sucking air out of a pipette she'd inserted into a test tube of blood.

A thin column of the red liquid arose. Swiftly, with a gesture she'd performed a thousand times, Denise removed the pipette from her mouth, covered the tiny hole with the tip of one latex-gloved finger, and then lifted it, allowing a small quantity of the blood to dribble into another test tube on the opposite end of the same rack.

Denise had no inkling of the origin of the blood in the first tube, no idea that it had been drawn from an Indian baby snatched from the Xingu reservation. She knew only that the blood in the second tube was that of Raul Oliveira, one of Dr. Bittler's patients.

Denise, like most of the employees at the clinic, was a thoroughly honest person with an impeccable record. And, like them, she was wholly unaware of how Dr. Bittler sourced the organs he used for transplants. In fact, the only people on his staff privy to that information were Bittler himself, Claudia Andrade, Roberto Ribeiro, Gretchen Furtwangler, Bittler's longtime secretary, and the anesthesiologist, Teobaldo Vargas.

Harvesting organs was not a simple procedure, but it was a good deal simpler than implanting them. It required fewer people, less expertise, and less time. And it was performed in one of two secret operating rooms, located under the building, accessible only from the parking lot.

Denise had no knowledge of those operating rooms, or of the adjoining oven used for cremating human remains, or of the holding cells that were used to keep the unwilling donors until their time came.

She *was* aware that the clinic seemed to have an almost unending supply of organs, but as far as she was concerned, the organs were obtained in ways common to the profession, if not strictly legal. She assumed it was a simple matter of her boss giving money to the families of the recently deceased.

No, it wasn't supposed to be that way, but this was Brazil. People with money had always enjoyed special privilege. That's just the way it was. It had been going on for so long that Denise, and most of her compatriots, didn't even think of questioning it.

The procedure she was performing that day was called a crossmatch. The objective was to determine an organ's compatibility. A so-called positive crossmatch was, in fact, a negative result for the patient. It meant that the available organ would probably be rejected by the body of the person who needed it. Each test was carried out with samples of refrigerated blood and each took about forty-five minutes.

The result of the first test had been positive. It appeared that the young patient, Raul Oliveira, had a shot at only two organs. He would have been out of luck if the second crossmatch had turned out the same way as the first.

But it didn't.

"Bingo," Denise said, irreverently, leaning back from her microscope. She peeled off her latex gloves, stretched her back, and picked up the telephone to report the result to Claudia Andrade.

ARNALDO AWOKE to the sound of music.

He had a pain in his head that surpassed any hangover

he'd ever known. His mouth was dry, his lips were cracked, and his vision was blurry. He sat up. It took some effort. He felt weak as a kitten.

When the area around him came into focus, it turned out to be a prison cell. At least that's what it looked like. The door was steel, with a little peephole. He was naked, but not cold. The room, in fact, was uncomfortably warm.

He tried to put two and two together. The big guy with the fucking Flamengo medallion had picked him up. He'd called Silva from the back of the van. He'd drunk something, eaten something, and then . . . and then he couldn't remember anything more.

The bastard must have drugged him. But why? What the hell was going on?

He started to get up, but movement made his head spin and he sank back onto the sheets, sheets only, no cover, no pillow, a thin mattress. He put his aching head in his hands and looked down. The floor was concrete, the metal bed frame fastened to it with bolts, bolts with large hexagonal heads.

The music went on. Something classical. It might have been an overture, the way it slipped from melody to melody. And the volume was turned up far too high. The sound was driving daggers into his head.

He stuck his fingers in his ears, lifted his head, and let his eyes sweep around the room.

There was a toilet in the corner, a stainless steel toilet without a seat. Next to it, bolted to the wall, was a sink, also stainless steel, with a single tap. No shower. No other furniture, only the bed. No windows. No indication whether it was day or night.

The music changed. A woman began to sing, but not in Portuguese.

It sounded to Arnaldo like some fucking German opera.

* * *

THE INDIAN baby's heart wasn't much larger than one of his tiny fists. Cutting it out was a delicate business, and it took Bittler longer than usual. When he'd finished, he told Teobaldo to go upstairs and anesthetize Raul Oliveira.

Three hours later, Raul, too, was dead.

Bittler's surgical mask concealed his nose and mouth, but not his anger. Claudia could read it in his eyes. He looked at the dead child as if it had displeased him and was deserving of punishment.

"Shock him again," he said.

"It's no use," she said. "He's gone."

"Shock him, I say."

So she did. The little heart contracted once. But only once.

"Damn," Bittler said.

"His parents are outside," Claudia said.

"You think I don't know that?" Bittler replied testily. "Go out there and lie to them."

"What?"

"Tell them we're finished. Tell them the operation was a success. Tell them he'll be in intensive care for the next twenty-four hours, and that we never allow family or friends into intensive care."

"They won't believe it."

"Why shouldn't they?"

"We've only been in here for the last two and a half hours. They must know that a successful procedure takes—"

"They don't know a damned thing," he snapped.

Teobaldo's eyes were twinkling above his mask. It was a rare thing for Bittler to lose his temper, and the anesthesiologist seemed to be enjoying the spectacle. Bittler glanced at Teobaldo, noted his amusement, and flushed. Then he took a deep breath and went on in a calmer voice.

"They'll believe you because they'll *want* to believe you. Tell them to go home and get some rest. Tell them we'll call them just as soon as his condition stabilizes. Come to me as soon as they've left."

TEN MINUTES later, Claudia found her employer in his office. She came in with a sour expression on her face. Bittler took it in with a certain degree of satisfaction.

"I was right, wasn't I?" he said smugly. "They believed every word."

"They're gone for the moment," she admitted grudgingly. She closed the door and leaned against it. "But it doesn't solve anything. We've won a few hours, nothing more. We can't keep them in the dark forever."

"A few hours is long enough," Bittler said. "Stick your head outside and tell Gretchen to summon Roberto."

Claudia shook her head.

"He's not here."

"Not here?"

"I wanted him to incinerate the remains of the Indian brat. When I couldn't find him, I asked Gretchen if she knew where he was. She said he didn't come in yesterday, and he isn't here today. She's called his cell phone repeatedly. She keeps getting his voice mail, and he doesn't call back."

Bittler frowned.

"There's no time to waste. We can't just sit around and wait for him to turn up. You'll have to do it yourself."

"Incinerate the Indian brat?"

"No. Teobaldo can attend to that."

"Then what?"

"Kill the Oliveiras."

* * *

"DR. ANDRADE," Ana Carmen said when Claudia showed up at the apartment unannounced. "Oh, my God, is there anything wrong?"

The chain was on the door, reducing the opening to just a few centimeters. Claudia could see little more than one of Ana Carmen's eyes. The eye was blue—and huge with fear.

"Raul's fine," Claudia reassured her. "Your place is on my way home. I'd thought I'd stop by and give you a progress report."

Claudia heard Ana Carmen breathe out a long breath and realized, only then, that she'd been holding it in. The eye was returning to normal size, but the woman still wasn't quite over her shock.

"May I come in?" Claudia asked.

"Oh, of course. Forgive me."

Ana Carmen fumbled with the chain and opened the door. She was wearing a bathrobe over a nightgown. Behind her, the corridor was unlit. In the dim light the smudges under her eyes looked like badly applied makeup.

Claudia crossed the threshold. Ana Carmen locked and chained the door. It was São Paulo, after all. One had to take precautions.

"Where's your husband?" Claudia asked.

"In the bedroom," Ana Carmen said, "trying to get some rest. Please, come this way."

Claudia followed her down a hallway lined with Indian artifacts: bead necklaces, feather headdresses, bows, arrows, spears, wooden knives, and some other objects she didn't recognize.

The hallway opened onto a small living room. Two armchairs, a sofa, and a coffee table crowded the narrow space. Watery sunlight spilled through the blinds and illuminated a painting on the opposite wall, a watercolor of some baroque church. Claudia approached the work, as if she were admiring it.

"Very nice," she said.

Beyond kitsch, she thought.

"We bought it on our honeymoon. The church is in Ouro Preto. You've been to Ouro Preto?"

Ouro Preto was deep in the mountains of Minas Gerais, a jewel of eighteenth-century colonial architecture.

"Yes," Claudia said.

"But you're not here to talk about travel or art," Ana Carmen said, obviously anxious to get to the subject of her son.

A good thing, too, Claudia thought, *because Ouro Preto is a boring backwater and that piece of trash is anything but art.*

"My husband and I are immensely in your debt," the baby's mother went on, "yours and Dr. Bittler's."

"And we're immensely pleased that we were able to save Raul," Claudia lied, going through the motions.

"I have to tell you, though, that the doctor's attitude toward the other children, the Indian babies, was something my husband and I found . . . well . . . shocking."

"I hope you haven't been talking about that, about where we got the heart for Raul."

"No, no, of course not," Ana Carmen said, wringing her hands. "Not even to my mother. Clovis wouldn't permit it."

"Wise," Claudia said.

"You can trust us. We'll never tell."

Not until you find out your son is dead, Claudia thought.

There was a door in one corner of the living room. It opened and Clovis came in. He caught sight of Claudia and his face turned pale.

"No," Ana Carmen said quickly. "He's fine. Doctor Andrade stopped by on her way home. She's going to give us a progress report."

Clovis's color returned, and some of the stiffness seemed to go out of his body. He looked down at his feet. He was wearing a tattered pair of his wife's slippers. One of them had the remnants of a pink bow.

Claudia saw it and smiled.

He caught her look and forced a smile of his own. "Yeah," he said. "Pretty ridiculous, huh? But we don't have a carpet in the bedroom."

As if that explained it.

Ana Carmen put a hand on Claudia's arm. "I'm being such a bad hostess," she said. "How about some coffee? You *will* drink some coffee."

"Coffee would be nice," Claudia said.

Clovis pointed at one of the four chairs in the tiny dining alcove.

"Why don't we sit there?"

Claudia reached into her bag and removed a metal box that had once held English chocolates. "I brought some cookies. They're to die for," she said, and almost smiled.

Clovis pulled out one of the chairs for her and took one on the opposite side of the table. A vase of wilting flowers stood between them. He moved it aside.

"I'm glad you came," he said. "I find it easier to talk to you than I do to Dr. Bittler."

"Many people do. He's a shy man. Sometimes it comes across as arrogance."

"Yes," he said. He picked up a dead petal from the table and distractedly rolled it between a thumb and forefinger. "The two of you have been doing this for a long time, haven't you?"

"Doing what?"

"Stealing organs."

Claudia crossed her arms and leaned back in her chair.

"Wherever did you get an idea like that?"

"I don't know. I just . . . I . . . well, frankly Dr. Andrade, I'm finding it very difficult to live with what I've done."

"Pangs of conscience?"

"Call it whatever you like, but now that Raul's procedure has been successful . . ." His words drifted off.

"Surely, you're not thinking of going to the authorities?"

"No, of course not," he said, his voice totally lacking in conviction, "but I'm not inclined to help you with any further kidnappings out of the Xingu reservation."

"You do recognize that Dr. Bittler only wants those Indians so he can save other lives?"

"I . . . I've been discussing the issue with my wife . . ."

"And?"

"You needn't look at me like that. I know I agreed to the scheme, but I feel differently now." He gave her what Claudia interpreted as a sly look. "I'd find it a lot easier to keep quiet if we just forgot about any future plans for the Indians."

Claudia removed the lid from the metal box, and pushed the cookies across the table to rest in front of Clovis. "We should discuss that in more detail," she said, "as soon as your wife comes back with the coffee."

THERE WAS a chance that one, or both of them, would refuse a cookie. Claudia was prepared for that. She had a 6.35 mm Beretta semiautomatic pistol in her purse.

The weapon proved unnecessary.

Chapter Forty-four

"WE GOT A BREAK," Danusa Marcus said. "No line on anyone we can bust, not yet anyway, but there's some indication that your namorada's hypothesis is correct."

"I already told you," Hector said. "She's not my namor—"

"Whatever," Rosa Amorim said. "Have you got a few minutes?"

Hector studied the two women who'd burst into his office without as much as a courteous rap on the door.

"For you two?" he said. "Always. Sit down."

Rosa sank into a seat.

Danusa remained standing, leaned over, opened the *Estado de São Paulo* she was carrying, and spread the newspaper out on Hector's desk. She tapped a manicured finger on the headline of an article: COUPLE FOUND DEAD IN APARTMENT.

"I saw this on the way to work this morning," she said. "The murdered couple are the Oliveiras, Clovis and Ana Carmen. Their names rang a bell. They were on our list of people to interview, but we hadn't gotten to them yet."

Hector took a moment to scan the article.

"Suspicion of poison, huh?"

"What it doesn't say," Danusa continued, "is that they had a baby boy, and that the kid needed a heart transplant. I spoke to one of the homicide guys assigned to the case. He told me Senhora Oliveira's mother had a key to their apartment. She was accustomed to talking to her daughter by telephone at least twice a day. Last night, after no contact since early morning, she went over there and let herself in. They were in the dining alcove, pitched over the table, dead. Her daughter was clutching her husband's hand."

"You go to see the mother?"

Danusa looked pained. "Had to, right? I didn't enjoy it."

"No, I'm sure you didn't."

"She lost her only daughter, and her only grandchild, and she's a widow to boot. Her husband died not six months ago, killed in a holdup for twenty reals in cash and a thirty-real watch. Sometimes, I hate this town."

"Her grandchild is dead, as well?"

"I was getting to that. Raul, his name was, born at Albert Einstein, up in Morumbi. Kid was less than two hours old when he was diagnosed with something called dilated cardiomyopathy, whatever the hell that is."

"Fatal?"

"Without a heart transplant, yes."

"And?"

"And Ana Carmen, that's the baby's mother, told *her* mother that they'd arranged for one, and that it was supposed to take place the day before yesterday. She also said there was something irregular about it, which precluded her from giving any more details. Irregular, that's the word she used."

"The plot thickens."

"Goddamned right it does. Now, get this: we can't be absolutely sure the kid's dead, but it seems like a safe assumption. We can't find any trace of him. We've called every single hospital and clinic known to be able to perform heart transplants. Nobody admitted to performing one on a kid called Raul Oliveira."

"Merda. How about the people at Einstein? What did they have to say?"

This time it was Rosa who spoke up.

"I talked to the cardio who did the diagnosis, a guy by the name of Jacob Levy. He says he put the baby's name on the list to receive a heart, but he has no idea where the case went from there. I think he's lying."

"Why?"

"Nothing I can put my finger on. Just a feeling. Call it a mother's intuition. My sons try it on all the time."

"I've learned to trust your intuition. You think this Levy is involved in the murder of the parents or the disappearance of the kid?"

"I wouldn't go that far. I talked to a number of other people at the hospital, did a little background check. Levy is competent and well liked. Compassionate is a word that came up often. I think he might have suggested a way for the Oliveiras to work around the waiting list and get a heart for their son. But there's no way he's going to admit that. If he did, he'd lose his license in a flash."

"Yeah, he would. Sweat him anyway. In the meantime, keep digging."

"We intend to," Danusa said. "So, like I said in the beginning, it looks like your namorada was right. Oh, sorry, she's not your namorada, is she?"

"No, she sure as hell isn't. We're friends, that's all. Who the hell is this Sylvie woman?"

"Told you. She's a friend of Gilda Caropreso's . . . and something a little more than that when it comes to Babyface Gonçalves."

"Well, she's misinformed."

"If you say so," Danusa said.

Rosa didn't say anything at all, but she looked at Hector as if he were one of her teenage sons, and she could see right through him.

Chapter Forty-five

PARAGUAY IS A COUNTRY about the size of California, ruled by dictators during most of its existence. Officially, the economy depends on agriculture and the exportation of iron ore and manganese. Unofficially, it depends on money laundering, smuggling, drug trafficking, and providing a safe haven for tax dodgers, criminals, and Islamic militants.

It was, therefore, an ideal choice of destination for Roberto Ribeiro.

His flight to Asunción, the TAM 8033, was scheduled to depart from Guarulhos at 10:30 AM. They arrived at the airport at 8:30 and Roberto checked in.

"I'll wait here until I see you pass the checkpoint," his mother said.

"It's only gonna make me nervous. Go home. I'll call you when I get settled."

"Don't be stupid. When they find out who I am, they'll tap my phone. Call your aunt Dolores. Here, I've made a note of her number."

She passed him a piece of paper. Dolores, not truly his aunt, was a close friend of his mother's. They'd turned tricks together all through their teenage years and right up until Dolores's marriage to a naïve accountant she'd met at a Sunday-morning mass.

"What do I tell her?"

"Just give her a number and a time to call. I'll get in touch."

Roberto pocketed the paper without looking at it. "Okay," he said. "Go."

She kissed him, held on for a while, and finally walked off, turning to wave several times before going out the door. He glanced at his watch. There was still time for a quick telephone call.

"WHERE THE hell are you?" Bittler asked.

He was angry. Had to be. It was the first time Roberto had ever heard him use profanity. "None of your goddamned business," he said.

It felt good to talk to the old bastard like that. He'd been eating shit for far too long.

There was a shocked silence at the other end of the line. Then, "What's happened?"

"The federal cops are what happened. They're onto me."

"How?"

"I got no idea. But you better get your place cleaned up before they show up on your doorstep."

"What did you tell them, you fool?"

"Fool, my ass, you sack of shit! I didn't tell 'em a thing. But that's only because they didn't catch me. If they do, I'll sing like a canary."

"Why are you telling me this?"

"Because I wanted to hear you squirm. You been treating me like a lowlife for years. Now the shoe's on the other foot."

Bittler started cursing. Roberto hung up on him. He hadn't been totally frank with the old bastard. He'd had another reason for calling. If Bittler got a chance to do some housecleaning before the federal cops showed up, the less evidence there'd be.

And less evidence would be a good thing for Roberto Ribeiro.

THE PASSPORT Ribeiro was using was, as his mother had remarked, a fine piece of work. The gold lettering on the green, cloth cover was faded and, in part, worn away. It bore visas from the United States and France as well as stamps for multiple entries and departures, all of which were genuine. In fact, the whole passport was genuine, except for the altered photograph and the pages with the holder's vital statistics. The document had been stolen at that very airport two weeks earlier and was the former property of a salesman dealing in agricultural products.

Ribeiro's new name was Eduardo Noronha, and his birthplace was listed as São Paulo. His mother had foreseen no problem with that and there wouldn't have been one had he not come up against a zealous young border-control agent named Renato Wagner.

Ribeiro, who'd never been abroad in all of his life, didn't know the drill. He handed over his new passport for perusal, but he didn't hand over his ticket.

"I need the ticket, too," Wagner said.

One of the tasks of the inspectors was to make sure that the visitor had paid his departure tax. The evidence of that was a stamp affixed to the ticket.

"Oh, *desculpe*," Ribeiro said, and reached into his pocket.

The one word was enough. Desculpe, sorry, had been pronounced with a slurry, sibilant "s." The only people who talked like that were cariocas.

Wagner double-checked the birthplace on the passport. São Paulo. He had it right the first time he'd looked. Something was fishy.

"You from Rio de Janeiro?" he asked.

"Born and bred," Ribeiro said proudly.

Wagner nodded. The dumb bastard hadn't even bothered to memorize his history. He glanced at the flyer that had been taped under the counter not two hours earlier. It was out of sight of the passengers, but in clear view of all of the agents.

"Uh-huh," he said, and pushed a button.

Chapter Forty-six

ARNALDO EXPECTED THE DRUG to wear off, but somehow it didn't. It was a mystery. They hadn't fed him, so he couldn't be taking it in that way. And he hadn't seen a single soul in all the time he'd been in the cell, so he didn't think they were injecting him.

And that was another mystery, the time he'd been in the cell. He had no way of knowing, no way of keeping track. They'd kept his watch. The single lamp in the ceiling never went off, so there was no way of distinguishing when it might be day and when it might be night.

The lamp was enclosed in a steel cage, so the prisoners couldn't get at it. Not that he would have bothered. The light was so dim that he had no problem falling asleep.

And that's about all he wanted to do. Sleep.

So, maybe that was the way they were doing it. Waiting until he was asleep, and then sneaking in and putting a mask over his face or a needle in his arm. Or maybe they were pumping in some kind of gas through the vent up near the light. Or maybe it was in the water. He doubted it was the water. There was just the one tap and it looked like a normal tap. They hadn't given him a glass. To drink he had to bend over the sink.

But drugging him they were. He was sure they were getting it into him in one fashion or another. There was no other explanation for the way he felt. He was dazed and disoriented. And he was in no condition to put up a fight when the two of them finally came for him.

It wasn't the carioca. It was a man and a woman. The

woman appeared to be in her early thirties and the man maybe a decade older. Both were wearing green medical scrubs. The gurney they'd brought was equipped with leather restraints that buckled around his upper torso, wrists, thighs, and shins. By the time they'd finished, he was all but immobile. The ride down the hall took only a few seconds. They wheeled him into a tile-walled room smelling of hospital and positioned the gurney next to a metal table surmounted by an immense surgical light.

"Your doctor will be with you in a moment," the guy in green scrubs said.

And laughed.

HECTOR COSTA stared into the mirror and rubbed the bristles on his chin. He didn't like the idea of being in the office unshaven. The bags under his eyes made him look as if he'd had a long night of drinking behind him. He splashed some water on his face, dried it with a paper towel, and returned to where his uncle was still working the phone.

"I'm going down to the padaria for breakfast and a razor. Want anything?"

"Coffee with milk and a buttered roll," Silva said, and started dialing the next number on his list.

HECTOR WAS sitting at the counter, reading the morning paper, and sipping *café com leite*, when his uncle stepped up behind him and grabbed his arm.

"We've got him," Silva said.

"Ribeiro?"

"He was trying to board a flight to Paraguay. They're holding him at Guarulhos. Come on."

There was a car waiting in front of the office, Babyface

Gonçalves behind the wheel. Babyface started rolling even before Hector had fastened his seat belt.

São Paulo shares with Bangkok the distinction of having the most serious traffic gridlocks in the world. Isolated incidents make those gridlocks even worse.

The isolated incident du jour was a tractor trailer whose driver had misread the height of a viaduct over the *marginal*, one of the belt roads that rimmed the city. The cab of the big truck passed under the Limão Bridge with more than twenty centimeters to spare. The forty-foot container it was pulling did not. The leading edge of the container hit the concrete abutment at a speed of almost fifty kilometers an hour, and stuck there, bringing the rig to an immediate stop and blocking one lane of traffic.

The driver, who hadn't been wearing a seat belt, had been propelled out of his cab by inertia. He'd flown through the windshield and come to rest on the other side of the dividing island, where he'd been promptly run over by a delivery van.

The driver of the van, in a desperate attempt to avoid the collision, had stood on his brakes and been rear-ended by another tractor trailer that had jackknifed over the entire road, blocking it in both directions.

When Babyface rolled to a stop, they had almost five kilometers of stalled vehicles in front of them. The traffic behind them was bumper to bumper, so they were effectively trapped. Television helicopters were converging at a distant point directly ahead. Silva, seated in front next to Babyface, switched on the radio. The accident was on all of the traffic reports:

" . . . expected to impede the free flow of traffic for at least the next four hours," the announcer said. "Drivers are advised to avoid the belt road at all costs. Seek alternative routes."

That was all Silva had to hear. He punched the button to shut the radio off, and he didn't do it gently. "Call for a god-damned helicopter," he said.

Babyface did. But it took almost thirty-five minutes to get there and find a suitable place to land. The spot chosen by the pilot was a construction site about three hundred meters from their car. Babyface stayed behind the wheel while Hector and Silva transferred to the aircraft.

After that, it was easy sailing. A ten-minute flight brought them to Guarulhos. A golf cart was waiting on the tarmac. They were met by a female agent with a federal police badge pinned to her black blazer. She brought them to the interrogation room, one level down from the arrival hall.

It was a windowless space with a television camera mounted high in one corner, a steel table, and four wooden chairs, all bolted down. There were two other federal agents in the room, both in suits, both with badges pinned to their lapels, both leaning against the wall, and both looking down at Ribeiro.

One of the federal agents was Antonio Moreira, the guy who headed the federal police assigned to Guarulhos. He was one of the first people Silva had spoken to after sending out the advisory e-mail. The other agent was a young guy who looked like he could have been Babyface's younger brother. If it hadn't been for the badge, Silva might have taken him for a teenage bystander.

"You got the wrong guy," Ribeiro was saying when Silva and Hector entered the room. He'd shaved off his mustache, streaked his black hair with gray, and ditched the Flamengo medallion, but it was him, no doubt about that.

He was seated at the table, sweating profusely, and shaking his head. It wasn't that hot in the room, but he was blotting his forehead with a handkerchief clutched in a meaty left hand about the size of a boxing glove. His other hand was cuffed at the wrist. A chain ran from the cuff to an eye-bolt welded into the top of the table.

"Crap," Delegado Moreira said, "You're Ribeiro. Stop denying it."

Ribeiro kept shaking his head.

"No way," he said.

Moreira looked up and smiled at Silva. He introduced the young guy as Renato Wagner, the man who'd spotted Ribeiro.

"Good work," Silva said, "but now I think it would be better if you left us alone."

Wagner frowned, but Moreira winked knowingly at Silva.

"I think we'll take a stroll down the hall," Moreira said. "You can't hear a damned thing from down there. The door to this room is steel. It has a way of dampening anything that happens inside."

He took Wagner firmly by the arm and led him into the corridor. Hector closed the door and leaned against it. Silva sat down at the table.

"Now," he said, "let's talk."

CLAUDIA WAS laying out her instruments when Bittler hurried into the operating suite. He wasn't wearing scrubs, a mask, or gloves. That alone was enough to tell her that something was terribly wrong.

"Teobaldo," he snapped to the anesthesiologist, "Leave us."

"I haven't got him completely stabilized," Teobaldo said, pointing at an unconscious Arnaldo.

"I don't care," Bittler said. "Go. I'll call you when we need you."

Once the door had closed behind Teobaldo, Bittler came around to her side of the operating table, leaned forward, and spoke in a harsh whisper.

"They're onto Roberto."

Claudia went to the double door and opened it. Teobaldo was bending over, his ear to the crack.

He looked up at her sheepishly.

"Go to your office," she said. "I'll call you there."

"And if the guy on the table dies?"

"He dies. Go."

When he'd taken off down the corridor, she closed the door and turned back to Bittler.

"Tell me," she said, "tell me everything."

BITTLER'S ACCOUNT of his conversation with Ribeiro made Claudia angry, angrier than she could ever remember. But she suppressed her rage, and stood listening to his rationalizations as if she accepted them at face value.

She recognized the game was over, recognized they'd lost, but the man in front of her, a man she'd once respected, was so blinded by self-importance and convictions of intellectual superiority he couldn't see the disaster in its true light. If he'd listened to her in the first place, it would never have come to this. Roberto would have been long dead. The debacle was *his* fault, Horst Bittler's fault, and no one else's.

"They haven't caught him yet," he was saying, "and with a little luck they never will. But we'll have to act quickly, just in case. If they do catch him, we can't count on him to keep his mouth shut. The records are a problem. They've been good enough for a superficial inspection, but they won't stand up to in-depth analysis. We'll have to destroy them."

"How about the others?" she said. "Gretchen? Teobaldo? That pilot you've recently taken into our confidence? What about them? What's to prevent one of them making a deal and selling us out?"

He considered that for a moment. "They're expendable," he said.

"And I am, too, I suppose."

He avoided her eyes.

"No, Claudia, of course not. I've always regarded you as my partner. Now, stop talking foolishness and let's get busy. God knows how much time we've got to do it all. A few days at the minimum, I suspect. Unless they catch up with Roberto. If that happens, they could be here sooner. We have to make sure that there's nothing, absolutely nothing, for them to find. First the records. We could—"

"Set a fire in the archives? Burn down part of the building?"

"Yes, yes, an excellent idea. Destroying part of the building would lend verisimilitude. And the holding cells? How can we justify the holding cells?"

"Claim that we intended to extend the clinic's services to the treatment of the violently insane? That we had the cells constructed for that?"

"No. No, they'll see through that in an instant."

"They will. But can they prove otherwise?"

"You're right. Proof is all."

But she'd only been toying with him.

"You're a piece of work," she said.

"What?" His eyebrows climbed almost to his hairline. She'd never spoken to him like that. He flushed a deep red.

"I said you're a piece of work."

"How dare you?"

"I told you more than once to get rid of Roberto. But, no, you thought you knew better."

"There was no reason to believe—"

"There was. There was every reason to believe that the man was a liability. You just didn't want to see it."

"I resent your tone."

"And I resent your actions. I spent years preparing to practice my profession, and now you've put it in jeopardy through your lack of judgment. What am I supposed to do with my life from here on in? Tell me that!"

"You're overreacting, Claudia. You'll continue as you've always done. I will endeavor to forgive your lapse in courtesy. Now, if there's nothing more . . ."

She shook her head in disbelief.

"Do you actually believe we can carry on? Just clean the place up and act as if nothing has happened?"

"We have the Kramer woman upstairs, waiting for her new heart. Get Teobaldo back in here and remove his." He pointed at Arnaldo's recumbent form. "Then, while the corpse is being dismembered, we can burn the body of the other Indian brat. But we'll have to clean his ashes out of the oven ourselves. Damn Roberto Ribeiro!"

"You intend to go forward? You intend to harvest this heart and then implant it in the Kramer woman? After what you've just told me?"

"Why not? They won't get onto us as quickly as all that. No use wasting what we have. Don't forget that we already have the Kramer woman's money. It's against my principles to give it back."

The man was insane. Strange that she'd never noticed it before.

Chapter Forty-seven

"I AM CHIEF INSPECTOR Mario Silva," the man in the gray suit said, "and you"—he put his finger on Roberto's chest—"are Roberto Ribeiro."

Roberto shrank away from the pressure of the finger and shook his head. "I'm not," he said. "It's a case of misshapen identity."

"The word you're looking for, you filho da puta, is mistaken, *mistaken* identity, not misshapen identity, and you *are* Roberto Ribeiro, and if you deny it one more time, I'm going to hurt you."

The cop came no closer; he didn't shout, he didn't bluster. But, somehow, Roberto felt as if the temperature in the room had taken a plunge. He looked into the man's eyes—blacker than coal—and shivered. Seconds before, he'd been sweating like a pig, and now he shivered. It didn't make sense. It was almost as if his body were responding on some primitive level.

"Personally," Silva said, "I don't think you deserve to live. The way I figure it, you've been complicit in the murder of dozens, maybe even scores, of people."

Roberto shook his head. "You got the wrong guy. I never even heard of—"

Silva hit him in the face with the back of his hand. The blow came so quickly, so unexpectedly, that Roberto didn't have time to raise his arm, or even turn his head. He put his free hand up to touch his nose. It wasn't bleeding and it didn't seem to be broken, but it stung like hell.

"Jesus Christ," he said.

"What–is–your–name?" Silva said, spacing out the words.

"Okay, okay, it's Roberto Ribeiro, but I don't know nothing—"

"Let's get something straight," Silva said, cutting him off. "I'd like to kill you, I truly would, and I—"

"Kill me? You can't kill me. You're a cop, for Christ's sake."

"Shut up and listen to me," Silva said savagely. Then he took a deep breath and went on in the same tone as before. "And I *will* kill you," he said, "if you don't tell me everything I want to know."

"I—"

"Believe me, Ribeiro. Believe me, when I say this room will be the last place you'll ever see, my companion and I the last people you'll ever meet, unless you respond truthfully to my questions. Truthfully, mind. If I catch you in a lie, even a little one, I'm going to hurt you again."

Roberto tried to swallow, but his throat was suddenly too dry.

"Don't make me work too hard to get the answers I need, Ribeiro. If you do, and you're not dead when I'm finished, then I'll kill you anyway. Do we understand each other?"

Roberto nodded.

"Honest to God," he said, "I never killed nobody."

He saw the cop's eyes narrow, and he flinched.

"I got to take a shit," he said, "really bad."

"Shit in your pants for all I care," the cop said. "Keep talking."

"I got to go, I'm telling you."

"Talk."

"It was *him*. Him and the woman. They did it. All I did was to . . . to help find people."

"Who's him?"

"Bittler. Horst Bittler. He's a doctor. He's got a clinic in Morumbi."

"Where in Morumbi?"

"Rua das Tulipas, number ninety-seven."

"And the woman?"

"She's a doctor, too. Claudia Andrade. She works with him."

"And the people?"

"Lots of people. I can't remember. Look, I'll tell you everything, just let me go to the shithouse before I—"

"What did they do to them? What did they do to the people you helped to find?"

"Kept them in cells under the building."

"And then?"

"Harvested them. That's what he called it, harvesting them. Like they was corn or something."

"Their organs? He harvested their organs?"

"Not all their organs, just their hearts. He only does hearts." Roberto's face was getting red with the effort of containing himself. "Let me go to the toilet," he said. "Please. I'm gonna lose it."

"Does Bittler have people in those cells now, right now?"

"Maybe."

"What do you mean, maybe?"

"Well, I . . . I talked to him. Told him you were after me. Told him I was on the run."

"And how, exactly, did you happen to know that? Know that we were after you?"

"I can't tell you. Look you gotta—"

"You'd *better* tell me. And I don't *gotta* anything. Not even let you live."

"My mother."

"What about her?"

"She lives across the hall. She told me that a couple of federal cops broke down my door."

"She own a cat?" the cop leaning against the door asked.

"Yeah, a cat."

"How long ago did you talk to Bittler?"

That from Silva.

"An hour or so ago. Maybe more."

"Okay, back to those cells of his. Who might he still have in there?"

"An Indian baby from the Xingu, maybe two."

"How did he pull that off?"

"There's this wimp who works for the FUNAI. He stole a couple of babies from some Indian tribe. One of them was supposed to be used for his sick kid. The other one was a kind of payment, or maybe a reserve in case the first one didn't work, I'm not sure."

"This wimp," the cop leaning against the door said, "was his name Oliveira?"

"Yeah. Oliveira."

"Alright," Silva said, "so there's a baby, maybe two. Anyone else in those cells?"

"I really gotta go. Now."

"Answer my question."

"Just some old . . . some guy about your age."

"And how did he get there?"

"There's this travel agency Bittler uses sometimes. They arrange trips for people who want to get into the States and can't get a visa. Every now and then one of them winds up at the clinic. They think they're going to Mexico, but they get harvested instead."

Silva leaned in close, got right into Roberto's face.

"Tell me more about this guy about my age," he said, his voice as cold as ice.

And that was when Roberto finally lost control of his bowels.

RIBEIRO KNEW the location and layout of Bittler's Clinic, and there was no time to lose. Ribeiro's presence on the raid would be a plus, but traveling with a man whose pants were full of excrement wasn't a pleasant thing to contemplate. Silva tasked Hector to take Ribeiro down the hall to the bathroom so he could clean himself up.

While that was happening, he called their pilot and told him to preflight the helicopter. Then he alerted ERR1.

The Brazilian federal police had four elite hostage rescue units (Equipes para o Resgate de Reféns) designated ERR1 through ERR4. The first of these, based in São Paulo, was composed of twenty-two men and two women. One of those women, Gloria Sarmento, commanded it. Gloria was a brilliant tactical leader, a crack shot, and highly skilled in jujitsu. She was also known to be absolutely fearless. Even Arnaldo Nunes, a *macho* to his fingertips and generally contemptuous of women bearing arms, was once heard to remark that Gloria had more balls than a pool hall.

Her first word to Silva was, "Where?"

"Morumbi," he said. "Ninety-seven Rua das Tulipas. A clinic belonging to a doctor by the name of Bittler."

From the way his voice echoed back to him, he knew she'd put him on a speaker phone. He could hear scrambling in the background, people assembling their equipment.

"What?" Gloria said.

"Hostage situation. An infant child, maybe two, and Arnaldo Nunes."

"Nunes? That Neanderthal? Man, I'd *love* to save his ass. I'd never let him forget it. Where are you?"

"Guarulhos. I've got a helicopter. I've also got a man familiar with the location."

"Bring him, and get him to make a sketch of the interior of the building. If he has any idea where the hostages are being held, tell him to mark it. If there are multiple possibilities, tell him to rank them and write in numbers. One for the most likely, two for the second most likely, and so on. I'll pick a staging area where you can land. My people will follow in a couple of vans. You have a cell phone?"

"Yes."

"What's the number?"

He gave it to her. She fired it back at him. He confirmed it.

"I'll call you in fifteen minutes," she said.

And hung up.

Chapter Forty-eight

THEY WERE ALREADY IN the air when Silva and Gloria spoke again.

"There's a vacant lot about a kilometer to the northeast of the target," Gloria said. "Tell the pilot to follow the river. When he's directly above the Morumbi Bridge, he should alter his course to three hundred and forty degrees. That will bring him in over the bluff. Look for a white cross and my helicopter. I'm already down. And tell him, for God's sake, not to fly over the clinic. The noise may tip them off. It's a large building with a mansard roof, parking lots in front and back, about three hundred meters beyond the landing site, the only house on the street without a swimming pool."

Silva relayed her instructions to the pilot, who asked him what the hell a mansard roof was.

In the rear seat of the Aerospatiale Squirrel, Hector was sitting next to one of the windows. Ribeiro was on the other side of the aircraft. There were two empty seats between them, but judging by the expression on Hector's face, it wasn't far enough. If the helicopter had had wings, Hector would probably be sitting on the tip of one.

Silva sympathized. He had one of the air-conditioning vents pointed toward his face, but even with his nose in the slipstream the smell of excrement was overpowering.

Ribeiro had his tongue between his teeth, a pencil in his hand, and was drawing on a clipboard. He looked up and saw Silva holding his nose, staring at him.

"It's your fault I smell like this," he said. "You shoulda let me go."

"How come it's taking you so damned long?"

"I'm finished."

Ribeiro handed Silva the clipboard. The work was crude, none of the lines parallel to one another. It looked like it had been drawn by a five-year-old.

"Where are the hostages?" Silva said, searching for marks or numbers and not finding any.

Ribeiro leaned forward. "I couldn't get it all on one sheet," he said.

"Don't do that!"

"What?"

Silva waved a hand in front of his nose to dispel the stench. "Sit back in your seat."

Ribeiro did.

"That's just the main floor," he said.

Silva flipped to the next sheet.

"That's the cellar under the building. That's where they take out the hearts and burn the bodies."

"*They*, huh? And you never did anything like that?"

"No, I told you. I never killed nobody. I swear to God."

"Can you get to the cellar from the main floor?"

Ribeiro shook his head.

"Only from the parking lot in back. There's a ramp that leads down to a door. You can see it right there." He extended a finger and started to lean forward again, but then he caught Silva's warning look and drew back. "Right there," he repeated. "Bittler made it that way on purpose, to keep it secret."

"Look," the pilot said.

Silva didn't have the eyes of an aviator, and it took awhile for him to locate what the man was pointing at: a white cross in the middle of what looked like a little park and, nearby, another helicopter. When they got closer, Silva could see the cross had been made with some kind of white powder.

Seconds later they were down and the white powder was all around them, kicked up by the wash from the aircraft's rotor. Silva disembarked, coughing and beating the powder off his gray suit. Gloria Sarmento, in black body armor and carrying a Heckler and Koch MP5 submachine gun, was waiting for him.

"Just to get something straight before we begin, Chief Inspector."

"Yes."

"You outrank me, but I'm good at doing what I do, and this is my show. I don't want you to interfere."

"I wouldn't dream of it," Silva said.

"Where are the sketches?"

"This one's the ground floor," Silva said, handing it over.

"How old is the guy who drew this?" Gloria said, studying Ribeiro's work. "Five? Six?"

"Only mentally," Silva said. He handed her the other sheet. "That's the basement where they keep the hostages."

"Access?"

"Only one way in. From the parking lot in back."

"Steel door?"

"I didn't ask."

"I'd better go over there and talk to that creep," Gloria said.

"Don't get too close," Silva warned. "He stinks."

GLORIA DIVIDED her people into two teams: Hammer One and Hammer Two. Hammer One was charged with breaching the perimeter and assaulting the main floor. Hammer Two, commanded by Gloria herself, would attack the complex beyond the ramp. She briefed them in the staging area, and then they all piled into the vans, Silva, Hector, and Ribeiro included. The guys sitting on either side of

Ribeiro wrinkled their noses and moved as far away as possible on the crowded bench.

The other female member of ERR1 looked at him and said, "Phew."

She was a perky brunette with short hair named Sarah Dimenstein. All the other members of the team were in full gear, but Sarah was wearing a skirt and blouse.

Gloria, sitting next to Silva, caught his expression and smiled. "Why shoot our way in," she said, "if we can do it with finesse?"

THE DRIVE to Bittler's clinic took less than a minute. They parked the vans out of sight of the guard at the main gate. The teams lined up on the sidewalk.

"You can follow us in," Gloria said to Silva. "From what that creep said, I don't expect them to do any shooting, but keep your head down anyway."

"I'll follow you around to the back," Silva said. "Whatever is down there is my major concern at the moment."

"Do me a favor," she said.

"What?"

"Get that nephew of yours to cuff the creep and chain him to something downwind."

SARAH APPROACHED the gate, carrying a small purse and wearing a microphone in her bra. The transmitter was in the small of her back. From their place of concealment, Gloria couldn't see the guard or the gate, but she could hear every word of his exchange with Sarah. And so could Silva.

"Help you?" the guard said, his voice tinny through the intercom.

"I'm trying to find this address," Sarah said.

They could hear the crinkle of paper. They knew she was

waving a sheet from a small notepad, holding it up. A few seconds went by and there was the whir of a motor and the squeak of hinges: the sound of the electric gate being opened. Footsteps approached Sarah's microphone.

Gloria smiled. "He's out of his hole," she said, "and away from the damned alarm button. We're in."

"Let me see," the guard said. They could imagine him extending a hand to take the paper, imagine Sarah reaching into her purse. And then, "What the hell is this?"

"This," Sarah said, "is a nine-millimeter pistol and *this*"— there was a short pause—"is my federal police ID. Turn around and face the wall."

ACCORDING TO the man stationed at the gate, there were two other guards inside the building. All three were municipal cops, moonlighting for a security company. They were there to protect the place from thieves and to keep undesirables like panhandlers and salesmen from molesting the staff and patients. Federal cops with a legitimate right to be there were something else again.

One of the other two guys on his shift, the guard who'd been on the gate said, would be watching the monitors hooked up to the security cameras. He'd be doing that from a small room under the main staircase just off the reception area. The other guard would be on his break, reading, sleeping, or watching TV up on the second floor. Provided the man covering the monitors hadn't seen Sarah's gun, it should be easy enough to disarm him, and the other guy should be even easier, since he'd be taken by surprise. And as soon as they were convinced that they were dealing with federal cops, and not a band of armed robbers, the guard who'd been on the gate added, they'd be sure to cooperate.

Ribeiro, now handcuffed to one of the metal pickets in

the perimeter fence, confirmed that the security men were unaware of the illicit activities that went on in the basement, probably not even aware that there *was* a basement.

Sarah strolled up the walk as if she had every right to be there. Once inside, she spoke to the guards.

The rest was, as Gloria later put it, a cakewalk. On the main floor, Hammer One found a functioning operating theater with a woman already anesthetized and ready to receive a new heart. Upstairs, there were patients recovering from recent operations.

The ward nurses were left to care for their charges, the remaining staff was lined up in the reception area. Ribeiro was called in to finger Teobaldo Vargas, the anesthesiologist, and Gretchen Furtwangler, Bittler's secretary, who, he said, were complicit in Bittler's and Andrade's crimes.

People wrinkled their noses and turned their heads away as Ribeiro moved down the line. When he pointed them out, Teobaldo tried to hit him, and Gretchen spit in his face.

A scrutiny of Furtwangler's Rolodex revealed the address of Manolo Nabuco, the pilot. A team was dispatched to arrest him at his home. Less than half an hour later, the call came through. They'd found him in bed with a teenage prostitute, both of them high on cocaine. He'd been taken into custody without a fight.

ARNALDO AWOKE to find himself staring upward into a battery of lamps. He blinked against the glare, tried to move a hand in front of his face and couldn't. His arms were still under restraint. A head poked into his line of vision, the face looking down on him.

"Oh no," he said.

"Oh, yes," Gloria Sarmento said, "sleeping on the job again, Nunes?"

"You!"

"Me."

"This is a nightmare," he said. "Please tell me it's a nightmare."

"There, there" she said, "you don't have to worry anymore. You've been rescued. You're safe at last. Now, just lie there quietly for a moment while Decio takes a picture of the two of us. I'm going to hang it on the wall of my office."

She brought her smiling face down and put it cheek to cheek with Arnaldo's. There was a flash as a strobe light went off.

"You shoulda let them kill me," Arnaldo said. "It woulda been more merciful."

GLORIA'S NUMBER two, a *gaucho* from Rio Grande do Sul with the unlikely name of John Fitzgerald Kennedy Carvalho, walked into the cremation room, saw the partially consumed body of a baby on the grate, and managed to make it back into the hall before he vomited. He went into the bathroom and washed his mouth out with water. Then he went back and sealed the door with yellow crime-scene tape.

An Indian baby, just one, was found sleeping on a cot in one of the cells.

SILVA WAS the one who found Bittler. The doctor was lying in a pool of his own blood, his body concealed behind the pump-oxygenator. His throat had been slashed from ear to ear. The cut was very clean, a sign that it had been made with an extremely sharp instrument. There was a look of surprise frozen on his face. Death would not have been immediate, but as a doctor, he would have known that his injury was fatal.

Later, a scalpel bearing traces of his blood, and Claudia

Andrade's fingerprints, was found among the medical instruments on a nearby table.

Paulo Couto, the chief medical examiner, who was famous for seldom speculating about anything, speculated that the scalpel was the instrument used to kill him.

Silva was convinced that it was Claudia who had done the job.

And Claudia was nowhere to be found.

Chapter Forty-nine

"CAN YOU SPARE ME ten minutes, Director?"

Sampaio put down his pen, motioned Silva forward, and smiled. "Well, finally," he said. "What have you got on the bastard?"

Silva crossed the threshold carrying a briefcase. "It's not about the minister's press secretary," Silva said. "It's about that organ-theft business."

Sampaio stopped smiling and picked up his pen.

"*Five* minutes. Five minutes tops, not ten."

Silva waited for his boss to look up again, but Sampaio didn't. The director circled an item on the page in front of him and appended a few words. The words ended in an exclamation point.

"I could come back later, Director."

Sampaio tossed the document into his out-box, picked up another one, and made an impatient gesture with the hand holding the pen.

"No, no," he said, "just get on with it."

"The anesthesiologist and that swine, Ribeiro, are being most forthcoming, trying to outdo each other to see who gets the best deal from the prosecutors. Turns out, there were three cemeteries in all, another even larger one in the Serra da Cantareira and a slightly smaller one near the reservoir in the hills above Cotia. There were false names on all the deeds and tax records, but in the end, they all turned out to be properties purchased by Bittler for the express purpose of burying his victims."

Sampaio kept writing.

"The victims were all strangers to Bittler and his friends. It's unlikely we'll ever be able to identify them all."

Sampaio didn't reply, didn't bother to look up.

"With the cooperation of Gretchen Furtwangler, Bittler's former secretary, we managed to track the Argentinian who ran the travel agency. He was lying low in Buenos Aires. The Argentinian federal police took him into custody about an hour ago."

Sampaio capped his pen and put it into the inside pocket of his jacket.

"And the woman? Any leads on her whereabouts?"

"No."

The director expelled a breath, removed his reading glasses, and rubbed the bridge of his nose.

"Too bad for you. Because I'm telling you right now, the press is all over this, and I don't intend to take the blame for allowing that woman to escape."

"No, of course you don't," Silva said.

Sampaio gave him a sharp look.

"And what do you mean by that?"

"You've delegated the task of capturing her to me. Only that."

The director chose to accept Silva's explanation rather than prolong the interview. He replaced his reading glasses. "Just as long as we understand each other," he said, "Now, if you're finished . . ."

"Not quite," Silva said. "Bittler owned that clinic of his for more than thirty years. I have reason to believe that he might have been experimenting with heart transplants before there was any chance of them being a long-term solution for anyone's health problem."

Sampaio glanced at Silva over the top of his half-moon lenses.

"That's ancient history. No one cares about ancient history."

"Before you jump to that conclusion," Silva said, "you might want to take a look at this." He opened the briefcase, extracted a photo, and slid it across Sampaio's desk.

"First," he said, "check out the inscription on the back."

Sampaio flipped the photo over and studied it.

"German?" he asked.

"German," Silva agreed. "It says, 'Beppo and I. Opening Day.' The handwriting is Bittler's. Now look at the image."

When Sampaio did, he was looking at two smiling men in white coats, arms on each other's shoulders.

"That's Bittler's clinic in the background," Silva said, "Bittler is the one on the left."

"Who's the guy standing next to him?"

"I got the photo when I searched Bittler's office. It was in a silver frame on the mantelpiece."

"I didn't ask you where you got it. I asked you—"

"Back in 1985, when I was working out of the São Paulo field office, we got a call from the West German federal police. I say West German because the Berlin Wall was still up in those days."

"You don't have to be so damned precise. Stop wasting my time and get on with the story."

"They'd searched the home of a guy named Sedlmeier, a lifelong friend of Josef Mengele's"

"Mengele? That Nazi doctor? The one they called the Angel of Death?

"Him."

"What did Mengele have to do with—"

"Bear with me. The West German cops found letters in Mengele's handwriting. Recent letters. They squeezed Sedlmeier. He claimed Mengele was dead. They didn't believe him. They squeezed a little more. He said Mengele was buried in Embu under a false name."

Embu was a small town about thirty kilometers from São Paulo, known to Paulistas for the art fair held there every Sunday afternoon.

Sampaio put the photo aside. "Okay, this is getting interesting. Maybe you'd better sit down," he said.

Silva sat and continued, "Sedlmeier claimed Mengele had been buried under the name Wolfgang Gerhard. The Germans asked us to check it out. We went to the cemetery, and there *was* a grave for a Wolfgang Gerhard. We got a court order and exhumed the body."

"And?"

"The guy in the grave wasn't Gerhard. The real Gerhard, the one who'd been issued a permanent resident visa, was a taller man, and younger. Next thing we knew, a whole raft of foreigners descended on us: Israelis, Americans, West Germans, pathologists, forensic anthropologists, security services, the whole lot. Some of them said the body was Mengele's, some of them said it wasn't. They would have kept arguing for years if the West Germans hadn't talked Mengele's son into contributing a sample of his DNA."

"Mengele had a son?"

Silva nodded. "Rolf. He admitted that the old bastard had been living here for years. Came over to visit him once, said they didn't get along, but we could hardly expect him to turn in his own father."

"And the body? Was it Mengele's?"

"It was. Turned out he died of a stroke while swimming in the sea off Bertioga."

Silva took another photo out of his briefcase. It was a black-and-white head shot of a smiling young man wearing an old-fashioned necktie and what appeared to be a black jacket. "Mengele," he said. "A photo taken in 1940. We got it from the West German police, and they got it from his war records. See that little growth on his face and the big gap between his front teeth?"

Sampaio nodded.

"Distinctive," he said.

"Now look at the first photo again."

The director put both photos side by side, looked from one to the other.

"Sure as hell looks like the same guy," Sampaio said. He started to rub his chin.

"Here's the clincher," Silva said. "Mengele had a nickname. The story is that he was a bit of a prankster in his youth. A circus passed through his town. They had an Italian clown."

"Beppo?"

"Beppo. The townsfolk gave Mengele the nickname, and the nickname stuck. He used it all of his life."

"I'll be damned," Sampaio said. "So Gerhard was Mengele, and Beppo was Mengele, and Mengele and Bittler were buddies?"

"Buddies, I don't know. Colleagues, certainly. Look at the white coats, the inscription."

Sampaio left off studying the photographs and cast a suspicious eye on Silva.

"And how come you just happened to recognize Mengele?"

"Because I saw his photos hundreds of times. The case

made a major impression on me. Nazi in our own backyard and all that."

"Okay. Hold on. Let's go back a bit. You figure Mengele helped Bittler to put this whole thing together, the clinic, the organ thefts, all of that?"

"We looked into Bittler's background. He would *never* have had the money to go into business on his own. But Mengele did. Mengele's family owned a big company that made agricultural machinery. Still does. They're loaded. The son admitted they sent the old man money. Not so much until 1978, and then, all of a sudden, a lot of it, more than two million deutschmarks in 1978, another eight hundred and fifty thousand in early 1979."

"What's that in dollars, or euros?"

"I don't remember, but, like I said, it's a lot, and we were never able to find out what he did with it."

"But now you figure—"

"According to the people we interviewed, the people that knew him, the old man wasn't into money. What turned him on was using human beings as guinea pigs. He would have needed a front man, a partner, someone who could give the patina of legitimacy to a clinic. Or maybe I should say a laboratory. He had kidney problems in his youth. Was fascinated with the idea of transplants."

Instead of looking shocked or somber, Sampaio broke into a broad smile. "Christ, what a story. The greedy young punk who's in it for the money and the world-class war criminal who likes to cut people up for fun. It's gonna be front-page news in the whole damned—"

He brought himself up short. The smile faded. "Who else knows about this?" he asked.

"My nephew and four other cops in São Paulo."

"Federal cops? People who ultimately report to me?"

"Yes."

The smile came back. "Get onto all five of them right now," Sampaio said. "Tell them they're to say nothing about this to anyone. I want to break this story myself."

"I rather thought you might," Silva said.

Author's Notes

The second half of Josef Mengele's life is shrouded in mystery, but he did, indeed, suffer a fatal stroke while bathing in the ocean off the Brazilian seaside town of Bertioga and his sobriquet *was* Beppo. It is equally true that he suffered from kidney problems in his youth, was fascinated by the idea of organ transplants, and was buried in Embu under the name Wolfgang Gerhard. The roles attributed to his friend, Sedlmeier, and his son, Rolf, are also part of the historical record. As of this writing, his remains are still lying in a drawer at the Instituto Médico Legal in São Paulo.

The first Portuguese explorers landed in Brazil in 1500, and the indigenous inhabitants of the country have been exploited, in one way or another, ever since. There were approximately five million native Brazilians at the time of the European conquest. Today, their numbers don't exceed three hundred fifty thousand, of which as many as forty thousand have had little or no contact with modern society.

Brazil is a place of many religions and many cults, with millions of people who actively practice more than one belief at the same time. Candomblé, for example, the Brazilian form of what is called Santeria in Cuba and Vodou in Haiti, often attracts the same people who frequent Sunday mass at the local Catholic church. Despite the condemnation of the Vatican, the two religions persist and intermingle, existing side by side in perfect harmony.

Wicca, much rarer in Brazil and much maligned as a form of witchcraft, is an earth-based religion in which the main belief is to do harm to none.

But Brazil harbors evil cults, as well. A case in point was the Superior Universal Alignment Sect, members of which were charged with kidnapping boys, cutting off their genitals, and sacrificially killing them. The cult's members included two doctors and the son of a prominent businessman, all well-to-do and all with political connections. It took eleven years, and intervention by the governor of the Amazonian state of Pará, to force a change of venue and bring the perpetrators to justice.

According to recent research, 79 percent of all Brazilians (the figure is higher for urban dwellers) live in fear that they or someone close to them might be a victim of violent crime. They have good reason. The murder rate in São Paulo is sixteen times higher than in Tokyo.

Countrywide, at least one million people live in shantytowns where the police are loathe to go.

The Comando Vermelho and the Primeiro Comando Capital (PCC) exist and are currently at war with the governments of São Paulo and Rio de Janeiro. They do, indeed, kill hundreds of policemen.

Rumors of murder for the purpose of organ theft persist. None have been confirmed.

São Paulo
February, 2007